Diana Appleyard is a writer, broadcaster and freelance journalist for a number of national newspapers and magazines. She worked for the BBC as an Education Correspondent, before deciding to give up her full-time job to work from home, a decision which formed the basis for her first novel, *Homing Instinct*. She lives with her husband Ross and their two young daughters in an Oxfordshire farmhouse. Her other novels *Homing Instinct*, *A Class Apart* and *Out of Love*, are also published by Black Swan.

D1369058

Also by Diana Appleyard

HOMING INSTINCT
A CLASS APART
OUT OF LOVE

and published by Black Swan

EVERY GOOD WOMAN
DESERVES A LOVER

Diana Appleyard

BLACK SWAN

EVERY GOOD WOMAN DESERVES A LOVER
A BLACK SWAN BOOK: 0 552 99934 2

First publication in Great Britain

PRINTING HISTORY
Black Swan edition published 2004

3 5 7 9 10 8 6 4 2

Set in 11/14pt Melior by
Falcon Oast Graphic Art Ltd.

Black Swan Books are published by Transworld Publishers,
61–63 Uxbridge Road, London W5 5SA,
a division of The Random House Group Ltd,
in Australia by Random House Australia (Pty) Ltd,
20 Alfred Street, Milsons Point, Sydney, NSW 2061, Australia,
in New Zealand by Random House New Zealand Ltd,
18 Poland Road, Glenfield, Auckland 10, New Zealand
and in South Africa by Random House (Pty) Ltd,
Endulini, 5a Jubilee Road, Parktown 2193, South Africa.

Printed and bound in Great Britain by
Cox & Wyman Ltd, Reading, Berkshire.

Papers used by Transworld Publishers are natural, recyclable
products made from wood grown in sustainable forests. The
manufacturing processes conform to the environmental
regulations of the country of origin.

To mum, the
intrepid traveller

Acknowledgements

To Bernie and Jane for being excellent travel companions, and to Abercrombie and Kent for organising a perfect trip to Peru. To Ross, Beth and Charlotte on the home front, to everyone at Transworld, especially Linda, and to Jo, Sheila and Vicky at A.P. Watt.

Chapter One

Persistence is a virtue, but not, necessarily, in an alarm clock. Its beeping tone, at first gentle and insinuating, was becoming shriller, its intermittent beeps forming into one long continuous ear-splitting wail. Without opening her eyes, she reached out to slam her hand down on its plastic flap. But her hand did not encounter a small inanimate object. It encountered human skin.

The skin was warm, and smooth. Very slowly, she opened one eye. Aha. Not a dream, then. Was that bad, or good? Gently she let her fingers rest on his back, feeling the warmth beneath. He flinched, as if a fly had landed, and, moaning softly in his sleep, he turned towards her and he too opened his eyes.

The eyes were chocolate brown, almond-shaped, his pupils and irises very clearly defined against the intense white of his eyeballs. Healthy eyes, undimmed by Western excess. Young eyes. He smiled at her, and, reaching out, he gently touched her face. She stared at him, shocked, as he slid a finger down her cheek, his smile confident and faintly teasing. He was comfortable with his nakedness, quite in control of himself, while she hunched the sheets up over her chest, conscious that her skin was not as smooth, not as flawless as his. She had much more to hide.

He lifted his hand from her face, and leant over, away from her, to switch off the clock. The hair in his armpit was black and silken. There was something slightly simian about him, she thought, with his jet black hair and dark brown eyes.

'What time is it?'

'Half past five.'

'Time to get up, then.'

'I think so, yes.'

He turned onto his back, and lay staring at the ceiling, easy and comfortable while she lay rigid with astonishment at what she had done. The sun was rising, but the heavy lined hotel curtains blocked out most of the light, so inside the room there was just a ghostly paleness, barely light enough to make out the features of the room. The wide double bed, its cover thrown off on the floor, a victim of the night. The pile of foreign currency on the dressing table, to be spent on this last day or rendered useless. Her necklace, removed by him. On the floor lay the duffle bag, half packed. Towels, T-shirts, a pair of damp walking trousers and her boots, covered in dried flaking mud, trail-worn, lay at the foot of the bed. There was so much to do, so much to organize, but she could not move. Her body lay immobile, paralysed by the extraordinary heaviness of spent passion, fear, and something very close to wild elation. In the night she

10

had woken, and felt only wonder at what had happened. Now, in this dawning light, she could think more clearly about what the effects would be. Only not, perhaps, yet. Not yet, while he was still lying warm and naked next to her. She would not have him for long.

I will stay in this limbo, she thought. I am caught, here, in a time which does not truly exist. This cannot be reality, because this is not my life. I have stepped over, into some kind of parallel universe because I cannot fully comprehend what I have done. This does not make sense. I will just lie here, and the world will go away.

'You must get up,' he said to the ceiling.

'Is that advice, or an order?' she said.

'I am telling you,' he said, turning back to her, a smile lighting his face, 'that as your tour guide unless you get up now you will miss your plane.'

'What if I want to miss my plane?' she said, quietly.

He said nothing. He knew she did not mean it. He knew they were in limbo too, and the movement they would both have to make would inevitably signal the beginning of the end.

But still she did not move. Moving meant breaking the spell. She felt as she had as a child, lying in bed at night, afraid, and hearing an odd creak on the landing outside. If I do not move whatever it is will go away, and, for a moment, the world stopped. Not moving was a way of not existing.

She had to get up. The world marched on. Just two rooms away her closest friends would be rising, murmuring to each other about the need for plastic

11

bags to protect damp clothing, what to do with the rest of their nuevo sols and dollars, airline tickets, passports. They were two women packing and tidying like proper middle-aged people ending a holiday, and she was lying in a bed in a foreign hotel with a naked man. How was she to move from this situation, back into normal life? Last night he had said that this night would be a memory they would have for ever, but it was all very well saying that when you were in the midst of passion, caught up in the fantasy. Now the cold light of day was beginning to shine on what had been, she shivered, an exceptionally reckless act by a woman who frankly ought to have known better. It was fine for him, he could get up and go, as he had done no doubt many times before, and shrug off the memory, but this was not the kind of thing she was used to doing. Not at all. She had to stop being part of this extraordinary fantasy and become herself once more, and work out how she was going to stop anyone, ever, from knowing. What had been their private limbo, this remarkable moment in time, would become public and the damage to her would be – what? Irreparable? She had never had a secret like this before. And that was all it could ever be. A secret.

He turned back to her, and lifted himself up on one elbow. In this pale light, he looked even more absurdly young. Like a child she would kiss goodnight. But he was still in charge, in charge of even this surreal situation. They had to break the spell, and say goodbye.

'You know, you have to get up.' He said the last two words forcefully, jokingly, like a threat. His voice was so beautiful. Heavily accented, perfectly phrased, like

Shakespearean English without the modern colloquialisms, so he would say, 'I think we ought to leave now,' instead of, 'We must go.' He had a round-the-houses way of phrasing sentences that was charming, sounding so polite and old-fashioned. If he interrupted a conversation, he would say, 'Excuse me. I wonder if you might consider,' or if they said 'Thank you,' he always responded, 'You're welcome.' He was so courteous, while all the time beneath his courtesy simmered a dangerous sexuality, like a light permanently flickering.

Can love lie? she thought. Can love, once experienced, be denied? Do you fool yourself about love, and think that you can choose? I used to think that. I thought that I would never again be vulnerable, because I neither wanted nor felt there was any room in my life for such an emotion, and, perhaps, I did believe that you simply grow out of the obsessive, white heat of love and find more practical compensations in the rest of your life. Instead of living in the clouds you walk firmly on the earth. But now, she realized, she had never truly been tested, had never been drawn into a reciprocated sexual attraction which, once set in train, sped powerfully towards an inevitable conclusion.

How condescending I have been, she thought. Imagining that I am above and beyond love. You are never safe, because it isn't about choice, as I thought it was.

A knock on the door made them both jump. She had a terrible urge to giggle, and pull the cover over both

13

their heads. Miguel held his finger to his lips like a naughty schoolboy.

'What?'

'Are you up yet?'

'Nearly.'

'We're going down. Do you want some breakfast?'

'Just coffee,' she called back, and was amazed at how normal she sounded. That was my voice, she thought, coming from a person I am not sure is me.

Still she lay there, but was restless now. What was the etiquette? Did she rise before him, or should she wait until he got up? Should they get up together, like synchronized swimmers?

Oh, this is silly, she thought. She lifted herself up, and threw the covers off her legs. He did not stir. Now another problem presented itself. It was still dim in the bedroom, but there was enough light for her to be seen and oh, it was a very different thing walking quite naked to the bathroom in the chill early morning light to falling backwards onto a bed in the darkness when it didn't seem to matter that her thighs were not perfectly smooth and her stomach formed neat rolls when she sat up. Now the world was patently no longer mad and normal things were happening outside this room and she was expected to walk, in all her imperfection, to the bathroom in front of a man who was, this is awful, almost twenty years younger than herself. I am a cliché, she thought, but I don't feel like one. I don't feel worldly wise, I feel very young, and inexperienced, and intensely vulnerable. That is the one thing love can do, she thought. It makes you vulnerable, and it changes you utterly.

14

His fingerprints would be there forever on her skin.

Get on with it, she told herself sternly. But then, out of the corner of her eye, she spotted a hotel towel draped over the back of the chair by the bed. Camouflage. Reaching out, while breathing in as hard as she could, she grabbed the towel and, rising, she slid it sinuously round herself, tucking one end into the fold so it stayed in place. Wordlessly, she padded awkwardly to the bathroom and closed the door, then leant against it, relieved.

They'd left the bathroom light on all night because that had been the last thing on their minds, and all night the electronic fan had whirred incessantly, but she had not heard it. Now, it sounded deafeningly loud. The light inside was so bright, a harsh yellow neon.

In the mirror, her face was very pale beneath the tan, the bags under her eyes accentuated by the pitiless lighting. She smoothed her fingers over them, willing them to disappear. Make me young again. Make me the person I see in my mind. She stared at herself. Surely last night must have left some visible mark upon her? But she looked just the same – only her eyes were full of the memory. She shivered, brushed by angel's wings. The mascara she had applied the evening before, ready for their big night out, the last night in Cusco, was smudged, accentuating the dark shadows caused by lack of sleep. All the alcohol they had consumed, although she had drunk less than Nic and Katie, had left the insides of her eyes pink-rimmed and there was a horrid metallic taste in her mouth. She stuck out her tongue. It was yellow at the back, and furry, like a small dead hamster.

It was very odd. She felt as if she had to tell herself to do things – arm, reach out and lift up toothbrush, fingers, squeeze toothpaste. Hurry up, hurry up, she told herself. He might just leave. He might get out of bed, dress swiftly, and go downstairs to say goodbye to her friends and then disappear, back to his own life, without leaving a ripple. Another night, another conquest. But surely that would be the sensible thing to do? Then she could dress, and make herself look less awful, and pack everything up into the duffle bag and check the room and do things she had done a hundred times before, the woman who tidies, a normal kind of routine, and then she would drink coffee and be picked up from the hotel and be driven out to the airport through the streets of Cusco where she would try outwardly to be calm and mature, while scanning the people on the streets, so familiar to him, searching hopelessly for his face amidst his people. Knowing that she had done a dangerous thing, and she alone would pay. She was the foolish one, imagining there could be anything more to this than the passing thrill of conquest for him. She knew that, rationally, yet through her ran so many sensations long forgotten, teenage sensations of excitement, daring, powerful attraction. They were feelings experienced at the start of something new, but this could not be a start. It was as if something at the base of her, something she had thought long dead, had been stirred, unleashing a spiral of feeling which made every nerve tingle. She felt so alive. How would he feel, now that he had possessed her so totally? Was that enough, for him? Was sex all it was? Could she just – forget, leave the

16

memory behind, like a parcel neatly wrapped in this foreign hotel room?

She rinsed the bottled water round her mouth, and spat into the sink. How good she'd been, drinking nothing but bottled water all trip, just as he recommended. It was such fun, letting someone else be boss, especially someone so much younger. Like being a child again, away from the responsibility of her life where she was always in charge, responsible, and making decisions. It was so lovely to have someone else there to make the decisions for them. He had a natural air of authority despite his youth, and he seemed at ease in every situation – lecturing them solemnly on the history of the Incas, chatting in Quechua with the porters, in brief conversation in Spanish with other guides they passed on the trail and with receptionists in the hotels, the women flashing looks and smoothing their hair while he joked with them. Being with him was like stepping into the sun. He was their leader, and they followed him, giggling like schoolgirls, unleashed from the pressures of their everyday lives. But they were playing at it, a fantasy with clear parameters, just for now. Only last night she had stepped outside those parameters and she had no idea where she stood, and how she should carry this on. She knew – and she leant forward to stare at herself firmly – she had to let go now. Now, before she made a fool of herself. Neither of them had any kind of choice, and her future was already quite complicated enough.

Quickly, she packed everything into her sponge bag. Her make-up was in the bedroom, so she couldn't even cheat and put some mascara, eyeliner and lipstick on in here and come out pretending this was her real face. Anyway, after last night, she had nothing more to hide.

When she stepped out of the bathroom, clicking off the light, his smooth brown back was bent over on the far side of the bed, as he pulled his trousers on. They were grey, with big cargo pockets on the side. Tog trousers, in breathable fabric. He loved Western clothes, his designer labels. They set him apart from the other guides on the trail. His back, though broad, looked somehow defenceless, childish. He stood up, doing up the button on the waistband, and she thought how perfect he was, and how incongruous they would look together. He was a beautiful young man.

He turned round, feeling her gaze on him. He said nothing, and the look on his face told her he would make love to her if he could. He had done that to her so often, when there had seemed no way anything would ever happen, and she had laughed to herself about it, though alarmed too, what does he think he is doing? His gaze was pure sexuality, a challenge, a very blatant statement of intent, from which she had ducked, and fumbled, and made excuses. Until last night.

Now she had to stop this fantasy or else she would go mad. It had happened, it was over, full stop. Part of her longed for him to leave so she could think, sit in silence and try and make sense of what had happened. But she didn't have that luxury, there was no time. She had to start building the connection to her proper life and she turned away from him, and started stuffing the clothes from the floor into the duffle bag, not in her usual careful way but any old how. She felt his breath on the back of her neck, felt the warmth of his arms as he held her tightly.

He said nothing, and she relaxed against him for a moment, so secure in his arms, enjoying the hard masculine feel of him. It had not been a dream, and it had not been wrong. But it had to stop.

'Please,' she said, trying to break free, trying to wrest back control against the strongest feeling inside, to turn, to kiss and lose herself once more in him and be a lover.

No. She reached down to push clothes through the neck of the bag, trying to keep her mind on mundane things, where were her sunglasses, her passport? He tightened his grip, so she could not move. His face was against her back, and she could feel his soft lips, insistent, where the towel had slipped, arousing her. But there was no time.

'Sash? We're going to be really late. Why haven't you come down yet?'

Katie's voice through the door, full of concern, jokily cross.

'You're not puking, are you?'

'No. I'm fine. I'm still packing. Give me a mo.'

She waited until the footsteps had receded down the narrow hotel corridor.

'You have to stop,' she said, pushing him from her. This was ridiculous. 'Go.'

The word came out more brutally than she intended. His arms gripped her even more firmly, then stopped, paralysed.

Grabbing her sponge bag, she shoved it into the

duffle bag, and then wrenched the clothes she'd been wearing the night before off the floor, where he had thrown them. They hadn't dressed up to go out, because there seemed no point if he was not to be there, and they felt far more comfortable in their fleeces, trekking trousers, and walking boots. Make-up was the big concession to the night out. They wanted to stay in the same clothes, their uniform for the trek, because that way it stayed with them and was not about to end.

With the clothes under one arm, she pulled away from him and walked into the bathroom. She dressed swiftly, pulled a brush through her hair, and then opened the bathroom door, just as the door into the corridor clicked shut. He had gone. She flicked on the main light of the bedroom. It was a normal room again, an anonymous hotel bedroom with a heavy flowery bedcover on the floor, towels by the bed and the blank black screen of the television below the mirror.

It was as if he had never been there. There was simply an indentation on the pillow next to hers, a small, polite mark from a head which had lain so close to hers when they finally slept, arms, legs, entwined, so she did not know where she ended and he began. How very different from Alistair, who slept as if she was not there and did not matter. She and Miguel, a man who was little more than a stranger, had slept as lovers. She and the man who had shared her life for eighteen years slept as strangers. She put her hand to her face. Her skin felt warm, caressed. She was beautiful, in that moment.

*   *   *

She knew their relationship was never going to be easy as soon as she first encountered him in the cool dark reception area of their hotel, where he was sitting in a large, sumptuous leather armchair, waiting for them, photocopied details about the trip spread out in front of him on the polished mahogany table. He had sprung to his feet, his hand outstretched, and she thought, 'Oh, no.'

There had been a sudden jolt, something she had absolutely not been expecting. He was so beautiful, so charming and so flirtatious. In a way, he was the cliché. How could someone with forty-two years of life experience behind her be vulnerable in that way? As she shook his hand she felt herself becoming flustered, her face red, and her hands shaking. He had caught her eye, and smiled at her, impossibly white teeth in his face, skin the colour of smooth milk chocolate. He's enjoying this, she had thought, he's well aware of the effect he has on women. But why me? Why single me out for that instant eye contact which says, 'I find you attractive'? Katie was younger, much more obviously pretty and far more flirtatious. It made no sense. Nicola was her usual matter-of-fact self and didn't even seem to notice the effect he was having on both her and Katie, who had caught her eye and flashed a 'wow' look at her. They would laugh about it later, when he'd gone. 'Good job we're all married,' Katie would say. 'But hey, bags I be the first to shag the sherpa.'

Sasha had hoped, while she walked the trail, that she would get used to him, and this attraction or whatever it was would wear off because it was deeply silly and it had nowhere to go. It would just be useful, as a joke between them, something to lighten the days as they walked the arduous trail, a girly joke they could share and laugh about in their tent at night. This doesn't happen to me, she had thought, as his eyes held hers for a beat too long. I am too old for this.

There. She surveyed the empty room. Everything's packed and all I need to do now is open the door, close it, walk downstairs, meet my friends and – go. Get on the aeroplane and fly to Lima from Cusco and then wait at the hotel there for almost a day and then get on the plane to Heathrow and be home after a long and exhausting flight, and yes, life will be a bit bumpy for a while but it will all settle down and I will go back to being my normal self and this will just have been a fascinating trip. A memory. Mine is not a life built for adventure, it does not allow for reckless things to happen. I have too many responsibilities and they are all at home, lying in wait for me, full of reproach at my two weeks of freedom. Nothing will have changed. We'll meet up for supper and look at the photographs and our husbands will tease us about shirking our responsibilities and groan when we say we are plan-ning to trek the Himalayas next year. No-one will look at me and think that Sasha, reliable, dependable mother-of-two Sasha, had spent a night of supreme and reckless passion with a beautiful twenty-four-year-old. The thought made her laugh out loud. Imagine the shock, the outrage. But this – this madness – will never happen again. It will be buried, and left, here. I have no choice.

She pulled the duffle bag up to her shoulder. It felt unbearably heavy. The poor porters, loaded down with three of these plus all the tents and the pots and pans. Not to mention the chemical loo. While the three of them had laboured along behind Miguel, the porters had sped on ahead to set up their lunch tents and then the camp for each night on the route, their flat brown feet in dusty sandals slapping along the paving stones of the trail, up and down the steep steps cut into the mountains, always at a jogtrot, never pausing or stopping for breath as the tourists had to do. Of course they had been born here, were well used to the altitude and their lungs were acclimatized to the thin, high air. They were sinewy and strong, with not an ounce of fat on their bodies, but their faces were prematurely lined with the grinding poverty in which they lived, the responsibility they had of bringing back the handful of dollars to make sure they could buy clothes for their children, and extra food not provided from their own meagre smallholdings tended by their wives while they were out on the trail.

They had passed many of these smallholdings while they walked, and, especially in the rain, she had wondered how you lived like that and smiled. The houses were a haphazard collection of stones, the floor inside the one- or two-roomed house earthen, which threw up dust in the summer, mud in the winter. Outside, a small pig squealed and ran about among the pecking chickens. The family llama grazed nearby, tethered and aristocratic. Children, dressed in brightly coloured handwoven jumpers and dusty shorts, played in the dirt, chased chickens or shyly held their hands out for a few sols, or, much better, dollars.

This was Miguel's world. True, he had a foot in the Western world, having been educated at university in Cusco and travelled outside Peru – a rarity for most citizens – but this was his culture. He was so proud of his country and he spoke passionately of his people and their history. He could talk, literally for hours, about thousands of years of the history of Peru, and tell the stories he had grown up hearing from his schoolteacher father, a musician and storyteller himself. They had sat at his feet in the candlelit tent, like rapt schoolchildren, as he weaved his tales of magical condors and great llamas in the sky which had saved warriors and foretold wars. I am an educated man, he told them, smiling, but one day I will become a *campasino*, a peasant, grow my hair long down my back and go to live on my family farm, build a house and marry the local girl who is promised to me. They had teased him about that, about the poor girl waiting at home for him in the hills, while he escorted trekkers along the trail. Did she think he would ever return? And he smiled and said, yes, she knew he would because she had been promised to him from birth. He enjoyed his foreign trips, to Europe, to America, but his heart would never leave. But would he marry? they persisted. He paused, teasing. Perhaps. If she was not so fat, he joked. They did not know whether to believe him.

And while he was speaking, in his heavily accented musical voice, with its odd idioms, he would catch her eye and send her that heavy, dangerous message again, and again. 'I want you. I cannot believe you do not want me. What harm will it do?' A message she had ignored until it became impossible to do so. 'Can you really resist me?' his eyes said to her.

Last night they had all joked that they could not let him go. He was 'theirs', and they were going to smuggle him home on the plane to England, like an exotic pet. But of course that would not work. He belonged here, as he said. He could never leave. He had a duty to stay here. His people. How often he used that phrase, how oddly. 'His people.' She remembered the night he had told her how in love his parents were, and how very much he wanted that for himself. While he talked, his eyes held hers and she thought, 'What are you saying to me?' He confused her, she could not work him out. Did he make a habit of this, singling out a woman in his party, testing his charm like the point of a blade against the skin, to see if she would yield?

Why, he said teasingly, did their husbands not mind them coming away on a trip like this, alone? Did they not miss them? Katie replied quickly that her husband would miss her, very much, but he knew this trip would make her happy and he wanted to please her. Nic said she and her husband often travelled separately as they had different interests and hobbies, and having been married as long as they had, they had no fear of separation. Sasha said nothing. Her life was much more complicated than that, and Miguel had looked at her quizzically. He knows, she thought. He knows why I am silent.

I wonder, she thought. I wonder if I was simply the easiest target, the most vulnerable? The thought made her shiver. But she knew in her heart it was not true.

There had been an instant connection between them, a chemistry, although she could not explain why. She was attractive, but not in Katie's league. She was no richer than the others and anyway he had shown no interest in their money. He had chosen her for his own mysterious reasons. Well, it was too late now. She could not undo what she had done.

She pulled the hotel door closed behind her, the computerized card in her hand. They'd settled up the bill the night before, which had been easy because they hadn't eaten in the hotel and had had no drinks. There was no time, arriving in a rush from the train from Machu Picchu, Katie so keen to get out and do that last bit of shopping for jewellery and soft alpaca sweaters and presents. A preparation, a way of smoothing their passage from this extraordinary journey into their lives at home. Then the last supper at the Inca Grill, convivial and noisy, all of them still high on the adrenalin of the trip, faintly hysterical at the thought of going home. Being here was like being woven into a fantasy, where anything could happen as normal life had been suspended. Now reality loomed and all three were unsure how everything they had been through on the trail would translate into the reality of their everyday existence. How could you go from the romance, the danger and the sheer grandeur of the Inca Trail to accepting a life of school runs and supermarket queues? How could you not be changed for ever by what you had seen and experienced? Sasha comforted herself with the thought that, at least, it would always be there, a time capsule in her mind, a space in which she only had to delve to see herself once more standing, looking out over a range of mountains stretching as far as the eye could see, snow-capped, remote, quite alone, on the top of the world. And everything she had to do, seemingly so important, or stressful, or worrying at the time, would be thrown into sharp relief for what it was – nothing – against that enduring vision.

All last night she had looked for him as they sat in the restaurant, the silent square overshadowed by the vast and ornate Spanish-built cathedral. No sign, no sign, until they returned to the hotel and he was there, waiting for her.

The corridor was empty, and silent. She walked slowly, borne down by the weight of the bag, her mind full of him. At the lift, she turned to look for him. There was no-one, a void with closed doors behind which room after room of travellers slept. The mirror at the back of the lift reflected a face caught between youth and age. Normally when she looked at herself she was checking for signs of age. Now she was check-ing for signs of guilt. It was a kind of progress, she thought, and laughed inwardly. Whenever she looked at herself from now on, she wouldn't look for im-perfection, but try to see herself through his eyes, the way he had looked at her last night. When he desired her. She had been wanted. Not useless. A man who looked like a god had wanted her.

She tucked her dark hair behind her ear, and smiled, her eyes bright, brimful of secret pleasure. She wished she'd time for a shower – she felt sticky and her skin smelt of his sweat. She brought the back of her hand up to her face and breathed deeply. Closing her eyes,

27

she could see him, as he entered the room, pushing her roughly back against the wall, frantic, male, overpowering. She was overcome with longing – why had she pushed him away just now? She might never be able to touch him again and the thought made her want to cry. She had not felt like this for so many years, the desperate need to be held by someone. It was the security and affirmation that you were needed, not just desire. She had forgotten how it felt, that all-consuming need to touch, to be entwined so you do not know where one ends, and the other begins. An attraction as powerful as addiction.

The foyer of the hotel was a bustle of activity. Other early morning travellers were milling about, checking their tickets and passports, tetchy at having to get up so early and querulous at the thought of the long flight home. In the middle a harassed-looking porter stood, trying to match up tickets from the security room with lost luggage. Most were American tourists in their impeccable beige trekking outfits. Next to them Sasha felt thrown together, untidy, but then at least she had actually walked the trail, rather than taken the train and done it the easy way.

The restaurant was tucked down a corridor away from the foyer, one wall ornately carved out of wood, looking out on a garden with a fountain in the centre of the hotel. This was one of only two five-star hotels in Cusco, but she didn't like it as much as the first they had stayed at, it was much bigger, more international, the immense reception area like an airport lounge. But then the first hotel had held the promise of the trip to come.

Katie and Nic were sitting at the far end of the restaurant, their bags at their feet, drinking coffee and chatting. They looked so resolutely normal that for a brief moment Sasha wondered if she had imagined it all. She fought a very strong urge to turn and run. He was not there, as she had thought he might be. As he had said goodnight to them last night, pretending that he was about to leave while she knew otherwise, he had said he would return this morning to bid them a final farewell and see them safely onto the minibus which would take them to the airport to fly to Lima. They didn't look up, not hearing her approach, and as she sat down, she realized her hands were trembling. She hid them under the table.

'Oh, hi. You made it, then,' Katie said ironically, looking at her searchingly, and she felt a blush rising from her neck. She couldn't meet her eyes because she felt as if she had 'I slept with Miguel' stamped on her forehead. Surely there was some visible sign of her sin? Katie and Nic were two of her closest friends, and to tell them would mean it would hang in the air, a forever-shared secret, making them partners in guilt. They would worry for her, want to discuss it, and she now realized that she did not want anybody, ever, to share this experience. It was just for her.

'Are you feeling OK?' Katie eyed her closely. Something was up. Over the week on the trail they had told each other everything, things they'd never told anyone before, and while having been an enlightening if traumatic experience, it made Sasha feel naked. She wasn't usually one for soul-baring, and letting down her defences to that extent made this very hard to hide.

Katie reached out and held her hand. To Sasha's horror, tears rose in her eyes. She felt suddenly overwhelmed – last night, the thought of going home, Alistair. Most of all she dreaded the loss of self, the person she had discovered was still in there, after all. 'You daft thing,' Katie said. 'It won't be that bad.'

'I know.' Sasha wiped away the tears, embarrassed. 'Don't set me off.' They both laughed, and Katie squeezed her hand, holding it up between them. 'Remember what we promised. Never again. Whatever you decide, we're with you.'

'Anyone fancy any more juice?' Nic pushed her chair away from the table. Katie and Sasha exchanged a glance. Now they knew what was going on, it was very hard to accept she could remain so calm and practical, as if nothing touched her. Her body language this morning was back to being defensive, studiedly matter-of-fact. But they understood that being organized to the last degree was Nic's way of coping with a double life.

As she walked away from the table, Katie leant forward and hissed, theatrically, 'Do you think she regrets it?'

'Sssh. What?'

'Telling us,' she said, urgently. 'I can't . . . Oh, thanks, Nic.' Nic put down two glasses of orange on the table and looked at her watch. 'We ought to be going.'

'I thought we were going to wait for Miguel,' Katie protested.

'Well, he's not here, is he?' Nic said. At first she'd been amused by Katie and Sasha's obsession with him, but now she made her irritation clear.

'No! But he promised. I wanted just one last kiss goodbye.' Katie ran her hands through her blond hair. 'Christ, my hair's sticky. Yack, I wish you'd let me have a shower. She is such a martinet,' Katie grinned at Sasha. 'But no, we were going to be late, weren't we? Now I have to fly home with a Cornish pasty on my head. I really cannot imagine . . . Oh, look! Here he is.' She arranged an attractive smile on her red-lipsticked lips and lifted her hair from behind her ears. Sasha's stomach fell away, as she half turned to look at him.

He was strolling towards them, moving easily between the tables, tight white T-shirt showing off his muscular chest and flat stomach, the grey baggy trekking trousers fashionably low-slung on his hips, a pale grey sweatshirt knotted carelessly around his neck. Sasha noticed how every woman's eyes in the restaurant followed his languid animal grace. When he was within feet of them, she hastily looked down, peering intently at the coffee cup she held in her shaking hands. There was a heat between them so intense she didn't need to look up to know how close to her he was standing. She felt him, with a primeval sense, and was faint with longing. God, how had she resisted him for so long? She concentrated hard on the centimetre of coffee left in the cup, composing herself, so she could look up without the face of a woman possessed. But as soon as she glanced up his eyes caught hers, and all hope of composure was lost. His mouth curved into a wicked smile, and his dark, almost black, eyes glinted at her from under his curling lashes. He should not be allowed out, she thought.

How could the other two not sense the signals flashing backwards and forwards between them?

'And how are you ladies this morning?' he said, his eyes holding Sasha's. That was how he talked to them, half-mocking, half-reverential, effortlessly and charmingly bridging the gulf between his authority and his employee status. He chivvied them, and teased, but on the trail they all knew he was in charge, because it was so dangerous with high narrow passes through the ravines, nothing between them and a sheer drop of thousands of feet. He made them drink a lot of water, forced them to rest even when they were not tired, looking out for any sign of altitude sickness. And always he was watchful for something which would interest them, a parrot with fantastic, rainbow-coloured plumage or the rare sighting of a wild black bear, a smudge of dark against the greens and browns of the far hillside. The perfect guide. Effortlessly he would swap between English and Quechua, speaking to the porters. He spoke eight languages fluently.

'No wine?' they had said, the first night, when the rudimentary eating tent was erected, and they'd squeezed in under the canvas flap, the rain drumming incessantly on the concave roof. The table was a small, wobbly square and they sat on canvas chairs close to each other around it, their knees touching. Sasha was careful never to place herself next to him, did not want to touch him. Even then, when the whole thing was a joke and something she was clearly imagining, she did not want to put herself in the path of temptation. Anyway, sitting opposite him, it was easier to watch him, watch the stunning whiteness of his teeth as he flashed his charming smile, watch how he controlled the conversation, brought them back to the subject when they veered off into frivolity, how he sat back with a half-puzzled, patient expression on his face when they started discussing friends they knew at home, when the conversation reverted to their usual pattern, of gossip and schools, children and love affairs among people they knew. He liked to be the ringmaster, staging each night, and Sasha suspected he even planned each topic of conversation to keep them entertained. He never had a night off, until last night in Machu Picchu, when he had stayed away from them.

He had been horrified at the suggestion of wine. 'How will we manage?' Katie said. 'No alcohol?'

'But no,' he said. 'We have a very early start each morning and you do not want to have drunk wine.'

'Do you drink much?'

'An occasional beer,' he said. 'I do not care for it. Do you drink at home?'

They looked at each other, not sure quite how much to reveal. They all liked to drink, for various reasons. Katie was a party animal, who liked to turn every night into a social occasion. She and Nic had wondered how their livers would cope over the two weeks. Nic drank wine with her husband every night too in a civilized grown-up manner, with no more than half a bottle on a weekday night. Sasha drank too, most nights, but worried far more than Nic or Katie about it. It worried her how much she needed a glass of wine, by seven or eight every night, and how she found it hard to think about anything else until it was in front of her and then she could relax. She knew that she used alcohol as a barrier between herself and Alistair, pretending it was a link, that they both enjoyed their bottle of wine in the evening and it gave them a chance to talk. In fact, it gave them a chance to become someone else. Alcohol smoothed out their edges and made them acceptable to each other. Then they could sleep.

'Have you time for a coffee?' Katie said, smiling at him winningly.

Miguel looked at his watch. 'OK. Why not?' He drew up a chair from a neighbouring table, and sat down next to Sasha. She had to physically stop herself from touching him, and as he reached forward for the sugar bowl he slid his foot against hers, the gentle pressure intensely sexual. 'We have about ten minutes until Ernesto comes to take you to the airport.' He looked at his watch again. 'Eleven minutes,' he said. Katie and Nic laughed. That was one of their jokes on the trail, how precise he was about timings and how he hated order to be disrupted. He was very methodical for a young man, which was part of his surprising maturity. One night Katie had said, lying idly on her back in her sleeping bag, bored stiff at having to go to bed at nine and longing for a drink, 'D'you think he's ever been really wild?'

'In what way?' Sasha turned over, with difficulty, onto her stomach. Lying in a sleeping bag was like being encased in a worm. It had to go with you wherever you went, and at night she would get twizzled up in it, knotted around her legs as she tried to get comfortable.

'You know, in a twenty-ish bloke kind of way. Going out getting pissed, picking up women, going to nightclubs.'

'Well, there aren't exactly many nightclubs in Cusco, are there?' she said, practically.

'But he's so controlled, don't you think? It's kind of spooky.' Katie slammed shut the book she was reading, a guide to Peru which managed to be both fascinating and very dull simultaneously, and put it down on the bumpy canvas of their floor sheet. 'He's so self-contained. I think he's got something to hide. He's a real dark horse.'

'What could he have to hide? A fourteen-year-old bride?'

'Quite possibly. I mean, why hasn't he got a girlfriend? He's gorgeous, and so clever. The local girls must be gagging for him.'

'He has a bride promised to him, remember. In his home village.'

A dreamy look came over Katie's face. 'Bet he finds her really boring, though. And have you noticed how fat the women get here? They're absolutely stunning as young girls and then, blam. They get married, have kids, and turn into little fat squat things with those voluminous skirts and wizened faces. Not much of a future for him, is it?'

'Why do you care?' Sasha said. 'We're only interested in him because we're trapped out here with him for a week. We'll forget about him the moment we get on the plane.'

'I wonder.' Katie was laughing now, her eyes wide.

'What?'

'I wonder what he would do if you did tiptoe down to his tent and unzip it and say, "Hi Miguel, did you really mean it?" I think he'd be horrified and he'd run a mile. I think he's still a virgin.'

'Oh, don't be silly. He's twenty-four. He's definitely not a virgin.'

'How do you know?' Katie peered at her closely, her head-torch shining in Sasha's face like an interrogation lamp.

'One little tip,' Sasha said. 'If you are planning to mosey on down to his tent and attempt to seduce him I would advise you to take that thing off your head. It isn't exactly sexy. It makes you look like a potholer.'

'I quite like it,' Katie said. 'It's like having your own personal light.' She aimed it at the wall of the tent. 'Now I can see. I am the light.'

'You are the stupid git,' Sasha said, turning over huffily. 'Now stop tormenting me with details of Miguel's existent or non-existent love life and let me read my book.'

'What are you reading?'

'*Bridehead Revisited*. It soothes me.'

'Blimey,' Katie said. It was a running joke between them that Sasha was the clever one, and Katie's brain was made of designer fluff.

'Miguel's got the hots for you.' Katie tossed this out casually.

'Utter rubbish,' Sasha said. 'If he's going to fancy anyone it will be you.' Katie smiled to herself. Of course it should be. She was much prettier, and she normally attracted men like moths to a flame, with her helpless wide-eyed act. But she was very good at picking up other people's signals, and it was Sasha he looked at. Odd, and rather fascinating.

'Will you two shut up?' Nic's voice was muffled

36

from the next tent. 'I am trying to get to sleep and all I can hear is you two going on like a pair of teenagers.'

'Goodnight Mum,' Katie called out.

'Goodnight children.'

'We're fine, thank you. Why, did we seem rather drunk last night?' Katie said, grinning.

'A little,' he smiled. 'But why not? It was your last night.'

'Will you miss us?'

'But yes, of course,' he said.

Nic regarded him sardonically. 'Until the next party arrives. Let's hope there are some young women for you.'

'You are young,' he said, mock-horrified, smiling. 'I cannot replace you just like that. We are a team.'

'I've forgotten something in my room.' Sasha blurted out the words clumsily, and stood up suddenly, knocking over her cup. He reached out and caught it, his reactions razor-sharp. His hand just missed hers. She could not be this close to him, and not touch him. She was galloping towards a precipice, and she was quite powerless to stop herself going over. Being near him was just prolonging the agony. Let the parting be swift, and brutal. It was no more than she deserved.

'I'll see you at the front door,' she said. Still she couldn't look at him, and she half walked, half ran out of the restaurant, her movement and dignity impeded by the heavy bag. Would he follow her? No. It would be too obvious. She looked back when she could no longer be seen, and he was leaning back on his chair, drinking his coffee, smiling, perfectly relaxed. How little he seemed to care, how little of himself he gave away.

She stood in the foyer, and took a deep breath. It was time to move on, and she had to collect herself. What had he said? That they had nothing more to prove, that last night would have to be enough for both of them. How? How could you have such amazing sex and then forget? A porter came up to her. 'Can I help you?'

'No, I'm fine,' she said. A familiar figure walked towards her. Ernesto, the guide who had brought them from the airport to their first hotel, and was now due to escort them back again, their holiday all but finished.

'Where are the others?' he said, smiling pleasantly.

'Just coming.'

'Let me take your bag.' He lifted the heavy duffle bag off her shoulder, and headed towards the minibus she could see parked outside the hotel. It was only a quarter to seven in the morning, but already the streets were filling up with people, children on their way to school in a ragtag of uniforms, women in traditional dress carrying babies, ready to position themselves around the main square to beg from the tourists, old men sitting on the edge of the pavement, rocking backwards and forwards as they smoked their pipes, staring into the sky. A small boy was herding a goat down the street, tapping its flanks as he made his way towards the market, and awnings were being unfurled, goods put out onto the street ready to entice the tourists into the network of stalls and tiny shops, stuffed to the rooftop with multicoloured handmade alpaca and wool jumpers, the endless fluffy toy llamas and beautiful Inca reproduction jewellery.

She made a last mental checklist of all her possessions, and unzipped her backpack to make sure she had her neat leather folder which contained her passport, airline tickets and schedule. She hurried behind Ernesto, and climbed into the minibus. She heard them approaching, Katie laughing, Miguel's low voice. The two women piled their bags into the back, and they too climbed in. Miguel leant in the door. 'A kiss,' Katie said. She leant towards him and he pressed his lips against her cheek, avoiding her mouth. 'Nic?' he said. 'I'll pass,' she said, smiling. 'But thank you so much. You have made this trip memorable,' she added, formally.

'I aim to please, as you know,' he said, his lips curling into a smile. 'Goodbye, Sasha.' She would have given anything to avoid this moment. Intensely aware that all eyes were on her, she took a firm hold of her galloping emotions and looked directly at him. His eyes were laughing, just as they had when he'd first taken her hand. He was telling her not to worry. That no-one would know, that it was their secret, that there was no point in remorse. It had been fun. They had both needed each other and that was enough. She would be strong, and she would be happy. His eyes also said that last night was remarkable, and she felt herself beginning to drown again in his wickedness. No, her eyes flashed at him. Stop. He smiled, and pulled her forward towards him, and she felt again his hot skin and the touch of his hand. 'Goodbye, Sasha,' he breathed into her ear. 'Thank you. I will not forget.'

Then he released her, and she had to stop herself from reaching out to hold onto him, curling her hand into a ball, the nails digging into her palm. He stood back, and started to slide the minibus door closed. She stared at him, desperate to memorize every contour of his face. Then he stopped, as if he had just re-membered something. 'My card,' he said, pulling his wallet out of his back pocket. 'Please hand on to your friends,' he said, giving them one each, 'and recom-mend me to anyone who is coming to Peru. I hope you have enjoyed yourselves, and I would love for you to come again.'

Sasha took the proffered card, and studied the embossed writing. It looked professional, and European. There was his email address, his mobile phone number. She looked again at his name, his full name. His eyes never left hers as he raised his fingers to his lips, as if to blow them a farewell kiss, or to bid her silence. Because he knew she understood, finally, just who he was.

'Ciao,' he said, casually. He let his fingers rest on his lips, while his eyes never left hers.

The door clicked shut, the barrier between them now physical, a reality. He was gone from her. It was as if she had stepped out of the sun, into a dark place. Never again. Katie leaned forward and peered at her around the seat.

'Was that desperately hard?' Her voice was teasing, but her eyes held a question.

'Don't be idiotic,' Sasha said, a surprising sense of calm flooding through her. 'And before you ask, no, I will not miss him. I am a very grown-up person who knows when she is a passing fancy. There will be someone else for him, on the next trip. You don't think

I'm that naïve, surely? Anyway, nothing happened. My conscience is quite clear.'

'You've really caught the sun this week,' Katie said, as Ernesto started the minibus. 'You look great.'

'Thanks,' she said, leaning back against the warmth of the seat, hugging herself, the joy of being so desired a deep glow within her. No-one could ever take this away, whatever happened. 'I feel like I have caught the sun.'

Chapter Two

'No, no, no. How much clearer can I be? No, no, no. N.O. I do not want my wife to go to darkest Peru, like Paddington Bear in reverse.'

Alistair's voice was joking, but the smile did not reach his eyes. He really did not want her to go, and Sasha knew he was on the point of losing control, of saying something awkward and truthful which would drop like a heavy rock into the smooth, polite surface of the dinner-party conversation. The fact that Katie was teasing him made him worse, he hated to be made fun of, even by someone so beautiful, and he was still raw from the previous night.

'The point is,' he continued, 'she is not going. You two useless, spineless articles may let your wives roam around the world pretending to be explorers, spending money and abdicating their familial responsibilities, but I won't.'

Around the table, uproar. It was Alistair being chauvinistically Victorian, taking a deliberately contentious stance towards the personal freedom of his wife, while both Nic and Katie's husbands wouldn't have dreamt of needing to give permission for a holiday. Their wives' plans for the trip were simply that, plans. To Alistair, the trip had meant just one thing – a desire for escape. Everyone but Sasha thought he was joking, that no-one could try to control another person like that. But she knew different. If she escaped his control, she might never return.

'You don't mean that,' Katie said, widening her baby-blue eyes in mock horror. 'How can you tell her what to do in this day and age? Sasha! Stand up for yourself. Don't be such a wimp.'

They'd all had a lot to drink, and the atmosphere was boisterous, convivial. Only Sasha hadn't drunk too much, aware of where the evening was heading and knowing that things with Alistair could too easily tip from joking banter into something much more dangerous. At the moment, it felt like they were living on a knife's edge, the slightest thing enough to tip the balance. Especially after last night.

He'd been drinking after work, just a couple, but enough to make him tetchy, quick to criticize. When he walked into the house, banging down his overnight bag on the floor, she knew from his face she should tread carefully. She retreated into the kitchen and busied herself opening a bottle of red wine. She heard him walk into the television room to find the children slumped in their normal position in front of *Sabrina the Teenage Witch*. 'For Christ's sake switch it off,' she could hear him saying, crossly. 'Can't you two think of anything else to do? I'm sick of coming in and finding you endlessly watching TV.' There was an indeterminate mumble, as they resentfully flicked off the television, and then Sasha heard Abbie bang up the stairs, followed by Emily's quick footsteps. Abbie's bedroom door slammed and she heard, 'No you can't. Use your own CD player. Tough.' She bent her head over the bottle as he walked into the kitchen.

'Have you got anything for dinner?' He took off his jacket and hung it over the back of a kitchen chair, taking out his wallet and cigarettes, placing them on the dresser. His entire body spoke of exhaustion and stress, his handsome face creased and weary, his eyes red-veined.

'Of course I have. A beef thing, it's in the oven. Horrid day?'

'Knackering. Then I met Tim on the tube and he suggested we go for a drink.'

'Fine.'

'What do you mean, fine? I don't need your permission.'

'I know you don't.'

'I invited them both for dinner tomorrow, we can manage eight round the table, can't we? What's this?'

She looked over at him, lifting two glasses down from the top cupboard. 'Just a bill, why?'

'You're not going to pay them, are you? Not when they've been three times and it isn't even fixed?'

Sasha thought, I will keep calm. 'I've told you. They can't find the problem, it just keeps locking out.'

'Well why the fuck are we paying them hundreds of pounds each time for them to tell us they can't find the problem?'

'I'll ring them tomorrow. Sit down and have a glass

of wine.' She handed him the glass, making sure her fingers did not touch his. He looked about him, subconsciously hunting for an outlet for the stress of the day. A day in which he'd been told another contract would not be renewed.

'Can't you make the kids clear up after themselves?' He gestured at the long kitchen table, the far end overflowing with the usual family detritus of newspapers, magazines, homework, catalogues and a tennis ball. 'Why are they still up, anyway? They've got school tomorrow, for God's sake.'

Oh go away, Sasha thought, looking at his tired face, his loosened tie, his trembling hands on the stem of his glass. Why do you take everything out on us? It is not our fault that your job is so stressful, that you feel every day is a constant battle. I have tried, and tried, to be a support to you, but you treat me as if my feelings are irrelevant, do not matter. When was the last time you asked me how I was? I am so tired of being your buffer zone. It was funny, how many of her friends thought she was so lucky to have attractive, amusing, dryly entertaining Alistair. But they never saw the man behind closed doors, never measured the gulf between them as they lay adrift in the marriage bed, each wondering the same thing but never saying it aloud. 'How much longer can I live like this and not go mad?'

Just looking at him made her tense, and she dreaded the sound of his key in the door. It meant she had to slip the mask back in place, and be a person she neither liked nor admired, the person he had formed over sixteen years of marriage. I could reach out to

45

you, she thought. But I daren't. I'm too scared of being hurt. Too much has happened, too much has been said over too many years to try to breach that gulf. They both knew what the underlying problem was. He still loved her but could no longer show it in a way which meant anything to her, had used her as the whipping boy for his worries and disregarded her feelings, until irreparable damage had been done. And then when he wanted her, needed her, she was not, could not, be there for him, and he could not take the rejection. To love, you must be prepared to be vulnerable to that person, she thought. It is a trust not to be hurt, and when that trust is broken and self-confidence has gone, you cannot expose yourself in that way again.

Instead of supporting each other, they chipped away at each other's foundations, but it brought them no pleasure. No-one won. They each thought they were the victim. They still made love, occasionally, but it was mechanical and cold. Each time he lost his temper with her, each time he said a hurtful thing, each time he took out his frustrations on her, a tiny piece of what remained of her love for him died and made her less vulnerable. And he saw this and her growing independence, her invulnerability, made him insecure, resentful and angry. She could not see how much he needed her and that he did not want anyone else. And so the merry-go-round turned, playing its sad, relentless music.

'I picked up some holiday brochures,' he said, gesturing at his bag back in the hall. 'Italy. I should think we can just afford it.'

Sasha said nothing, and bit her lip. That would

46

make plans for Peru even more tricky, if he wanted them to go on an expensive summer holiday. She would be the selfish one, spending money on just herself. Five years ago she had thought that a holiday would make everything better, but it was only moving one set of problems into a different environment. And she dreaded holidays more than anything else, because it was a time when you should be happy. I long for peace and freedom, she thought. Space in which I can lie in the sun, alone, and not have to take anyone else's feelings into account. I just want to *be* for a while, on my own.

'What do you think about Italy? The girls would love it.'

'Fine.'

'Can't you show a bit more enthusiasm?' He was watching her carefully.

'All right.' She lifted the casserole out of the oven, and levered off the lid, a puff of steam escaping. She took the plates from the top shelf of the oven and put one down in front of him. 'Yes. Italy would be very nice,' she said, cautiously.

'Nice?' he goaded her.

'What do you want me to say? It would be fantastic, wonderful, marvellous? Thank you so much for thinking of us?' The words slipped out, frustration at not being able to say what she really felt, that two weeks trapped in a villa with him, trying to pretend to be happy, would be absolute torture. Holidays were a merciless exposer of the flaws in a relationship. She regretted the sarcasm immediately. She had handed him the free gift of a catalyst.

'Oh for fuck's sake,' he exploded. 'Why are you so impossible? I thought, I really thought, that you'd be pleased I was trying to arrange something we could look forward to, but that isn't good enough, is it? I have no idea what you want. What do you want? I say I'm planning a holiday for us all and you hit me with bile. You tell me I don't talk to you, that I don't spend enough time with the children, that I'm too wrapped up in my own problems and don't give a shit about anybody else and yet when I make an effort you make me feel like a complete idiot, as if I'm forcing you to come away with me. Don't you want to? What do you want to do? Go on holiday with a girlfriend? Take the children away on your own? I'm their father, for God's sake, I want to be with them. Or maybe you want to go on some self-awareness holiday with a load of dykes to crap on about how useless men are.'

She looked at him pityingly. She knew exactly what he was trying to do. He was being deliberately sexist and outrageous to provoke a reaction from her, but he'd done this so often, trying to snatch her up into a whirlwind of emotion to force that inner person out, that vulnerable person he needed her to be. She was not falling for that one. Staying calm was the best revenge. 'I'm sorry,' she said. 'I didn't mean it to come out like that.' If she said nothing, did not react, they would eat, and watch television, and sleep, and she could look forward to the modicum of happiness she had carved into her life, the children, the house, the garden, their friends.

'Maybe I should just leave. Maybe we're just prolonging the agony.' She stared at him, shocked. He had called her bluff. She never wanted him to go this far. It was better for the children to have him here, whatever the cost.

'Don't be stupid, I don't . . .' She was amazed he had said it.

'Don't you? You're so desperate to get away, on this irresponsible, phenomenally expensive Peru trip, but you have no interest in planning a holiday for us. Our life. Do you remember what that is, or is it not important any more? I'm so tired of you being so selfish and useless. You think it's perfectly acceptable just to fuck off on some whim and leave me in the lurch for two weeks at a fucking awful time at work . . .' He banged the plate in front of him down on the table. There was a stunned silence.

Abbie stood in the doorway. 'Do you two have to shout all the time?'

'I wasn't shouting, darling,' Sasha said. 'Daddy and I were just having a discussion about the summer holiday.'

'It didn't sound like it. It's like living in World War Two. Can't you just talk to each other like normal people?' She looked at them, her beautiful face deceptively calm.

That was it, really, wasn't it? Sasha thought. They should be able to talk to each other like normal people but they couldn't. Everything meant something else, a subtext, a flashpoint.

'Have you tidied your room?' Sasha said, trying to keep her voice steady.

'Oh, that matters, doesn't it?'

Alistair said nothing, staring down at his paper. He

49

wants this to be my fault, Sasha thought bitterly, although I didn't start any of it. She moved forward, but Abbie stepped away swiftly, her arms wrapped around her thin body. 'I just wish . . .' she said.

'What?'

'I just wish I could live with parents who weren't constantly at each other's throats. I wish I could just leave.'

'Abbie, don't be ridiculous, it was just a silly little argument.'

'He called you useless.' Her voice was bitter, appalled.

'He didn't mean it, it's just one of those things you say . . .'

'I think you're pathetic,' Abbie said, clearly. 'Grovelling round him to try to keep the peace.' Alistair took a long drink of wine and turned a page. Abbie looked at him savagely. 'You let him get away with it. I wouldn't take that crap. Why do you let him walk all over you?' Because of you, Sasha thought. Because of you.

'This isn't your battle,' she said.

'Isn't it?' She glared at both of them, and turned to go, her too-long jeans slapping on the wooden hallway floor, leaving behind her a silence in which the truth hung in the air, but could not be said.

'Thanks so much for your support,' she said, angrily, to Alistair. He was sitting, his arms patiently folded over his striped work shirt. He had achieved his objective, he had forced her to react. Now he was prepared to be magnanimous in her defeat.

'I'm not going to interfere,' he said, with irritating

calm. 'If you think it's fine for the children to talk to you like that then you can take the consequences. I've had it up to here. Time and time again I have said that if you aren't prepared to give them any kind of discipline then they'll speak to you in any way they like. They have the better of you, and they know it.'

'You started all this!' she shouted. 'If you hadn't started this row by saying such appalling things to me then Abbie wouldn't have heard us fighting. She has a right, you know, to express her opinions and she isn't going to take the crap I will. You can't treat her like you treat me, she's not just another me coming through who can be bullied. If you carry on behaving like this you will lose her.' And me, she thought. She took a deep breath. Oh, sod it. She had every right to let go. 'You cannot barge in and create a drama and then just retreat and blame everyone else. All you can see are your problems, your bloody business, and you think you can make it all right by offering me a little holiday like some ditsy stupid housewife. Day after day we are expected to walk on eggshells around you because you are the one with the big problem, you are the one who matters. I've had it. Do you really wonder why I want to escape from you? Being with you is like living with . . . like living with a dead person who just sucks in the happiness around him and turns it sour. You're dragging me down with you and I am so very tired of pretending that everything in our lives is OK, when it's . . .'

'How you love drama,' he said, with the same agonizing, infuriating calm, and made as if to reopen the paper. 'If you've finished, can we eat?'

'Jesus wept!' she yelled, and, picking up his wine glass, she hurled it to the floor. Tiny shards of glass flew everywhere, red wine splattered the walls, the table, the newspaper. Like blood. Sasha leant back against the dresser, gasping. Part of her was horrified at what she had done, part of her felt a huge sense of release. Alistair sat and looked at the tiny daggers, glinting on the floor. 'I guess that says it all,' he said. 'Excuse me.' He folded the paper, stood up with exaggerated calm and stepped over the shattered stem of the wine glass, lying at the foot of his chair. 'You are a madwoman,' he said, as he passed her. 'You should get help.' She could smell the red wine on his breath, the sweat from the tension of the day.

Brushing up the shards of glass, her heart still beating wildly, she thought, maybe he's right. Maybe I am mad. He makes me mad. Oh Christ, I have to get away. I have to be on my own or I will kill him. But I'm letting the children down. How will they cope? Then she stopped, her hand poised over the dustpan. She breathed in deeply, to still the chaos and let sense return. That's what he wants me to think. He wants me to feel so guilty I will not go to Peru. He's provoked this drama to get his way. He made me do it. He is not going to win. She brushed with renewed ferocity. No way. I'm fucking going if this is the last thing I do. He will not win.

Abbie, in her room, heard the shattering glass and then her father's heavy tread on the stairs. She lay on her bed, clutching her ancient elephant, the elephant she'd loved for all of her fifteen years. She was not coming out, they were both lunatics. The sooner they

. . . no, she didn't know if she felt that. She didn't know what she felt, apart from turmoil.

After last night Sasha knew she had to tread very carefully. All day she had been planning her line of attack, how she was to bring up the subject of Peru and present the trip to him as a fait accompli, somehow backing him into a corner so he could not refuse or make it impossible. If she did not go she would go mad, she had to have it to look forward to, to hang onto in the ensuing months. She would have the support of Nic and Katie, surely Alistair would not refuse to discuss it in front of them? She'd thought about cancelling the dinner party, but then it was hardly the first time they'd invited people round and not been speaking to each other. In many ways it was easier, because Alistair would be forced to talk, to be civil. If they were on their own he would ignore her completely and find a way of making her punishment complete. It was so childish, so infuriating, and she knew how to deal with his silence, they were wise to each other's tricks. Now she just ignored him back and got on with her life. It was the perfect reaction, because it infuriated him more. It was only embarrassing when he ignored her in front of someone else.

We are digging a hole, she thought, as she bashed the steaks and made hollandaise in the blender. We are gradually digging a hole in which to bury our marriage. The thought left her oddly cold. Maybe he has tested my emotions so far they no longer feel the pain, she thought. I am becoming immune to him. Inhuman. I am losing my ability to feel. He provokes me to anger to get a reaction, because he cannot bear my indifference. I will focus on the trip, she thought. That is all that matters. It will put clear water between us and the madness will calm, and then perhaps I will be able to see clearly enough to make a sensible decision. I cannot make a decision when I am living in the midst of this. I need to look at it from afar, put it down and get away so I can breathe and it cannot hurt me. Away, I will be safe.

'Why,' said Nic in her calm, reasonable voice, 'can't you take two weeks off and just enjoy being at home with the kids? I don't see why it is such a problem.'

'I can't just take two weeks off from the business, not at the moment,' Alistair said. 'Not so Sasha can have a bit of a holiday.' He laughed, but no-one laughed with him.

'But the children are at school all day,' Katie pointed out. 'You could work from home. Lots of people do.'

'Not possible,' Alistair replied, giving her a look which said 'case closed'.

'I'm with Alistair,' Tim said. 'I for one would love to take two weeks away from the office and mess about with the kids, but it can't be done.'

'You'd be useless anyway,' Tim's wife Carol said, looking at him affectionately. 'You don't even know how the washing machine works. I'd come home and find filthy children living off McDonald's.'

'I don't know what century you all live in,' Nic said, testily. Sasha looked at her in surprise. It wasn't like Nic to be snappy, but she seemed a bit on edge tonight. But then Carol could be exceptionally annoying – she had a high, girly laugh and hung onto Tim all the time, as if he might balloon away. Even at the dinner table she stroked his hand, picked fluff off his jacket and smoothed down his hair. It was exceedingly irritating and Katie said she treated him rather like a large hamster. An investment-banker hamster, Sasha said, making them both laugh. Every woman should have one. When the trip had first been mooted Sasha had made the mistake of mentioning it to Carol, who said it sounded rather like fun. As soon as she'd said it Sasha regretted it because she knew that after a few days alone with Carol she would have to boil her in oil. Nic had reacted quite out of character – she'd said no way, and that if Carol was going she would back out. Sasha then had to lie to Carol and say there were no seats left on the plane.

'I'm not being unreasonable, am I?' Alistair said, smiling around the table, trying to gather support. Katie thought how attractive he was. Sasha thought, you bastard. 'I'm in the middle of building up a business which is extremely stressful, although my family fail to see that, and I simply cannot take two weeks off because my wife says she is bored and fancies walking the Inca Trail. Frankly, wouldn't we all like to just take two weeks off and get away? When I dare to say that it is inconvenient I am hounded for being unreasonable and even chauvinistic.'

'But I never complain when you go off,' Sasha said, calmly. I will play the game, she thought. I will let our friends think this is just a little tiff, a minor inconvenience.

'That's work. That is different.'

'You go on golfing holidays sometimes,' she said. 'That isn't work.'

'Only for a weekend, not two whole weeks,' he said, and his eyes glinted at her through the candlelight. Do not push it, they said. You may have your friends around you, but I am not going to be manipulated in public. 'What do you think, Johnny?'

Nic's husband regarded him coolly over the top of his wine glass. 'I think you're being a bit of an asshole,' he said. Katie snorted into her wine.

'Thanks, mate,' Alistair said. 'Remind me to back you up next time you need support.'

'Well, I really don't see why it's such a big deal,' he said. 'Sasha's paying for it, isn't she, Nic tells me?'

That was quite the wrong thing to say. Alistair's face clouded. Because she could afford it, she had her father's money, the money she had wanted to use to help Alistair's television production business when it hit trouble, but he would not let her because he was going to do it on his own and he did not need her family's support. So it just sat in the building society, not a huge amount, but enough to make their lives more comfortable. Money she would not have dreamt of frittering away on clothes or whatever because that was not her way. It should have been for something proper and useful, life-building, but Alistair had refused her help so often, when Katie first brought up the subject of the trip she thought, 'Why not? Why not spend a bit of it on escape?' He would not take the money because he had something to prove, something he had struggled with all their married life. The need to be more successful than her father. He measured himself against her father's financial success and his failure, in his eyes, was the touchstone of his insecurity. Sasha told herself it could not have mattered less to her, that she did not judge him in that way, but sometimes she wondered if she lied. She had not, after all, married her father.

'The point is it isn't just a holiday,' Katie said quickly, her antennae telling her to change the subject. 'It's a challenge. A real challenge. I've always wanted to go to Peru and walking the Inca Trail sounds so killingly romantic.' Her husband Harvey smiled at her fondly. Sasha was envious of their marriage – in all honesty she found Harvey a bit leaden, and she often thought him an odd choice for vivacious Katie, who brought the sun into any room she walked into. But they seemed so calm together – he had two older children from his first marriage and Sasha suspected they hadn't had children together because Katie was, to all intents and purposes, his adored and indulged daughter. She did not work, made his house beautiful and skipped from fun thing to fun thing while he followed on behind, picking up the bills and ensuring she had no responsibility but to be gorgeous and amusing.

Nic and Johnny seemed never to row either – they made her and Alistair look like bickering children. Perhaps she was the only person at this table with a crap marriage. She was too ashamed to confess the full horror of their lives to Katie, who was probably her closest friend. Nic was a close friend too, but there was something remote about Nic which didn't encourage total intimacy, and she always made Sasha feel not quite formed, a child, while she was the wise grown-up.

'Anyway,' Katie continued, 'it is a great shopping opportunity. Think of all the new trekking clothes we'll need, and there are fabulous things to buy in Peru.'

'And there we have it,' Alistair said. 'This is all about shopping. Shopping at high altitude. Nothing to do with walking or a challenge at all.'

'An element of that,' Katie said, smiling. 'And why not? They have the most fabulous fabrics and designs.'

'But it isn't just that,' Sasha said, passionately. They all stopped talking and looked at her. It wasn't like Sasha to sound passionate, she was normally so controlled. 'It isn't just about getting away from our responsibilities.' Alistair looked at her ironically, his eyes watchful.

'It's about doing something really extraordinary when you have the chance. I mean, imagine walking through the gate of the sun and looking down on Machu Picchu. The lost city of the Incas. Hardly any-one ever has that opportunity in their life, and we do.'

Katie applauded. 'Hear, hear.'

'For goodness sake, we're all getting on, aren't we?' Sasha continued.

'Speak for yourself,' Katie interjected.

'We need to grab whatever opportunity we can. It's like,' she floundered, embarrassed. 'It's like trying to fulfil a dream before it's too late.'

Alistair refilled his glass. 'You grow out of dreams,' he said. 'Some of us live in the real world.'

'But that's so sad.' Katie was beginning to sound a

little maudlin. Harvey looked at her. She'd had enough to drink. Time to go home.

'What I mean,' Sasha continued, 'is that we can't just give up, can we? We can't just think that the best and most exciting part of our life is over? Surely it's just beginning, now the children are a bit older and can look after themselves more. I feel like this is the time of life to actually get out there and do something before old age sets in. I'm so tired of being normal. I want to be out there, doing something a bit wild. Why not?'

'Break free, you mean?' Alistair said, biting each word. Nic and Katie exchanged a quick look. 'Throw off the old responsibilities and maybe do something far more interesting?' Alistair's voice was low, and dangerous.

'I didn't mean . . .' She tried to backtrack. She had said far too much. Somehow she had to rescue this.

'Oh, I think you did, didn't you? What you meant was that you want to change your life. That you are unhappy and you want to go off and find yourself. And you don't want to involve your family in that, this is just about you. How lovely it must be,' he continued, his voice bitter, 'to have the freedom to just up and go.' Katie looked at him, horrified, as if a mask had slipped. This was a side of Alistair she hadn't seen before.

There was an uneasy pause and then Nic said, 'That wasn't what Sasha meant. This isn't anything to do with being unhappy.'

'Allow me the luxury of knowing what my wife means,' he said, coldly.

'No,' Sasha jumped in, acutely aware of the embarrassment around the table. An embarrassment mixed with shock that something unpleasant, and truthful, had been said. Mankind, after all, cannot bear too much reality. 'I didn't mean I was unhappy, of course I'm not, I just meant that I want to try something that is a real physical challenge. It has nothing to do with wanting to change my life or anything like that.' She tried to laugh, to lighten the atmosphere, to make such a suggestion ridiculous. A private row had been made public, and no-one quite knew how to save the situation.

'Is that what you really feel?' Alistair said into the silence.

'Of course,' she lied. And of course he knew she was lying.

'Cheese,' she said. 'It's on the dresser in the kitchen. Nic, would you give me a hand?'

Emily was sleeping with her face on her toy rabbit, her arm thrown over its plump pink fluffy body. 'She's still a baby,' Sasha thought, smoothing the thick, wavy dark hair, so like her own, from her face. How much she would miss her, if only for two weeks. But it would do Emily good, because she was so dependent on her mother, and Sasha had kept her a baby for too long. Abbie resented it, and it caused friction between them. She said it was high time Emily grew up and became more responsible, and why did she have to do everything about the house when she was at home while Emily did nothing? It was a major source of arguments and Sasha could see her point, but couldn't stop herself trying to hang onto Emily's childhood for as long as she could. Maybe it meant that she did not have to face the next stage of their life, the stage in which the children would grow up and go away and she and Alistair would be left alone, together. And instead of building blocks towards that next phase of their life, they were intent on smashing them down until there was nothing left but ashes of hope.

What should she do? Maybe you could live a half-life. Maybe she was expecting too much and she should simply be grateful for what she had, a comfortable home, good friends, the children. Very few people kept love, real, passionate love, in their lives. They could ride these current storms and make a truce. It was not impossible. She and Alistair had loved each other once, and maybe that had to be enough and she would never again experience what it was like to be wanted, admired, caressed. To be made to feel unique and beautiful.

'You got what you wanted, then.' Alistair took off his trousers and let them fall to the floor on his side of the bed, in a pile next to his socks and underpants. She would pick them up in the morning and hang his trousers back in the wardrobe as she always did. She glanced at him, as he pulled back his side of the duvet. Shoulders, still broad, legs, still toned and muscular. Only his stomach gave away his age, a stomach he sucked in when he looked in a mirror, passed a hand across it, as if to make it go away. They both still slept naked, but had long since lost the unconscious touch of each other's skin and their bodies no longer sought each other for security in the night.

'You humiliated me sufficiently in front of our friends to make me agree.'

Sasha picked up her book. She was too exhausted to argue. It was two in the morning, but she still needed to read for a while in order to let her mind settle and fall asleep.

'How convenient that Nic just happened to know of an au pair who can look after the children for two weeks. I don't suppose you worked that out beforehand, did you?' His voice dripped with sarcasm. Actually, Sasha thought, we hadn't, but she could not summon the energy to respond. What did it matter, what he thought? She was going.

'Don't make it something more than it is,' she said, mildly. 'It's just a holiday.'

'Oh, I won't,' he said. Then he switched off his bedside light and turned, pulling the duvet away from her. 'But this is the last time you pull a stunt like this.'

Chapter Three

'You can't seriously be thinking of wearing those? With your stomach? Please, Mother, get real.'

Sasha turned this way and that in front of her full-length bedroom mirror, surveying the hipster jeans she had bought in a rush of blood to the head.

'It's just too grim,' Abbie said, her head critically on one side. 'You'll have to give them to me.'

'I will not,' Sasha said, defensively. 'They cost me a fortune thank you very much, and you're not getting your mitts on them. I think they look very cool.'

'Accept it, Mother. Revolting. You need to have a flat stomach for jeans like this and no-one in a month of Sundays would ever describe your stomach as flat. Look,' she said, poking at Sasha's midriff. 'Rolls of flab. Yuk. Cellulite city.'

'I do not have rolls of flab,' she said, sucking in her tummy and stretching herself up in front of the mirror. 'I think they look perfectly fine.'

'I think they look lovely,' Emily said, hanging about behind her.

'Creep,' Abbie said.

She hadn't been sure all the way up to the till but something was possessing her in these weeks before her departure, an air of unreality which made abnormal things possible, all normal restraints flung out of the window. Alistair was barely talking to her, but that was OK – there was a threatening air about him, as if he was cooking up some way of getting even, but she was too excited to care.

They had had an absolutely brilliant time in London, both children infected with their mother's new-found daring, leaping into cabs – they usually took the tube as it was so much cheaper – blowing money on lunch at a ritzy Italian restaurant instead of going to a sandwich bar as they normally did. Usually Sasha shopped for cautious fashions aimed at her age group, but something had come over her in the teenage shop, a kind of mist which said, 'Why not?' They'd gone in there for Abbie, who died for its clothes, and Sasha had said she'd treat them to one outfit each as she was spending so much on herself. It was her money, but even so she was reluctant to add yet more fuel to Alistair's fire when they slunk back into the house laden with bags, flushed and replete with the ecstasy of shopping.

She'd never owned a pair of hipster jeans before. Jeans were utilitarian clothing, not for having fun in, and she saved hers for gardening or walking the dog. These jeans were different – they said 'wild child'. Or, as Abbie would have it, 'wild crone'. They were half denim, half velvet, kind of like riding chaps, with a velvet trim around the low waistband and hem. They called to her, catching her eye, seducing her with their coolness. She hadn't even tried them on in the shop, worried they would make her look as she feared, a forty-two-year-old woman trying to snatch back her youth in a butterfly net. She'd just grabbed them off the hanger, checked the size and bundled them under her arm before marching to the till with Emily in tow, making sure Abbie could not see her and demand to inspect what she was buying. Abbie was her ruthless style guide and refused to let her wear anything she deemed remotely 'embarrassing'. Abbie had such a thin skin about her, what she wore and how she acted in company.

Basically, Sasha thought, if Abbie could have forced her into a full-length burka and persuaded her to take an oath of silence she would. Everything Sasha said, wore, and did was wrong. She was like some kind of thought police, lurking about waiting to pounce, to prove that she, Abbie, knew far better. Maybe it was something about the transition from child to woman, but God, it was murderous to live through. Having a husband who thought you were a madwoman was bad enough, but having a daughter whose present sole aim in life seemed to be to make her feel inadequate in every way put the tin lid on it. Thank God for loving Emily, her one-child fan club. Ever since Abbie had entered the teenage years, Sasha had found herself increasingly the family fall guy.

What a lot of crap I have taken, she thought suddenly. Why am I such a doormat? What do I have to lose? Abbie was right. Why should she let Alistair get away with being so bad-tempered, so controlling? I should have nipped it in the bud years ago, stood up to him, she thought. But for the sake of family peace she had sacrificed her own integrity. However, now was not a time for internal debate, for decisions. All she could focus on was the trip, and she did not want to think beyond it.

Whenever she saw her reflection she tried to catch a glimpse, a fleeting ghost, of the girl she had once been. The real her, who could do or be anything she wanted. The girl to whom nothing bad was going to happen, whose father would always make it better. She had never been close to her mother, and she and her father had formed a close bond, much more intense than most fathers and daughters. An only child, she'd been brought up by him to believe that she could be whatever she wanted to be, because she was loved so much. In marrying Alistair, she had sub-consciously sought out another alpha male who would look after and protect her. Only it had turned out that he was not her father. The insecurity of his own family life made him a much more needy and complicated person than she had ever envisaged. It had taken her sixteen years to recognize the fact that she felt cheated. And then, five years ago, her father had died and her security blanket had been ripped away. She was no longer someone's child.

'Katie's got a pair quite like this,' she said, turning round to look at herself from the back.

'Katie is thin,' Abbie said. 'And younger than you.'

'They'll be fine,' Sasha said crossly. 'All my T-shirts come down over the waistband so you won't see my stomach.' She lifted up her jumper. Actually, her tummy didn't look that bad. OK, so it wasn't washboard-thin like Abbie's with hip bones which stuck out like little shark's fins, but there wasn't too much of an overhang.

That was the trouble with teenage daughters. Especially teenage daughters who were taller than you, with long blond hair, smooth pale skin which didn't need make-up and legs up to her armpits.

'What else did you buy?' Abbie said, rooting about in the plastic bags clustered on the bedroom floor.

'Never you mind,' Sasha said, making a grab for them.

'God, you have spent a lot of money. Dad is going to be furious.'

'It's not Dad's money. He won't mind.'

'Yeah, right. Look at all this.' Abbie pulled out all the trousers and tops she had bought from the out-doors shop while Abbie had borne Emily off to buy cheap jewellery. 'Trekking trousers, fleeces, jumpers, T-shirts . . . hey, these are quite cool,' she said, holding up a pair of beige trekking trousers with big pockets on the side, baggy at the ankles. 'I'll have these after you've finished with them.'

'I might not be coming back,' Sasha said, idly. 'I might be captured by the Shining Path and you'll never see me or my trekking trousers again.'

'No!' Emily's face was full of fear. 'Don't say that!' Her face crumpled into the tears which had never been far away since Sasha had announced she was going to Peru in a month's time. Emily didn't know where Peru was, although her mother had tried to show her on the spinning globe which lit up at night in her bedroom. She just knew it was a very long way away and it was a very different thing knowing that your mum was safely tucked up in bed with your dad from thinking of her thousands of miles away. Plus the fact that Daddy was even more bad-tempered since Mum had said she was going, and Emily had very finely-tuned antennae for relations between her mum and dad. Most of the time they seemed to rub along OK although they didn't hold hands at all like her best friend Ellie's parents did. Mummy said not all mummies and daddies held hands in public, it was a private thing. You hold my hand, she pointed out to her mum, in the street. That was different, Sasha replied. Now her mum, the mum she relied upon to be always there and know where everything was, wouldn't be, and she would have to be looked after by a woman she didn't know. It was a nice thought, to have her father all to herself at the weekend, but there were fears there too, about Daddy's ability to make the washing machine work and find all her games kit and cook her food she could eat. Actually, he'd told her secretly that they would eat out at restaurants, which was very exciting. He said they'd make Mummy sorry she was missing out on all the treats he had planned.

'Of course I'm coming back,' Sasha said, bending down with difficulty to hug her. Oof. These trousers weren't awfully comfortable when you bent down and her knickers rose up at the back, making them both visible and uncomfortable.

'Gross,' Abbie said. 'Put your big knickers away.'

'Well, what pants do you wear with them?'

Sasha said, turning to look up Abbie's long slim body.

'A thong, of course,' Abbie said disdainfully. 'Nobody but you wears big pants any more.'

'A thong,' Sasha said crossly, 'is not an adequate knicker. It's like wearing dental floss. I don't know how you bear them.'

Abbie started to laugh. 'Actually, that's a really sad idea. You'd look like a Chinese wrestler from behind. Forget I ever suggested it.'

'How I ever dare set foot outside this house without wearing a biological warfare suit which covers me from head to toe I'll never know,' Sasha said, wearily.

She hid her new clothes in the wardrobe in the spare room. She didn't think it was any of Alistair's business, what she bought with her own money, but she did not want to deliberately provoke him. As she opened the door, all her other purchases fell out, all the foreign, exciting items she'd never had call for before, and just looking at them gave her a sense of trepidation and wonder. The walking stick, an absolute must, Katie said. Her friend Rosie had trekked part of the Himalayas the year before and said she would have fallen off the mountain without it. The super-high-tog de luxe sleeping bag, bought at vast expense from the specialist camping shop. The sleeping mat, guaranteed to give you a sound night's sleep. It didn't look awfully thick to her, but the important part was the fact that she would be sleeping on it alone. It was all hers. All of it was just for her. The backpack recommended by her travel company for carrying bottles of water and cereal bars to keep them going on the trail, and the head-torch for reading at night. She devoured all the literature the travel company sent to her, and carefully ticked off all the items on their 'must-have' recommended list. Even buying anti-diarrhoea pills seemed glamorous and exciting.

Katie had leapt into the preparations with her customary gusto and was spending money like water. Nic said you really didn't need to buy everything on the list and was taking it much more calmly. But Sasha and Katie had had very enjoyable boozy lunches going over everything they needed to take and reassuring each other that they would definitely be fit enough. Definitely.

'How fit is moderately fit?' Sasha said, looking at the travel brochure for the umpteenth time while Katie went to get them a coffee in Starbucks the week before. 'No, no chocolate brownie for me, thanks. Do I look any slimmer?' she called to Katie, who was manoeuvring her way back to the table with two containers of coffee in her hands. Katie paused, and looked at her critically. 'Much,' she said, while secretly thinking that she didn't look any different at all. How lovely it was to be a size eight when all around you were twelves.

'I should be. I have been going to aerobics three times a week and yet I still look exactly the same. I think I have reached my plateau weight. Or should I say gateau weight?' she said, gazing longingly at the chocolate decadence cake.

'I haven't been to any,' Katie said smugly, smoothing

her jeans over her slim thighs. 'I'm sure I will be quite the most unfit person on the trip. I'll have to be carried up the trail by some hunky Peruvian guide.'

'Are they hunky, Peruvian men?'

'No idea,' Katie said, picking the chocolate off the top of her cappuccino. 'Actually, I think they're rather small. Anyway,' she said, leaning forward and squeezing her elbows together with excitement, 'we're not going for the men, are we?'

'Certainly not,' Sasha replied. She hadn't even thought about that. 'The thing I'm most looking forward to is waking up without someone asking me where their socks are. That, and not having to worry about, well, anything. Like have you loaded the dishwasher, and does the boiler need servicing and have you picked up the dry cleaning and is there any petrol in the car . . . you know, everything that isn't really anything but just builds and builds into an impossible towering list you never get to the end of. I'm just sick,' she said, 'of everything, absolutely everything in that house being my responsibility. I just want to be able to shut the door and bugger off. Let someone else be in charge for once.'

'Do you think it will change us? Make a difference?'

'In what way?'

Katie looked sad for a moment, an unaccustomed melancholy flitting across her face. 'No reason. I guess both of us need a break. I know it sounds mad but I feel like a teenager again, setting off on my own.'

'I know what you mean. This is the first time in what – twenty years – that I have been away on holiday without Alistair. I usually dread holidays, I really do. It's like everything you have to do at home, only magnified. All the packing, and the worry about leaving things behind and then when I am there, I worry that we're not having a good enough time spending all that money and Alistair and I never want to do the same thing at once and we usually have a row about how much freedom Abbie can have and . . .'

'God, Sasha, chill, for heaven's sake. Sometimes I think you take life far too seriously. Is everything between you and Alistair OK? He seemed a bit, well, tense, when we came for dinner. Is he fine about you going now?' She looked at Sasha searchingly.

'Oh fine. Really. I'm not making it up. He just likes to beat his chest occasionally, that's all.' She glanced away from Katie.

'It must mean he really loves you,' Katie said. Sasha looked up in surprise. 'To mind you going so much. Harvey can't seem to wait until I've gone.'

'But he adores you.'

'I know. It's a bit odd, isn't it? I sometimes think I'm too much of a responsibility for him.' She laughed, a strange, bitter sound not like her normal laugh at all. 'Anyway, come on, get the brochures out. I want to go through the itinerary again. Aren't these names impossible? Runkurakay. That's just using up letters, it's not a real word. Huayllamba,' she said, trying to get her lips and tongue around the word.

'Wasn't that a song?'

'Ha, ha.'

Chapter Four

It was pitch dark when she rose, as silently as she could. The alarm clock said four a.m., and she had made sure that everything had been packed the night before and stood neatly to attention in the corridor by the front door, ready for a quick getaway. The day before she had tried to assuage her conscience by going through the house like a whirling dervish, clearing out the larder, doing all the washing, stocking the fridge and changing the sheets ready for the au pair. Maybe Alistair would have an affair with her. She'd met her several times and she was pretty, although she had a very annoying high-pitched voice and screechy laugh. Emily thought she was lovely, Abbie thought she was unspeakably vile and had already nicknamed her 'hyena breath'. She would make her life hell, Sasha was sure, but that was their problem.

The previous night she'd made agonized phone calls to Katie saying, 'Do we need malaria pills? Are you sure? I've got two types of altitude sickness pills, will that be enough?' while Alistair lurked about with a martyred air, peering into the breadbin in the hope of finding it empty, and opening and shutting the fridge door with a despairing sigh.

Nic had worked right up until yesterday, packed in an evening and warned them both about taking too much, but it was so hard to know what to take to a country which had such a vastly different climate according to the region. Lima, which was on the coast, would be hot – up in the thirties – so they would need swimming costumes and warm-weather clothing like shorts and T-shirts. The first hotel they were due to stop at, briefly for one night, had a swimming pool, and Sasha thought the idea of arriving after such a long flight and being able to flop into the pool would be heaven. Then, once they flew to Cusco the following day on a short hour-and-a-half flight, they would be arriving in high altitude with a much cooler temperature, around the mid to low twenties. Once they were actually out on the trail and walking through the rainforest, the air would be cool and damp, even in May, with the possible threat of showers. At Machu Picchu, up at two and a half thousand metres, it would still be cool and the nights would be positively chilly.

Emily and the dog were determined to impede her packing – Bob the black Labrador sat firmly in the canvas bag, which was more than mildly inconvenient, with an expression very similar to Alistair's. Maybe they were thinking of forming some kind of martyrs' society while she was away, and she'd come back to find the house littered with hair shirts and birch twigs. Emily had been less direct in her protest, but kept trying to 'help' by folding her clothes into lumps and suggesting things she really had to take, like glittery hair clips and beanie babies. Sasha said she appreciated the thought but six beanie babies might not be the most useful thing on the trail, compared to a walking stick and sleeping bag.

She was treading carefully, though, because Emily was very emotional about her going. She could easily put up with Alistair and the dog's male martyrdom, but Emily's worried little face and big eyes made her heart turn over. Maybe it was a selfish thing to do, because she could have used the money to take them all on holiday or buy lots of new clothes for them . . . No. Just for once, she was doing this purely for herself, and she must not feel guilty. Katie said she was fed up with Sasha agonizing about the selfishness of the trip and if she mentioned it once more she would have to stab her. Sasha thought that was all very well with a husband like Harvey, who was being incredibly helpful and had even been out shopping with her for head-torches and whatnot, an act which for Alistair would have been the equivalent in pleasure of eating his own hair.

The thought that they were about to walk the Inca Trail seemed quite impossible. She had bought lots of books on the subject and started out with great enthusiasm, determined to absorb as much information as she could, but then she overloaded herself and got bored with it. Katie, she felt, was not treating the trip in quite the same way. Most of her research so far had been poring over the 'Peruvian Connection' catalogue containing unbelievably expensive alpaca sweaters, pashminas and coats. Sasha wasn't sure about the Peruvian fashions – they looked a bit too hairy for her, and there was a touch of the poncho about the clothing. She hadn't worn a poncho since she was about seven, and even then she remembered feeling like a small colourful bat. It wasn't very practical for riding a bike in, either. She doubted the poncho was ever really likely to swing back into fashion, and probably a good thing too, given that the only person ever to look remotely sexy in one was Clint Eastwood.

She'd even left out her new sunglasses to wear, which was rather mad in the dark. But she could wear them in her hair, and wearing sunglasses in her hair made her feel exotic and glamorous. Exotic and glamorous was exactly how she wanted to feel. Not like herself. A new person who did exciting things like this and climbed onto a plane at a time when she was normally hunting lost shoes.

She crept into the bathroom, closing the door with extra special care because she did not want, above all, to wake Emily. She'd said goodbye to her the night before, and that had been bad enough, with Emily trying to keep a brave face on it with her bottom lip wobbling and her eyes filling up with tears. Alistair wouldn't go away when she was putting Emily to bed, and hovered behind her saying, 'Don't be silly, Emily, Daddy will be here,' until Sasha wanted to slap him. He'd even cooked them both a meal, a disgusting chicken dish with floury lumps in the sauce. They ate it in queasy silence, neither of them quite sure what to say. She found herself constantly saying 'Thank you,' as if she were at a hotel. They could not meet each other's eyes.

In the bathroom she brushed her teeth with his toothbrush because she'd packed hers, and splashed cold water on her face. As she held her hands under the taps, she saw that they were shaking. They hadn't drunk much wine the night before, it couldn't be that. Then she realized what it was. It was excitement. It was the type of excitement she'd felt as a child, waking up on Christmas morning, or being woken by her parents in the early hours to set off on holiday. Grown-ups don't get that kind of excitement, and she thought the feeling had gone for ever. But this morning her heart was beating faster, her nerves were tingling and she couldn't stop smiling to herself.

Tiptoeing back into their bedroom, she drew on the clothes she had laid out the night before. Alistair lay fast asleep in bed, one arm thrown up over his head, his hair, blond, fading to grey, on the pillow. In sleep he looked so much more the man she had married, before disappointment had set in. He seemed oddly vulnerable. Looking down at his sleeping face, she suddenly felt immensely sorry for him. Maybe — maybe she didn't give him enough. Maybe he deserved more. No, she shook herself. For two weeks she was not his wife. She was herself and she did not have to think of him or worry about what kind of mood he was in. Trying not to clink, she slid on the bracelets she'd also left out, bracelets she wouldn't normally wear in the day because they'd get in the way. She'd even painted her nails and toenails the night before, again an entirely superfluous gesture but one which made her feel good.

She pushed the sunglasses up into her hair and turned to go. She looked back at Alistair. Should she kiss him goodbye? No. She might wake him.

Quietly, she eased the bedroom door to, wincing as it brushed over the carpet. Just as it was closing she heard his voice, little more than a whisper. 'Sasha, don't . . .' Hurriedly she pulled the door shut.

She couldn't help going into Emily's room. The beanie babies lay scattered on the floor, alongside lots of felt tips with no lids. She picked them up, put the tops on and found a pencil case for them. Next to Emily's bed was a drawing. She must have done it just before she went to sleep. It was a picture of Sasha, with hair like Barbie and a great gash of red lipstick, standing next to a small brown bear with staring eyes. 'Have a lovely time in Peru. I love you, mum. I will miss you SO MUCH,' the words 'so much' underlined several times. Around the words were huge hearts. She picked it up and folded it carefully to put in her backpack. Then she bent, as gently and quietly as she could, to kiss her daughter's cheek. Emily's long eyelashes fluttered at the kiss, but she did not wake. 'I love you too,' she breathed, so the words would form part of Emily's dream. She hesitated by Abbie's door. It was firmly closed, and to push it open might waken her. Abbie had given her an awkward hug the night before, and told her gruffly to have a good time and buy her lots of presents. Sasha had said to her, 'Look after Dad,' and Abbie had given her an ironic look, which plainly said, 'As if you care.'

* * *

Downstairs, Bob's tail thumped in the darkness. 'Ssh,' she whispered. There was no time for a coffee, and anyway Katie would probably give her one at her house, where they were due to rendezvous, as Katie had elected to drive to the airport after Nic picked her up from home. She pressed her lips against his warm head, felt his paw lift and gently place itself upon her arm. 'I'll miss you too,' she said, and he leant his head against hers, his tail thump, thump, thumping in the dark. 'Be good. No sticks in the house, OK?' She felt his reproachful eyes on her. He knew she was leaving. As she closed the kitchen door, she heard him sigh, circle, and then lie down again. Life went on. They could all do without her. They would carry on at their normal pace, while she stepped out into the extraordinary.

Chapter Five

'Put the kettle on will you darlings, I'm still in the shower.' Katie's voice floated down the stairs as Nic and Sasha hovered at the bottom, not quite sure what to do with themselves. As they'd driven up the long drive to Katie's house they saw all the lights were on. No creeping about for her – Harvey was up too and busying about in their floodlit circular drive, making sure her bags were neatly packed into the back of the car. Nic raised one eyebrow at Sasha and said, enquiringly, 'Did Alistair get up with you?'

'No fear, I did everything I could not to wake him. You?'

'Hardly,' Nic said, dryly. 'I'm not sure it's even registered with Johnny that I'm leaving today.'

'I wish I had that kind of husband,' Sasha said. 'I've an awful feeling I'm going to pay for this for a very long time. But,' she said, shaking herself, 'I'm not going to think about that. I haven't been this excited for years. Are you?'

'I will be when I get there. I can't say I'm looking

forward to the flight.'

'It sounds mad but I'm even looking forward to that. Just think! Eleven hours of justifiable sitting down and reading magazines, with drinks and food being brought to you without anyone asking you where something is, or handing you sweet papers and making you do word searches or play I spy. Heaven.'

'I hope you still think so at the end of eleven hours,' Nic said.

Katie wandered down the brightly lit staircase, her hair wet from the shower. 'The cafetière's in the cupboard under the sink. Help yourselves, will you, I've just got one more bag to finish packing.'

'How many do you have?' Nic said, a smile playing around her lips.

'Just three, why?'

'I thought we were only supposed to take one. It took me hours last night to fit it all in. How are you going to carry them all?'

'Oh, I'll manage,' Katie said, airily. 'Anyway, I need room for all the things I'm going to buy. Oh fuck, fuck, I've forgotten tweezers.' She turned and ran back up the stairs, immaculate in black leather trousers, high-heeled boots and a tight-fitting beige cashmere sweater. Nic was wearing a large blue fleece, trekking trousers and her walking boots.

'Do you think she's actually got any walking clothes?' Nic said, when Katie was out of earshot.

'The very latest,' Sasha replied, with a smile. 'The most expensive, the very best.'

The kitchen was a futuristic dream – Katie had

superbly combined the beams and period detail of the eighteenth-century house with a dramatic contemporary look. At one end of the vast gleaming pale oak table was a stainless steel double-door American-style fridge, next to it a pewter Aga. The cupboards were very pale wood, the work surfaces granite. 'It's a bit like the *USS Enterprise*,' Nic said, who hadn't been in Katie's kitchen before.

'I know, isn't it amazing? I've never seen it messy.' Sasha opened the cupboard under the sink. The doors slid back on runners, almost taking her kneecaps off. 'Wow. Look at all this.' On one of the trays were bags and bags of coffee, every type known to man, from Colombian to French to Italian. On the next level down was the spotless gleaming cafetière.

'The grinder's there, just by the kettle,' came Katie's voice from behind her.

'No instant?' Nic said.

'Leave my house,' Katie said, smiling at her. 'Ghastly poison.' Pushing Sasha aside she pulled out a bag of coffee beans, expertly tipped it into the grinder and switched it on. The noise was deafening. Then she poured in the boiling water.

'Right darlings,' she said, pouring the thick dark coffee from the cafetière into three mugs and tipping in milk from a jug. 'Salut!' They obediently clashed mugs. 'Hope we get something stronger on the plane.'

'Drinking makes the effects of jet lag ten times worse,' Sasha said primly.

'I hope you're not going to be like this all holiday,' Katie said. 'Boring cow. Live a little. What do we have to lose?'

'To the Inca Trail!'

'And all those lovely Peruvian men,' Katie said. 'What? What did I say?'

Sasha had thought she might catch up on her sleep on the way to the airport, but in fact she was far too excited. She felt very alive. It was like being at the top of a waterfall, not really certain you would survive the drop but knowing you were sure as hell going over. It was such a leap into the unknown – she had never been to South America before, and although she'd read up about it, she had no real idea what to expect. Guidebooks gave you the history, but they couldn't give you the sight, sounds and smell of a country.

Standing minding the bags at the airport while the other two went off to find a coffee shop which was open at that time in the morning she wondered, not for the first time, how they were going to get on as a three-some. She had been the common link initially – she and Katie had been friends for four years, as Harvey was Alistair's lawyer and had helped him set up his business. When she first met Katie, she wasn't sure they would be friends, and had dismissed her as little more than a trophy wife. She was very much a man's woman, and a bit too girly and flirty for Sasha's taste, the sort of woman who got men to carry suitcases for her. She was too effortlessly pretty, too, well, spoilt. She also seemed to have an incredibly naïve outlook on life. But once Sasha got to know her, she realized that her apparent obsession with clothes, shopping and the way things looked was simply window dressing. Behind the somewhat brittle superficial façade was a very real person, a person who was immensely kind and the most loyal of friends. She was also brutally honest, and did not suffer fools gladly. Some of Sasha's other friends could not understand why Sasha was friendly with her, because they felt she was hardly her intellectual equal. They were probably, Sasha realized, jealous of the fact that Katie always looked so amazing, had such a beautiful house and a top-of-the-range sports car, a jealousy they masked in condescension. Sasha did wonder why she and Harvey had not had children. Harvey had two, a boy and a girl, now at university, from his first marriage. Whenever Sasha gently probed Katie swiftly changed the subject, and Sasha deduced it was a sensitive subject and left it alone. Quite possibly she couldn't have them, and compensated with buying things.

Nic she knew through school – Nic's youngest son was in the same class as Emily, and Sasha and Nic had been members of the parents' committee at the same time. If there was anyone Sasha really admired it was Nic. She seemed to effortlessly run her life and that of her three children – they never forgot their musical instruments or games bags, and Nic never appeared flustered. Sasha, who had been known to take the girls to school in her dressing gown, wondered how the hell she did it, and worked full-time too, as a university lecturer. She and Johnny seemed the epitome of a happy couple, smoothly rubbing along together and bringing up polite, well-balanced children who always did their music practice and never forgot their home-work. Nic and Katie hadn't known each other at all until Sasha introduced them two years ago, and they had amazed her by getting on like a house on fire. So well, in fact, that soon they were meeting up independently of Sasha, and she felt rather jealous and left out. Katie, she felt, confided in Nic in a way she didn't confide in her, and it made her cross. When they met up as a threesome, she felt as if they knew secrets she didn't, and it was like being fifteen again and left out of the gang. But she was not going to be childish on this trip, and obsess.

Both women seemed very certain of who they were, secure in their own skins. Sasha didn't feel like that – she knew she adapted her personality to whom she was with, blowing in the wind. It was something she despised about herself, this lack of confidence, and it was something she recognized she had done at school – tried to be the person she thought her friends wanted her to be. It was an odd feeling, as if you were simply a blank sheet on which other people wrote. I lack definition, she thought. And Alistair did not help.

They waited in the roped-off section leading to the check-in, each clutching a polystyrene cup of coffee. They were flying KLM, and there was an hour-long stop in Amsterdam and then in Aruba in the Caribbean, where the plane refuelled.

The queue moved forward and Katie wheeled her enormous suitcase forward with it, her two other bags on a trolley. Nic and Sasha each moved their own solitary canvas bag along the ground with their feet.

'What have you got in there?' Sasha surveyed the matching luggage in wonder.

'Clothes. Toiletries. The usual.'

'How are you going to carry it on the trail?'

'There'll be porters, or I'm sure we can leave some of our bags at the hotel. We're going back to the same hotel in Cusco, aren't we, at the end of the trail?'

'Don't talk about the end yet,' Sasha begged.

Katie made them order wine on the plane, because, as she argued, it was almost lunchtime. It made Sasha feel light-headed, irresponsible.

'At this time,' she said, looking at her watch, 'I'm normally walking the dog.'

'What an interesting life you lead,' Katie said, looking out of the window. 'I'm normally in the gym listening in to everyone else's gossip.' She had a great stack of glossy magazines on her lap, but wanted to chat. Sasha was too excited to read. She felt like she had been let loose.

'I'm normally sitting in a tutorial group trying to drum some information about European history into a group of very hung-over students who can hardly keep their eyes open,' Nic commented, without lifting her eyes from her novel.

'Which of us has the best life?' Katie said, suddenly, as if the thought had just occurred to her.

'What are you on about?' Sasha giggled.

'I feel that Nic must have because she has the proper career, but then you have your art. I don't really have anything much.'

'But you have a fantastic life!' Sasha said. 'I envy you like hell. Anyway I don't have my art, you know I haven't painted anything for yonks. There never seems to be any time, and anyway as Alistair says it's not as if it makes any money. You don't seem to have to worry . . .'

'What, because Harvey takes care of me?'

'Yes, I suppose so. And you always seem so positive.'

'I actually feel rather purposeless. I suppose that's why I wanted to go on the trip so much. It makes me feel . . . you're going to think this is silly . . . but it makes me feel as if by doing something so different I can rediscover the person I used to be. Before I got married.'

'I feel like that too,' Sasha said. 'What about you, Nic?'

Nic lifted her head. 'I haven't thought about it that deeply,' she admitted. 'To me it's just a chance to do something out of the ordinary. Test myself.'

'You're not escaping, then?' Katie said.

Nic looked momentarily startled. 'From what?' she said, uneasily.

'Escaping, you know, from normal life.'

'Oh, that. Yes, I suppose I am. I don't feel I have anything to prove, though. I don't need to "find myself".' She laughed, as if the idea was ridiculous.

'I've got something to prove,' Sasha said. 'I need to prove there's still a real person in here. Someone I like.'

'What on earth do you mean?'

'I just feel that I'm defined by everyone else,' she said. 'Yes, I will have another drink, thank you. Dry white wine. Thanks. I feel I'm defined by being the children's mother, and Alistair's wife. There was so little to me between stopping being someone's

87

daughter and then becoming someone's wife, and I suppose never really getting a career off the ground didn't help. A job makes you who you are, rather than always being at everyone's beck and call. I think of the children leaving and I think, Christ, who will I be?'

'You don't stop being a person just because you're married,' laughed Nic. 'I don't feel like that at all. I don't think marriage or having children changed me, and I certainly don't feel defined by being Johnny's wife. That's crazy, the old "woman as victim" theory. Surely you stay the same person you've always been.'

'You're lucky,' Sasha said. 'You're not married to someone who has spent most of our married life trying to change me into someone he'd like more.'

Katie looked at her oddly. 'Is that how you feel about Alistair? He's always seemed fairly easy-going to me – a bit of a temper, certainly, but you seem happy.'

Sasha was quiet for a moment. She felt guilty. Only hours into the trip, and already she was painting him as a monster. 'That was too strong. No, it's much more about me. I feel, well, I feel like I've never really fulfilled my potential and if I don't get started now it will be too late.'

'What do you want to do?' Nic said, closing her book and looking with concern at Sasha.

'Honestly? I'd like to paint, but there's so little potential in it really, hardly any artists make any money at all and if I do work, it ought to contribute to the family needs. But then Alistair tells me childcare would cost so much . . . it's a bit of a running battle. I'd really love a career, though. What about you, Katie? What would you do?'

'I used to work as a fashion buyer – you know that,' she said. 'But there's not much point when we don't need the money and Harvey likes to know where I am. Then there's so much to do with the house, having to organize the housekeeper and gardener.' She waved her hand, vaguely. 'That's the deal, I guess.' That was a strange word, Sasha thought.

'What do you mean?' Sasha asked. Katie took a long drink of wine and looked at her challengingly.

'That isn't part of the deal between me and Harvey,' she said. 'You have no idea why . . .'

Nic caught Sasha's eye. 'Oh no,' Katie continued, 'I'd need a lot more of this to tell you the full story.'

'Everyone's life is a bit of a mystery, isn't it?' Sasha said. 'I don't think you ever know what goes on in other people's marriages or their lives. I mean, I've always envied both of you, you seem so . . . so settled. So happy. Whereas I seem to spend my life feeling that I'm never quite good enough. A bit useless, I suppose.'

Nic laughed. 'Settled? I'm not sure I would say that. Happy, possibly. Whatever that means. But I don't think you can take anyone's life at face value.'

'OK, you're boring me now,' Katie said, and picked up *Hello!* 'Time for celebrity trivia. I didn't come away to bare my soul. Not that there's anything to bare.'

Chapter Six

Perhaps it was something to do with the novel she'd been reading before she slept, but her dream was a curious and disconcerting one. She dreamt she was in a room in an anonymous hotel, and it was very early in the morning. She wanted to rise from the bed, but something was holding her down, there was a heavy weight on her legs. She could see nothing, but the weight was insistent. She wasn't scared – in fact the pressure made her feel secure, sexual. She relaxed against it, and slowly she was aware of a warm breath on her neck, and her mouth opened. Now she could feel him, and his face came into view – he was a man she had been in love with, twenty-two years ago, at art college, a fellow student, the first man ever to really unlock the door of sex for her, when it had become pure pleasure rather than an uncomfortable favour. Her arms came up around his muscular brown back and his mouth covered hers as she felt him move against her. Even as she dreamt, she felt she was awake, it was so vivid, and she called out his name.

She woke with a start, sweating, her heart beating wildly. Where the hell was she? It took seconds for her breathing to slow down, her eyes to focus. Of course. She was on the plane, surrounded by sleeping people. The light inside the plane was a dull grey, punctuated by little pools of yellow light where people could not sleep, and had put their overhead lights on to read. Next to her Nic slept soundly, her head thrown back, her mouth open, guidebook open on her lap. She turned to look at Katie who was sleeping too, her head resting on the inflatable neck rest she'd brought with her. Even in sleep she managed to look neat. Sasha shifted her legs uncomfortably, worrying about DVT. The plane was full of murmurings, the murmuring of hundreds of people sleeping, the hum of the aeroplane engines.

She looked up at the screen charting their flight progress with a yellow arrow. Halfway. Halfway between Aruba and Lima, with five hours still to go. God. She felt restless, and wanted to get up to go to the toilet, but worried about waking Nic. No, she really did need the loo. Carefully, she folded the airline blanket resting on her legs, and attempted to untangle the wire from the little black headphones, still plugged into the socket on her armrest. At her feet were a jumble of magazines, her backpack and the useless little airline pillow. She felt uncomfortable, trapped, and recognized the first stirrings of claustrophobia. She gently started to lift herself over Nic. 'Sorry,' she breathed, as she banged against her legs. Nic murmured in her sleep, then turned over, awkwardly, in the narrow space. Sasha stood up thankfully in the aisle. What an unnatural thing it is, she thought, to be trapped in a metal tube flying above the earth. The air had an odd, metallic taste and was chilled. Not real air. Her head felt fuzzy, and she regretted the bottle of wine, she should have stuck to water. Limbo, she suddenly thought. This is limbo. Maybe that's what the spirit world is – thousands and thousands of souls endlessly orbiting the earth in metal tubes. What a loony thought.

In the toilet, she took out the sponge bag she'd put in her backpack, containing her toothbrush, tooth-paste, make-up and hairbrush. 'Be brave,' she told herself. 'Nothing bad is going to happen. You are safe.' Sometimes she got these odd, nameless fears, a kind of free-floating anxiety which made her heart beat faster. She'd experienced it a lot in her early twenties when she was just starting off, working in a gallery. She'd been unsure of herself, suddenly surrounded by free-dom and not knowing what to do with it. Looking back, she'd only really felt secure again once she married Alistair and she was part of a family once more, even if it was a rather volatile, immature family. And now she wanted to rediscover the freedom she had feared when she was her own master. Was there ever to be a stage in her life when she would think, 'This is perfect' and feel happy in her own skin? Get a grip, she said firmly to herself, look forward, not back, without fear.

Carefully she underlined her eyes with black kohl pen, and then put on some lipstick. She brushed her thick dark hair, and looked at the effect. She had good skin, not lined apart from around her eyes, with freckles across the bridge of her nose. An outdoor face,

92

attractive without being beautiful. Lightly tanned, with slightly slanting dark brown eyes, her waving hair cut in an easy shoulder-length bob. She had a wide, mobile mouth, and good teeth. Her father's hair and eyes, her mother's tendency to put on weight around the stomach and hips. Gee thanks, Mother. Great genes to inherit. When she raised her eyebrows the frown lines were there, but they were a natural part of her face. She couldn't bear the thought of Botox – fancy allowing yourself to be injected with a paralysing toxin. She wondered if Katie had had Botox, her forehead was so smooth. Quite possibly. There was a gentle knock at the door. She shook herself, gathered up her things in the narrow confines of the toilet, put them back in the bag, zipped it up and then slid the metal catch back. The man waiting stood aside to let her pass. 'Thanks,' she whispered.

Two Peruvian women had placed their toddlers on the floor to sleep, swaddled in coats and blankets. How good they were being – she was sure that both her girls at the same age would have toddled about all night, or cried. She had a sudden vivid memory of being on holiday with Emily in France when she was just two, and they were staying in a hotel. Emily, as usual, had woken at about five, and cried. Sasha sat on the edge of the bed and rocked her, but she wanted to be at home, where she could play with her toys and see her familiar things about her. She'd ended up walking the deserted streets with Emily in the pushchair, cross, tired and resentful at being what felt like the only person in the whole world to be awake. Why couldn't Alistair help her more with the children? But that night he had taken them out to a wonderful seafood restaurant, in recompense, and they'd chosen the banquet, and introduced Abbie to the delights of mussels and king prawns. She could picture Alistair as he was then, tanned, cheerful – he'd worked for a broadcasting company at that time, before he struck out on his own.

What had been the turning point for them? Was it Emily's birth, and the fact that she didn't sleep which put so much stress on her and meant they played musical beds all night for three years, or was it the year later when he resigned to set up his own company and suddenly the reality of no steady monthly income hit them? She should have stuck to her guns and got a job then as she'd wanted to, it didn't matter what she did as long as she brought in extra money to the house. A local estate agent had offered her part-time work which would have fitted in with the children's school, but no, Alistair didn't want people to think she had to go out to work to support the family. He saw her attempts to help as a slight to him. Crazy, in today's world, but that was what he was like. She hadn't fought too much because she did genuinely enjoy being at home with the children, pottering about the house and making a home. There must have been a catalyst to things going so badly wrong, she thought, as she made her way back to her seat. Because they had loved each other so much, at first. She tried to sleep once more, in a position where her legs were comfortable and her back didn't ache. Had she been as supportive as she could have been? Well, it was too late now. The damage had been done.

Chapter Seven

Trying to get through customs and passport control at Lima airport brought home to them most forcibly the fact that they were entering a very different world. After the bland efficiency of Heathrow, with its international adverts and endless gleaming corridors, coffee outlets and shops, Jorge Chavez Airport was a shock. It had all the bones of an international airport, but none of the organization. The Spanish-looking staff were harassed, sweating, and instead of an orderly queue passing through the barriers there was a scrum, with people waving their passports above their heads, jostling, desperate for immediate attention. The three of them looked at each other, bewildered, and clutched their backpacks tightly. It was a big relief when their bags appeared on the carousel, and they could try to get out.

'This city, it is crazy.' Katarina, their travel company's representative in Lima, gestured out of the window and the minibus she was driving swooped across the road, into the path of one of the hundreds of ancient taxis which thronged the wide streets, horns blaring. 'Eight million people, and not enough work to go round. They do these things – look, this man at the side of the road, filling in the hole with stones. He has made that job for himself, to make a dollar. You see them in the banks, they are cleaning the floor, they do not work in the bank. They do it just to make a dollar. Idiot!' She blared the horn once more. 'It is a mad place, but I love it.'

They stared out of the window, speechless. Numb with jet lag, they felt pitched into an alien world, drunk with the heat, the noise, the colour. The route from the airport was anarchy, with no road markings, just three lanes of traffic racing each other as they hurtled the seven kilometres into the main city centre. It was hot, so hot that the pavements shimmered in the heat, and the people they could see were either native Indians or dark-skinned Mediterraneans. They wore an odd mixture of dress – some wrapped in traditional multicoloured woollen ponchos or blankets, with battered trilby-style hats, others in Western jeans and T-shirts. Clouds of dust were thrown up by the constant stream of traffic, most of the cars old Mercedes, minibuses or Toyotas, some with exhausts hanging off, the windows wound down to allow dark arms to gesticulate wildly at the incompetence of fellow drivers. It was brash, noisy and irresistible. A few young men in suits and ties jostled along the street next to old men herding cows and goats. It was a mad mixture of the old and the new, part Third World, part Western. They were heading towards their hotel, the

Plaza, in the Miraflores district, the rich part of the city where the wealthy Westerners lived and the tiny percentage of Peruvians who made serious money.

'Our economy, it is still not under control, but so much better,' Katarina said. 'I earn eighty dollars a month – how much is that in your currency?'

'About fifty or so pounds,' Nic said.

'My rent costs me forty dollars and this is a good job, this travel company is very good to work for.'

'Do many women work?' Sasha asked. Her head ached from the noise of the traffic, and she longed to have a shower and lie down in a quiet hotel room. Peru was going to take some getting used to. It bombarded her senses, too foreign, too loud.

'My generation, yes, who live in the city. But outside, in the mountains? Not proper jobs. They tend the crops and look after the livestock and the children. They have very poor lives, they build their own houses and they live off the land. In the city now it is good for women like me, we have the choice. I went to university, but my family had to pay, it was very expensive. Very few can afford to go to university, and not everyone goes to school, especially those living in the *barriadas*, the shanty towns. They come down from the mountains to find work but there is no work. They make their homes like this –' she gestured at the rows of corrugated iron shelters lining the side of the highway – 'and they try to get work. If they have the money they buy an old car, they make a taxi.'

Katarina spoke English with a strong Spanish accent, and she had explained that nearly everyone in Lima, the cosmopolitan capital city, spoke Spanish.

Only the peasants, the people from the mountains, clung to their traditional language of Quechua for everyday use. The majority were bilingual. She was very proud of the Western influence on Lima, and said that many millions of foreign investment had been poured into the rich areas of the city, like Miraflores and Lima Centro.

'The peasants from the hills,' she said, dismissively. 'They come here and they piss in the streets. It is our big problem,' she continued. They all looked shocked at her words, but Katarina shrugged. 'It is a fact. Our population here in Lima has doubled – doubled – in thirty years. They see the bright lights but there is nothing for them here. They just create these slums and their children are starving.'

'What about the Shining Path?' Sasha asked. 'Are they still active?'

'Not so much a threat any more. In 1999 the Government destroyed the stronghold of Sendero Luminoso in the Huancayo region, and now there are just scattered cells. Don't worry,' she said, turning to look at them, her pretty brown face creasing into a smile. 'You are not in danger. You will not be kidnapped on the trail! It is very safe.'

'Thank God for that,' Katie said.

'What about cocaine? Is that still a problem?' Nic asked. She sounded as if she was researching one of her history lectures, and Katie and Sasha smiled.

'We are making progress there too. It is on the decline, but so hard to stop entirely – it is industry, you see, for the people in those regions like the Huallaga valley. They have been making it from the coca leaves for many, many years and their lives and the lives of their children depend upon it,' Katarina said sadly. 'There is still much work to do, to provide enough jobs for all the people who want to come here.'

Sasha felt exhausted, having been awake for almost twenty hours and having effectively lost a day. What an odd thing it was, to lose a day. The weariness of her body added to the sense of unreality as she sat, a camera, passive, recording, as they drove along the wide highway towards Miraflores. Why did so many people want to come here, to all this pollution, dirt and noise after what was presumably the clean air of the mountains? The faces of the country people, the Andeans, were so unlike the city dwellers that they seemed a different race entirely, their features flat, their skin darker, much closer to their native Indian roots. Katarina, a native of Lima, looked almost entirely Spanish, her features and dress European.

The city racing past them was a bewildering mixture of architecture – tall, colonial-style buildings of ornate stone stood next to derelict tenements which were little more than piles of rubble. Fly-posters proclaiming such products as 'Inca Cola!' were splashed over any available wall space. Neon signs for beer winked above the buildings.

There seemed no rhyme nor reason for the traffic – if a taxi was hailed, it would dive across four lanes, and swerve to face the other way in an elaborate U-turn. 'It's like the Wild West,' Nic said, amazed.

'Many deaths on the roads in Lima,' Katarina said. 'The worst are the *combi colectivos* – you see, these little buses? They compete for customers all the time, they barge in front of each other to get the fares. Madness. Look now – you see the church? Finest church in Lima.' It was extraordinary, a baroque building with an elaborately carved wooden façade.

'You must be careful if you go out on the streets,' Katarina said. 'The pickpockets are very bad now, and there is much crime. If you want to go out tomorrow morning, before your flight, you ring me and I will come and pick you up.'

'All I want to do is flop into a swimming pool,' Katie said. 'And then I want to sleep for a week in a proper bed.'

'I'd like to see Lima,' Sasha said. She was beginning to perk up, energized by the sights and sounds around her. 'It's a fascinating city.'

'This is the main square, the Plaza san Martin.' It was a large, grand square, dominated in the centre by a huge fountain. 'And now we go to Miraflores.'

Gradually, the intriguing mixture of the old colonial buildings and the prefabricated slums that had sprung up between them disappeared, giving way to streets which could have been part of any major Western city. There were tower blocks, restaurants, cafés, bars and clean, wide pavements along which well-dressed European-looking people strolled. Along the front, by the sea, were beautifully tended gardens flanked by serried rows of palm trees, almost too immaculate to be true.

'It's like a film set,' Sasha said.

'Very beautiful, no?' Katarina said proudly. Sasha thought privately that old Lima was far more beautiful to her, and much more interesting. This could have been anywhere.

'These flats,' Katarina said, waving at a smart high-rise apartment, 'cost many, many hundreds of thousands of dollars. I would love to live there. It is my dream.'

It was midday, and the pavements glittered in the heat. Out on the sea, like tiny moving dots, were surfers, riding the enormous waves. It put Sasha in mind of pictures she had seen of Copacabana beach in Rio. It was a far cry from the *barriadas*.

'Fabulous restaurant – you must go there, if you have the time when you come back to Lima at the end of your trip,' Katarina said. They followed her gaze and saw an elaborately carved pier, with a domed building in the centre like an exquisite wrought-iron jewel in the ocean. 'La Rosa Nautica,' she said. 'The best seafood restaurant in South America.'

'We must go there,' Katie said, 'when we come back.'

'That will be our last day,' Sasha said. It was an impossible thought.

'Now we are here.' Katarina stopped the minibus in front of a tall gleaming tower. Two liveried doormen jumped forward and slid open the door.

'God, isn't it hot?' Nic said. Stepping out of the air-conditioned minibus was like stepping into a furnace, and they all blinked in the blinding sunshine.

'Leave your bags, they will get them.'

They followed Katarina's slim figure in her beige suit into the cool marble interior of the hotel. It was very grand, with a vast flower arrangement dominating the foyer. They felt grubby and travel-stained.

'Sit.' She motioned them towards a chaise longue. They obediently sat, while Katarina handed over their passports at reception.

A smiling young man in a smart blue uniform came towards them with a tray. 'Fresh orange juice,' he said. 'Thanks,' Nic and Sasha said, gratefully.

'No gin?' Katie said.

Their bags were hung onto a carousel-style trolley – Sasha and Nic's duffle bags looked rather out of place – and they were escorted towards the lifts, having said goodbye to Katarina, who gave them her card, and said they must ring her if they needed anything. In the lifts Katie said, 'Well, I'm going to have lunch, several glasses of champagne and then I am going to sleep.'

'Sounds good to me,' Nic said.

Despite several drinks at lunch, that afternoon Sasha could not sleep. Although she had been up now for over a day she tossed and turned in the wide hotel bed, unable to stop everything she had seen this morning flashing through her mind, like a speeded-up film. Eventually she doubled up the bolster pillow – why didn't they give you normal pillows? – and, propped up, read her guide to Peru, fascinated by the way the country had changed, how it seemed to be split between two cultures – the Andean population, clinging to their ancient ways and beliefs, and the go-ahead modern Peru, as typified by Lima, chasing the mighty dollar.

Nic and Katie were sharing a room – as they were three, they had decided to stay alternative nights sharing rooms, so everyone would have a chance of privacy. At the foot of the bed was a big TV screen, and, fed up with reading, she flicked it on. She surfed her way through numerous Spanish channels, which primarily seemed to be game shows or situation comedies with hysterical canned laughter, until she came to CNN. She lay and idly watched American news for a while, and then felt guilty about failing to immerse herself in the local culture. Only here, in Miraflores, there didn't seem to be much local culture in which to immerse yourself, it was Westernized, sanitized, made perfect for what the tourists would expect.

After half an hour she decided to go for a swim. After all, this and the hotel in Cusco would be the last bit of Western luxury they would have for well over a week, so why not treat herself? For so long, at home, she had been desperately wanting to have all this space and time for herself, and now she had it, she didn't quite know what to do with it. She felt surrounded by emptiness, alone.

'What floor is the swimming pool on?' she said, aloud. 'Now I am talking to myself. It must be the jet lag.'

The effects of the champagne at lunch were wearing off, leaving her with a headache. A swim would cure that. She unzipped the bag, and rooted about for her swimming costume. After putting it on in the bathroom she wrapped herself in the hotel dressing gown and then took one of the big fluffy white towels from the heated towel rail.

'Isn't this awful,' she said, giggling, still a bit drunk. 'What a terrible life I am leading. All these tricky decisions.'

The swimming pool was on the roof of the hotel, and when the lift opened she saw glittering turquoise water, flanked by sun loungers and parasols. Several staff stood about attentively, and there was a canopied bar at the far end of the pool.

Quickly dropping the dressing gown onto a lounger, she dived in. It was blissfully cool, and she turned and floated on her back, staring up at the cloudless blue sky. 'I'm here,' she said to herself, her voice unnaturally loud with her ears underwater. 'On the other side of the world, and no-one can get at me. I am quite, quite free.' Then she turned over and swam several lengths, trying to swim away the champagne, earning herself exercise Brownie points she could use as an excuse for a delicious dinner. The challenge of the trail seemed a long way off.

She fell asleep, finally, in the sun, and woke with a burning face and red knees and toes.

That night, for the first time in many, many years, she got drunk, really drunk, without the fear of anyone telling her off, or holding it against her. She was beholden to no-one. They started with cocktails – outrageously expensive in the hotel bar – and moved to champagne, and then to wine, and then to liqueurs and then back to cocktails in the bar. They held each other up in the lift, and cried with laughter, and fell out of the lift onto the floor. The next morning Sasha woke with a blinding headache, but no-one to make her feel she had done anything bad.

Chapter Eight

'Welcome to Cusco,' Ernesto said smoothly, ushering them through the rudimentary customs. 'Did you have a pleasant flight?'

Sasha had been sick in the toilet, so it had not been very pleasant at all. She smiled bravely at him. 'Fine.'

'First we will go to the hotel, you can relax and have lunch, and then I will pick you up at two. Will that be all right? There is much to see.'

'That'll be lovely,' Sasha said, holding her throbbing head. 'I can't wait.'

From the window of the plane as they approached Cusco she had seen the city fanned out beneath her in a wide valley surrounded by tree-covered mountains, the warm terracotta tiles of the roofs reflecting the sunlight. The walls of the houses were whitewashed with exposed stonework, and the soft terracotta of the roofs was interspersed with the dome of a church's bell tower, the city watched over by a huge white figure of Christ. Written into the hillside were the words 'El Peru' in enormous letters. Their flight had also taken them directly over the ruins of the ancient Inca fortress, Sacsayhuaman. Katie had managed to drift off to sleep again but Sasha had sat, queasily, not daring to read or close her eyes because the world spun. Nic hadn't drunk as much as they had and she sat doing the *Telegraph* crossword from yesterday.

As the flight progressed, Sasha watched as the sprawling suburbs of Lima gave way to a mountainous region, the slopes covered by dense vegetation. There were glimpses of small towns, but overall it was very sparsely populated. Katarina had told them that eighty per cent of the population now lived in the major cities, an amazingly high figure given the traditional agricultural history of the country, where people depended on their own crops and livestock to survive. No wonder so many of the native people felt like a fish out of water in Lima. But still they came.

Ernesto, their guide in Cusco, was a very serious middle-aged man, wearing, despite the warm sun, a Western-style black wool overcoat with the collar turned up. He had a severe side parting and very smooth black hair. In the minibus he solemnly handed them all a bottle of San Antonio water. 'You must drink,' he said, 'at least four bottles of water a day. We are very high here, over three and a half thousand metres, and your body will take a while to acclimatize. We will take it very slowly this afternoon and you must tell me if you feel dizzy or sick at all.'

Cusco was a very different city to Lima, much smaller,

with a population of only about three hundred thousand people, swollen by tourists. The cobbled streets were steep and narrow, very different to the flat, wide open highways of Lima, giving it the feeling of a medieval city, intimate and almost Dickensian, full of hidden-away shops and small alleys. The people seemed more relaxed than in Lima, and children in dusty shorts and T-shirts waved at them as they drove past. Many of the adults were dressed in traditional Andean Indian clothes, handwoven blankets around their shoulders and trilby-style hats pulled low on their dark-skinned foreheads.

'This is the Plaza de Armas,' Ernesto said. 'The main square of Cusco.' It was a wide, cobbled square, dominated by a huge ornate cathedral with a large bell tower. The red-tiled buildings and whitewashed walls gave the city a faintly Mediterranean air, as did the hacienda-style archways which formed an arcade in front on each building, creating shade from the high sun. People sat on benches, or strolled through the manicured gardens in the middle of the square. No-one seemed in a hurry. 'This is the Spanish-built cathedral,' he said. 'And on this side is the smaller Iglesia de la Compania de Jesus.' Both were exquisitely beautiful, and they craned their necks to cast a last glimpse of them as the minibus rattled up a small side street, before pulling up in front of two large ornate wooden doors. 'The Hotel Monasterio,' Ernesto said proudly. 'The newest, and one of the finest hotels in Cusco.'

Solicitously he ushered them from the coach into the cool dark interior. 'This is a bit of all right,' Katie said. 'I think I'm going to like it here. Do we have to actually, like, trek at all? Can't we just stay here and say we've done it?'

'Tempting,' Sasha admitted.

The hotel was set around a sixteenth-century cloister, and had once been a monastery. The serene, cool atmosphere was enhanced by the background music, a monk's chant. All their bags were piled up in reception, and then they were led, through the plush bar area with deep leather seats, to their rooms.

'This is just fabulous,' Katie said, bouncing up and down on the bed. She turned over onto her stomach. 'You know, I really thought we were going to be roughing it even though we'd booked the best hotels either side of the trek, but this is amazing.' The walls of the room were stone, contrasting with the elaborate, embroidered curtains which swept to the floor, and the twin beds were covered in matching gold velvet fabric. It was like the interior of a very wealthy gay bishop's palace.

'What do you think the food will be like?'

'Not guinea pigs,' Sasha said, picking up the information brochure. 'Did you know that's the national dish? *Cuy,* they're called.'

'How mean,' Katie said, opening her backpack and rooting around for make-up.

There was a knock on the door. Sasha called, 'It's open.'

'I,' said Nic, swaggering slightly, 'have a royal suite with the biggest bathroom you've ever seen with two toilets. Do you think they've got us mixed up with someone else?'

'Who cares?' Katie said. 'Let's have lunch.'

They ate in the courtyard, surrounded by flowers, enjoying the warmth of the sun. The temperature was by no means as hot as Lima, more like a pleasant English summer day. Sasha leant back in her chair, the sun on her face, and felt, for the first time in a long while, utterly relaxed. She felt newly-minted, expectant, irresponsible. Nobody here knew her except Nic and Katie, she could be anyone she wanted to be. The food, as Katie predicted, was Western, without a roast guinea pig in sight. They had pasta, and one glass of very good dry white wine, which they thought was extremely restrained. Walking back to the room though, before the afternoon's tour, Sasha felt lightheaded and thought she must take an altitude-sickness pill. She had been warned it might give her odd tingling sensations in her hands or feet, but better that than keeling over and having to go home. She'd read that altitude sickness could be no joke – in the most extreme cases your lungs could collapse. The only way back down the trail was being stretchered by the guides – it was too mountainous for helicopters to land, and the only possible treatment was to descend.

Her heart gave a tiny lurch of fear – what if she wasn't fit enough, what if that happened to her and she let Katie and Nic down? They'd probably all have to go back and that would be the end of the trek. It was a horrible thought, and she tried to banish it from her mind. She'd be fine, surely, as long as she took it slowly. But they had over sixty kilometres to cover, sixty kilometres on a trail which wound up and down higher mountains than she'd ever climbed before. Well, the first mountains, in all honesty, she had ever climbed.

Ernesto had said he would meet them outside the hotel, and the moment they stepped out of the gate two small boys ran up to them, shoving postcards of Cusco at them. The first one, who looked about eight, had an appealing, cheeky, handsome face.

'What is your name?' he said to Katie.

'Katie. What is yours?'

'Antonio. You are very pretty lady. You like David Beckham?'

'What?' she said, laughing.

'David Beckham. Manchester United. I like very much. I will remember your name,' he said, firmly. 'Now you buy postcards. Only two dollars, very good value.'

'Let me see.' Nic took hold of them and began to flick through them.

'Go away!' Ernesto came running across the street, flapping his arms at the boys, who grabbed the postcards from Nic and beat a hasty retreat.

'Do not encourage them,' Ernesto said. 'We have a big problem with beggars here in Cusco and we are trying to stamp it out. Once you have spoken to them, you cannot get rid of them and they are a nuisance to the tourists.'

'Why aren't they in school?' Sasha asked.

'Not all children go to school,' he said. 'They

110

should, but often it is the parents who keep them off school, because they can earn the money from the tourists. There are orphans too – some sleep in the square at night – and they can live only by begging. We have no real welfare system, you see, although there are charities who give them food and shelter. But they prefer to be independent.'

They began the tour on foot. As they walked, Ernesto gave them a potted history of the city. 'It was founded,' he said, 'by a leader called Manco Capac around 1200 AD. But it really came to importance much later, in 1438, at the time of the great Inca leader Pachacutec. He conceived the idea of expanding what had been quite a small town into a great ritual city, built in the form of a puma, a sacred animal at the time. The head is the fortress, Sacsayhuanan, a place called Pumacchupan where the two rivers merge is the creature's tail and between these two sites is Koricancha, the temple of the sun, which is the repro-ductive centre of the Inca universe. You see, here on the door of the cathedral?' He pointed up to the great ornate door. 'There is the puma head – a pagan symbol carved by the local people to uphold the old beliefs.' He ushered them into the vast interior of the cathedral. They all stopped, and gasped in amazement. It was unbelievably ornate, one wall decorated from floor to ceiling in beaten silver leaf.

'Minimalist,' Katie murmured.

'When the Spaniards, led by Francisco Pizarro, arrived here in 1553, they set up a puppet emperor on the throne, Manco Inca. Quickly they tried to impose their Christian beliefs, but the native people did not

111

want to give up their pagan gods. They worshipped the sun, Inti Raymi, and in making this cathedral so impressive, so ornate and full of beautiful things, the conquistadors were saying, "Look how awesome our God can be? See what riches he brings?"' Ernesto turned to them with a wry smile. 'The local people took the religion, on the surface they gave up their pagan beliefs, but even now, in the mountains, they still worship their own gods. These symbols, like the puma head, are a little rebellion.'

'But how were the Inca defeated if there were so many more of them?' Sasha asked, staring up at the high, domed ceiling with its elaborate tracing. She liked the idea of them sneaking in their own symbols, under the noses of the bossy Spanish.

'Pizarro had swords, cannons and cavalry,' Ernesto said. 'And the Spanish had treachery. They worked on the Inca leaders. They flattered them, and promised them great riches from Spain. They captured the Inca leader Atahualpa, and they said they would free him if he filled the ransom room at Cajamarca with the famous Inca gold. Over six months he did so, but still he was brought to trial. Then they said he would be burned alive as a pagan or he could convert to Christianity and be strangled. Understandably, he chose Christianity, was baptized – and then they killed him. The Spaniards took the gold treasure, and shipped it back to Spain where it was melted down.'

Nic shuddered. 'How awful. What a terrible waste of so much history.'

'Savage times,' Ernesto said. 'Our country's history is written in blood.'

'And what are you?' Nic said, then, feeling she had been a little blunt, 'I mean, do you count yourself as a native, or Spanish by heritage?'

'I am Peruvian, of course,' he said, proudly. 'We have our independence, we are, you know, no longer a colonized nation. But I am a *mestizo*. I have mixed blood, as have so many people in Peru today. Come. I take you to the Koricancha, the temple of the sun.'

Inside the thick stone walls the air was cool. 'You see here,' Ernesto said. 'This is the prime example of Inca stonework. These great blocks of andesite fit so perfectly together, without mortar, they can never be destroyed. They would take many hundreds of men to move. When we have an earthquake, many, many houses in Cusco fall but not the Inca buildings. They understood, you know, how to build to withstand an earthquake. Their science and engineering was way ahead of its time. That is why their windows are trapezoid – the weight is at the bottom, and many of the outer walls of the buildings are curved. Before this temple was sacked by the conquistadors there were four small inner sanctuaries, the walls covered in beaten gold, and filled with fabulous treasures. And here, beneath this trapezoidal window, at the summer solstice, the Inca leader would sit as the sun's rays shone on his costume of beaten gold and priceless jewels. On solstice day, June 21st, the sun will shine exactly through that window, to this day.'

Sasha closed her eyes and tried to imagine what it must have been like to have seen the Inca Lord, sitting on his throne, covered from head to toe in gold armour and jewellery, his proud face topped by a gold helmet and rainbow-coloured feathers. You'd have to be pretty masculine to carry off that kind of get-up, but then the Inca Lord must have been a fierce sort of person and would not have taken any sniggering at the elaborate nature of his attire. It must have been an awesome sight, with the sun reflecting off all that gold – no wonder, as she had read in her guidebook, that the people believed their Inca Lord was the son of a god, the descendant of the Sun King.

Ernesto was very keen on his walls, and in the hot sun, they all began to flag. Ice-cold gin and tonics seemed more and more appealing, as did a bit of light shopping. From Cusco, they drove in the minibus to the fortress of Sacsayhuanan, which stood high in the hills above the city. From the plane it had been impressive, but close up it was an incredible sight. There were wonderful views from the hill, looking down over the ancient city. What remained of the fortress were rows of huge, sloping walls, made up of interlinking blocks, like jagged teeth. They were built in a curious zigzag shape, which Ernesto told them was to represent the deity of lightning. What was so amazing about these walls, he said, warming to his favourite theme, was the fact that they held together without any mortar, like the temple of the sun, each block perfectly matched to the next, and so they had stood, withstanding battles, earthquakes and storms. Even now, the tallest stone stood twenty metres tall, dwarfing the tourists wandering beneath.

Standing close to the walls, Ernesto caressed them as he gave the history of the fortress, and Sasha, catching Katie's eye, had to stifle a giggle. This man had a wall fetish. 'What do you have in your culture to compare with this?' he continued, searching their faces for signs of awe. Sasha quickly composed her features and gulped. 'Nothing,' she said, in an oddly high-pitched voice. 'Nothing at all. British walls – well, they simply cannot compete. Can they, girls?' Nic and Katie shook their heads solemnly. 'I am glad you are impressed,' Ernesto said formally. 'Let me show you some more examples. Follow me.'

Katie sidled up beside Sasha. 'If he asks you if we want to see another ruin please say no,' she hissed in her ear. 'I mean, it is magnificent and all that but if I see another example of trapezoidal architecture I will scream. I haven't bought anything for two days and I am getting withdrawal symptoms. We'll get all this history on the trail. Can't we just go back to the hotel and sunbathe?'

'Reading really crappy magazines and drinking gin?'

'Exactly.'

Nic, who was walking on ahead with Ernesto, turned round and shot them a disapproving look. Katie and Sasha put on expressions of polite interest and trotted after them.

'Oh look – aren't they sweet!' Katie said. In the car park beyond sat a small group of women and children, accompanied by an embarrassed-looking white alpaca with red tassels in its ears. The women and children were dressed identically in local native costume of red, orange and blue patterned skirts, topped with a similarly multi-coloured little cape made from hand-woven wool. On their heads were curious flat hats, from which hung small red pompoms. The alpaca's tassels also had pompoms on them, a detail which clearly added little to the animal's innate sense of dignity. They were sitting immobile, a living photo opportunity.

'Take my picture with them,' Katie said. 'I know it's a cliché, but please.'

As she approached the group, a wizened hand shot out from under one of the women's capes. 'Ten dollars,' she said, in a very clear voice.

'Ten?' Katie said, in wonder. 'Two,' she suggested.

'Three.'

'The benefits of capitalism,' Katie said dryly, taking a roll of dollars out of her money pouch.

Having got the money the women and children obediently stood to attention and smiled, the oldest woman giving the alpaca a sharp tug on its rope to make sure it looked straight at the camera. It looked decidedly miffed. After taking the photograph, Sasha reached out her hand to stroke it. It snapped at her fingers. Ernesto, approaching them from behind where he had been chatting to Nic, laughed. 'They can be grumpy,' he said. 'The llamas are gentler.'

'What's the difference?' Sasha said.

'Alpacas are smaller, their necks are shorter and their wool is much smoother, much less coarse. Alpaca wool is very soft, like cashmere. But a llama makes a wonderful pet and work animal, you know,' he said. 'They are very loyal. If you feed them, they will never go away. The village people use them not just for wool but to carry provisions in the mountains. However,' he added, smiling more broadly, 'a llama knows its own mind. If you put any more than twenty kilos on its back it will sit down and refuse to move.'

'Effective,' Katie said.

'And inconvenient too,' Ernesto said. 'Once a llama is sitting it is very hard to move.' Sasha warmed to llamas. It was a perfect form of protest – quiet, non-violent but deadly in its effectiveness.

Back at the hotel, too late to sunbathe and feeling stuffed to the gills with culture, they collapsed into the leather chairs in the bar. A waiter appeared bearing a tray. 'If that is coca tea I do not want it,' Katie said. They'd each been given a glass on their arrival at the hotel, having been told it was the perfect antidote to altitude sickness. It was like drinking warm feet. Sasha and Nic had got it down somehow but Katie had absolutely refused to drink it, declaring she placed more faith in good old Western medicine. She'd gone off to get her pills, saying at least they didn't taste like Harvey's socks, which made Nic and Katie feel even more nauseous.

'What now?' Nic looked at her watch. 'We've got two hours until that guy comes to tell us about the trail. What did Ernesto say his name was? Miguel? He's going to be here at seven, before dinner. I'm exhausted. I think I'm going to have a lie-down, and I want to read up about everything we've seen.'

'What about you?' Katie said to Sasha.

'Go on,' she said. 'I'll come out shopping with you. If I absolutely must.'

The moment they stepped out of the door they were accosted by Antonio. 'Hello Katie,' he said cheerily,

117

while keeping a wary eye out in case Ernesto came flapping round the corner. 'Now you buy my postcards. I have done very bad business today,' he said, making a sad face as if he was about to cry. They looked at him stoically. That didn't work. He whipped the sad face off and put on a happy one instead, beaming flirtatiously up at them.

'Go on then,' Katie said, rooting in her money pouch.

'Thank you. Where do you come from?'

'Near London in England.'

'England. David Beckham.'

'We know.'

'Manchester United.'

'I support Burnley myself,' Katie said.

'Who Burnley?'

'Who indeed?' Sasha agreed. 'Come on. He'll keep us all night.'

They walked off down the street. Antonio ran beside them. 'You want your shoes shining?' Sasha looked down at her suede walking boots. 'Not really.'

Just yards from their hotel was an alleyway which led into a warren of stalls. Antonio stuck to them like glue, chattering about football. 'Please make him go away,' Sasha said, wearily. 'Go away,' Katie said. 'OK,' he said, quite happily. 'I see you later. I will wait for you.'

'I bet you will,' Sasha said.

The stalls were piled to the rooftop with goods, from sweaters to socks and Peruvian hats. Pan pipes hung on the walls and there was a bewildering range of silver jewellery. Llamas were a predominant theme. 'Is

118

there anything without a llama on it?' Sasha asked a young woman sitting behind a counter, nursing a small baby wrapped in a colourful blanket. She looked at them uncomprehendingly, and then produced a white fluffy toy llama.

'Apparently not,' Katie said. 'God. Everything is so cheap. You'd pay a fortune for this in the UK.' Soon she had ten gorgeous soft pashminas spread out over the counter. 'Baby alpaca,' said the woman, smoothing it lovingly with her hand. 'Very soft. You feel.'

'Poor thing,' Sasha said.

'They don't kill it, stupid,' Katie said. 'Sasha, please stop hanging about over my shoulder. You're putting me off. Look, I'll take ages. Shall I meet you somewhere? What about the Inca Grill, that restaurant on the far side of the square? I'll see you in half an hour.'

Unwanted, Sasha wandered out of the shop. She planned to buy a few things too, but did not have Katie's feverish desire to do it all now. There was plenty of time, and anyway they had another night in Cusco at the end of the trek. Nor did she have as much money to spend.

The light was fading as she walked out into the street. The sun was sinking behind the mountain, casting long shadows across the wide square. Waiters were carrying tables into the restaurants, ready for the evening custom, as the air was chill, and the lights from the shops and bars cast pools of light on the pavements outside. Solemnly, the great bell in the cathedral tolled and Sasha paused for a moment, taking in the scene.

She felt very calm, serene, as she stood and watched

119

the tourists, the beggars and the shoeshine boys moving about the square. There is a mysticism to this place, she thought. Ernesto had told them many people came to Cusco because they believed it was the navel of the world, the heart of Pachamama, Mother Earth. From the temple he had said dozens of *ceques*, power lines similar to ley lines, radiated out towards more than three hundred and fifty sacred *huacas*, which were special stones of pagan worship. There was a sense of peace about the city, and Sasha had the odd feeling that she had come home. She hadn't felt it in the ancient cathedral but the sensation of peace and spirituality was here now, all around her in the twilight air.

From nowhere came the sound of pan pipes, the first time she had heard them in Peru, drifting up to where she stood. A small group of men were playing, she could see, in front of one of the many restaurants around the square. It was the perfect music for Peru, she thought, haunting, lilting, natural, the sound of the wind in the mountain trees, soaring like the condor into the wide open sky and then falling into the deep ravines where the rivers snaked around the base of the mountains. The music of another time, a music which spoke of legends, an ancient time when man had been bound so closely to the earth, dependent on its beneficence for life itself.

She shook herself as a ghost ran through her. I have been here before, she thought.

Chapter Nine

She drifted down the steep cobbled street, stepping aside to avoid a group of young women, dressed in colourful traditional costumes with what looked like lampshades on their heads, giggling amongst themselves as they hurried through the darkening streets, one holding a baby alpaca which nestled in her arms like a puppy. Sasha shivered. It was getting chilly, and she hugged her warm fleece jacket around her. A taxi blared its horn as she stepped out into the square, swerving to avoid her. There were far fewer cars on the streets of Cusco than Lima, adding to its more peaceful air.

'You buy something from me?' A middle-aged woman squatted on the street corner, in front of her wares. They were laid out on intricately detailed rugs made of tough cotton, in deep reds, oranges and yellows, the colours of the sunset. She was weaving as she spoke, with swift, deft gestures, while at the same time reaching out with one hand to restrain her child, a four-year-old boy, who was drawing on the pavement with a stone. While she wore the traditional costume of a wide, embroidered skirt and wool poncho, her thick black hair in a plait down her back, he wore a blue and white football shirt, stained with dust, and a pair of shorts. He had no shoes on his feet.

Sasha paused to look at the goods she was displaying – at first she had been riveted by how many different things there were, the colourful jumpers, the socks, the warm hats with earflaps and the silver jewellery, but she was quickly realizing that nearly everyone seemed to stock the same things. But then they made them themselves, the crafts passed down from generation to generation.

'I like you,' the woman said. 'You have a nice face. Very pretty. You American?'

'English,' Sasha said, flattered despite herself, and she bent down to pick up a bracelet of beaten silver, inlaid with an attractive orange stone. She tried it on. It gripped her wrist, rather than being fastened by a clasp. 'It's lovely,' she said. 'How much?'

'Five hundred sols,' the woman said.

'That's . . .'

'Fifteen dollars.'

'Ten.' Sasha turned it round on her wrist. Now she did want it, quite badly. It kind of fitted her new identity.

'Twelve.'

'OK.' She reached into the pocket of her trekking trousers, and pulled out a roll of dollars. The woman eyed them in wonder. It suddenly occurred to Sasha that the money she carried casually, to do a bit of shopping, was probably more than the trader earned in a year, and she felt guilty about haggling.

* * *

Gently, she touched the bracelet as she walked away, towards the restaurant. It pleased her, and made her feel one step closer to Peru, now she wore a part of it around her wrist. Around her milled the other tourists, mostly young backpackers, from England, Germany, America and Australia. They had bought heavily into the culture too, with alpaca hats with long, drooping earflaps, scarves and jumpers. Everyone here had a uniform, of baggy trousers, big walking boots, backpacks and warm fleecy jackets, with at least one item of Andean clothing, usually a hat. There was a fine line, she thought, between fun Andean headgear and looking like Deputy Dawg. She found a table, and ordered a beer. Around her was the hum of many conversations, and she did not feel alone. She felt quite, quite content, all anxiety gone. Full of a peaceful anticipation about the week ahead, a sense of belonging in this foreign place.

They'd stayed too long in the restaurant, chatting, as Katie pulled out all her purchases like an excited child, beautiful scarves, jumpers, and jewellery. Typically she had managed to find a more expensive shop which exported many of its goods to London, where they sold at three times the price. This fact gave Katie a great sense of vindication, because of course she was not spending wildly, but getting a bargain. She was actually saving money.

They had to run up the hill to the hotel, and Sasha's chest felt like it was on fire. You could not take the altitude for granted – it squeezed your chest, made your lungs feel half their normal size and left you gasping for air. When they walked into the hotel foyer, at ten past seven, she had to pause by the door, feeling faint. When she'd got her breath back she followed Katie into the bar. She could see Nic sitting chatting to a man with very dark hair, just visible over the back of the armchair.

'There you are!' Nic said, irritated. 'Come on. Miguel's had to wait because there's no point going through it all twice.'

As she approached the table, he stood up, and turned to them. He was tall for a Peruvian, and broad-shouldered. When he was facing them, she found herself running her hand through her hair, loosening it, lifting her fringe away from her face, and she was aware that she had stopped breathing just for a second. It must have been the altitude, but she felt as if she really might faint.

He reached out his hand to her, smiling, motioning her to sit down.

She looked down, away from him, confused, aware that she was going red and wanting to hide it from the other two. What on earth had come over her? So what if he was astonishing-looking?

'You must be Sasha,' he said. 'I am very pleased to meet you. Now sit, and let me tell you about the trip. I have many details to tell you, and I do not want to keep you too long. We all must sleep well tonight. Your last night in a bed.'

She lifted her eyes to his, and it was as if an electric shock ran through her. His eyes held hers for too long, telling her that he felt this connection too. No, this was

124

not possible. He was, what, in his twenties, and must be well used to women staring at him, but his eye contact said this was unusual for him, he too was surprised, and pleased. Her hand flew to her bracelet, and she firmly squeezed it tighter around her wrist.

He leant back in his chair, as a waiter hovered behind them. Miguel turned, and said something in rapid Spanish. Then he flashed a charming smile at them. 'A drink?' he said.

'I'll have a gin and tonic,' Katie said, not taking her eyes off Miguel.

'I'll have the same,' Sasha said.

'Tea,' Miguel said, in English. Sasha now felt very embarrassed at having ordered alcohol. 'Tea for me too,' Nic said. You would, Sasha thought.

'Now ladies,' he said, spreading the notes out in front of him. 'I hope you are all fit and ready for the trail? We have sixty kilometres to cover, and some of the trail is very steep. I hope you have all been exercising. You will need to keep up with me, and I am very fit.' He laughed, as if he was joking.

'Oh yes,' Katie said, lying smoothly. Nic regarded her sardonically.

Sasha tried to concentrate on her notes, but the words were blurring and she couldn't stop herself from sneaking glances at him. He was quite unlike anyone she had ever seen before. His skin was a smooth, pale chocolate and his teeth were very white, small and even. He had a small nose, and wide-set deep brown eyes. His hair was thick, jet black, and stood up away from his face, waving, down to the back of his neck. He was clearly more Andean than Spanish but it was not a truly Indian face, although he had the high cheekbones and the slightly hollowed cheeks of a native. His lips were fuller, more European than the other native Indian men she had seen. It was an aristocratic face. His hand moved over the paper, and she noticed his fingers were long and artistic, with short, very clean nails. She found herself wondering what it would be like to be stroked by those fingers, and startled, mentally gave herself a quick shake. What was she thinking of? He had a wholesome, almost preppy look, despite his dark skin and black hair, accentuated by his clothes – a soft grey wool crew-necked jumper and fashionably baggy trousers. Around one wrist hung two copper bracelets and dark brown beads. He looked like a student, but he had an air of authority about him too, seeming firm and very much in charge of the situation. Katie's foot was pressing against hers, and she suddenly realized she must be staring. She coughed, and bent her head, while she sensed Katie shaking with suppressed laughter next to her.

'You find something funny?' he said, looking at Katie with a smile.

'No, nothing,' Katie said, quickly. 'It's just that I had been dreading the trek a little and now I'm not. I know we will be in good hands.'

He smiled down into his notes, and when he looked up once more, she found his eyes on her. Why her? Why not Katie, who was reaching forward to touch his arm, perched on the edge of her chair, smiling at him and giving him little looks out of the corner of her eyes, running through the full repertoire of her flirtatious skills?

She must be imagining it. She tried very hard to concentrate as he reeled off the details of the trek, the ruins they would see, the type of clothing they should take with them and how far they would be travelling each day. He had a beautiful voice, she thought, his words oddly phrased, almost overly polite. He had an inflection of Spanish but there was something else there too, something European, possibly French?

'You speak perfect English,' Nic said.

'Thank you,' he said. 'I was taught at the university here in Cusco, and I have travelled in your country and in America. I have also spent some time in France.'

'Have you?' Sasha said, surprised, then realized she sounded rude. 'It's just . . . you look quite young.'

'I am twenty-four. I love to travel, and I am fortunate in that my parents can afford to help me.'

'How many languages do you speak?' Katie said, interested.

'Eight.'

'Eight!'

'It isn't difficult,' he said. 'I have an ear for languages and I like to learn about other cultures. It is my passion. You will teach me much, will you not, about the British culture, on our trip? We will have much time to talk. I must not always lecture you,' he added, smiling. 'You will be my teacher too.'

Sasha took a gulp of her gin and tonic, and tried to think of something sensible to say. She wished she'd put on some make-up before she'd gone out with Katie, and then caught herself. What on earth did it matter what she looked like, he was only there to be their guide and she was sure it wouldn't make a blind bit of difference to him if she had lipstick on or not.

'Any questions?' He sat back in his chair, and lifted one leg over the other, so his foot rested on his thigh, just above his knee. He was wearing trainers, with no socks, and his trousers had ridden up to reveal a brown ankle.

'It sounds awful,' Nic said, 'but where do we go to the toilet?'

He grinned. 'A very practical question. We have a chemical toilet that the porters will carry. It is a big luxury, on the trail. But there will be showers and proper toilets at several of our campsites.'

'Will we share tents?' Sasha blurted out.

'You have two tents,' he said, and Sasha felt the blood rising in her cheeks. Whatever had made her say that? 'So two of you must share. The other will be alone.'

'Now,' he said, gathering up his details from the table, and draining his cup of tea. 'I will not keep you any longer. Please read and digest,' he smiled at them, 'the details of the ruins you will see on the first day because I will be testing you.' He laughed. 'Not really. But I hope you will find the stories fascinating. I study history as well as languages, you see, so I am quite passionate about my country's past. I hope you do not find me too passionate – you must tell me if I bore you. Once I start talking . . .' He opened his hands in front of them, a helpless, charming gesture.

'I'm sure you won't,' Katie said, quickly.

'I see you tomorrow then, bright and early. We must leave at six, to drive to Chilca where we will join the trail. Sleep well.' As he said this, he caught Sasha's eye, his voice lingering on the last words. He knows perfectly well I won't, she thought. This flirtation was absolutely not going to happen. What a nerve, she thought. Perhaps he's doing it just for fun, to see how she would react. Well, she was not going to react. She was not going to be affected by this, because how could it be for real? Things like that did not happen to her. She was well past that kind of infatuation. It was just pleasant, really, and rather exciting to have a beautiful young guide to escort them, rather than some dull middle-aged man like Ernesto. It simply made the trail, already exotic and mysterious with the promise of Machu Picchu at the end, even more glamorous.

'Another drink?' Katie said. 'I don't know about you lot but I need one. He's fucking gorgeous! It's a good job we are all old married women, but bags I be the first to shag the sherpa.' Nic looked at her disapprovingly. 'Oh come on,' Katie said. 'Even you must admit that he's going to brighten things up quite a lot.'

'I suppose so,' Nic said, a smile starting to play around her lips. 'I can appreciate his looks in a purely aesthetic kind of way.'

'What, as opposed to wanting to rip his clothes off? As for you, Sasha,' Katie continued, leading them towards the bar, 'your tongue was practically stuck to the table.'

'No it wasn't,' Sasha said, crossly. 'I didn't think he was that amazing. He had very – very small teeth. There was something a bit monkeyish about him too. Anyway this is silly. He's never going to look at any of us, he's probably got some divine Peruvian girlfriend waiting for him at home. It's his job, isn't it, to be charming? We've got to like him so the trail is a success and his company are happy with him. It's costing us enough. He was just doing his job.'

'Well, that's it then,' Katie said, laughing in disbelief. 'If that's the only criticism you can make I am going to have to keep a very firm eye on you, especially when it's your turn to have the single tent.'

'What about you?'

'Oh, I've far too much sense and anyway he's too young even for me,' Katie said airily, waiting for them to say he wasn't. When they didn't, she continued rather crossly, 'Anyway, God knows what you might pick up. I'm sure they have AIDS out here.'

'I don't think he's like that,' Nic said. 'He seemed rather old-fashioned to me. Rather a gentleman.'

'Anyway,' Sasha said, lifting herself onto a bar stool. 'We're worlds apart.'

Sasha lay in the bed next to Katie, turning over constantly to try to find a position in which she could relax and let her mind drift into nothingness. She tried putting one hand under the pillow and spreading her fingers, while making her feet flop. That usually did the trick. Nope. She turned on her back, and stared at the dim ceiling. She felt – what? Stirred up, and whenever she thought of him she had a moment of faintness, when she drew in her breath suddenly and had to tell herself to breathe. It must be the altitude, it was making her a bit mad. She found herself memorizing his face, tracing every line, every curve of his cheek. She thought of his dark eyes, burning into hers. You daft bat, she said silently to herself. Think of something else, very dull. She tried to think about emptying the dishwasher. About filling the car with petrol. About taking money out of the cashpoint, standing in a queue in the dry-cleaners, being too early to pick Emily up from school and having to wait in the car, ironing, putting the cover on the duvet . . . nope. Her mind kept leaping back to him, like a salmon. She lay, in a foreign bed in this most exotic of countries, and felt on the threshold of something quite new and potentially very dangerous indeed.

Chapter Ten

'I'm never going to be able to decide what to take,' Katie moaned, sitting on her bed surrounded by jumpers, knickers, socks, plastic bags full of suntan cream, medicines and cotton wool.

'Just put your trekking things in,' Sasha said, wandering out of the bathroom in knickers and bra, holding her sponge bag. 'Look, it's only for four days, and then one night at the Sanctuary Lodge.'

'But that's it,' Katie wailed. 'I want something lovely for that night, as it will be a celebration, but I cannot find room for extra shoes. I can't go out in walking boots, can I? Why did Miguel have to be so strict about only taking one bag?'

'He was very firm about it, wasn't he?' Sasha giggled. 'He is very strict about things. I think he's going to lick us all into shape.'

'You wish,' Katie said, grinning. 'But I've got so many things it's impossible to choose.'

'You shouldn't have brought so much, then. We can only wear one outfit every day on the trail anyway.'

'But they all match,' Katie said, laying things out. 'Look, this scarf goes with this shirt, this shirt goes with these trousers . . .'

'Does it really matter?'

'Of course it does,' she said. 'I can't feel comfortable if I'm not feeling good about the way I look.'

Sasha had never really thought about this before. Of course if she was going out for the evening she considered what she was going to wear and made an effort to look pretty, but for everyday things, well, she just slopped about in whatever came to hand, often trousers and a jumper from the previous day. Most mornings she took Bob out for a walk after dropping Emily off, so there was no point putting anything nice on. But Katie always looked immaculate. Sasha really couldn't be bothered, there was no-one to impress anyway, only Alistair, and he never seemed to notice what she looked like. The only thing he did moan about was the grey pants she dyed in the wash, but then there was no way she was going to truss herself up in sexy underwear like a performing elephant for him. Wearing sexy underwear just made her feel embarrassed, and she had long since given up buying it.

But, in fairness to Katie, she had, for once, thought long and hard about what she was going to wear this morning. She had packed her duffle bag the night before, in a matter of ten minutes, while Katie looked on amazed – 'How can you be that quick? It takes me hours,' – and left out the clothes she'd had in her mind all along, her favourite pair of grey trekking trousers, the ones Abbie had wanted. They were low-slung on her hips, fashionably so, and she would wear a tight white T-shirt with them, a cashmere navy blue crew-necked jumper knotted around her neck. Without consciously realizing it, she was copying him. And her necklace from Abbie, the one with navy blue and white terracotta beads, and her amber earrings, not very practical on the trail, but they made her feel more glamorous. She even quite liked the boots because they looked right with the big baggy trousers, with thick, heavy soles. She'd carry her waterproof coat knotted around her waist, because there was very little you could do to make waterproofs look in any way chic.

She'd risen early, before Katie, and had a shower, washing her hair. Once Katie was awake she dried her hair upside down, to give it more body, and when she flicked her head back and looked in the mirror, she was really pleased at what she saw. Her hair looked glossy and stood away from her face, waving down to her shoulders. She kept thinking she ought to have a fashionable short cut and be a bit more 'out there' – after all, long hair on older women could start to look a bit sad. But she could never find a style that suited her as much as simple shoulder-length hair, all the same length apart from two shorter strands at the front which framed her face.

Her skin looked lightly tanned and healthy, and the sun in both Lima and Cusco had brought out her freckles. Her dark brown eyes, which all too often at home looked red-veined and tired, shone. She outlined them in kohl, and put on some mascara. It was probably a silly thing to do as the washing facilities would be rudimentary on the trail, and she'd end up with black smudges like Chi-Chi the panda. But she did it anyway as it brought out her eyes, and then smoothed on some lipstick. Not too much, because she didn't want the others to think she was tarting up. It would be so easy to look silly in front of him, and anyway by the time she'd packed she had managed to convince herself she was imagining it and that when she saw him this morning she would notice all the imperfections she had not seen the previous night, he would be by no means as good-looking and he would treat her in exactly the same way as everyone else, which would prove it was all in her head.

'Katie, it is now twenty to six. We have not had a coffee, our bags were supposed to be ready in reception at half past five for the porters, and it appears to me that everything is not in your bag, is it? It is all over your bed.'

'Oh fuck off,' Katie said, grinning amiably. 'Give me a hand then.'

'You don't need this –' Sasha picked up a crushed black silk skirt Katie had been about to put in her bag – 'and you certainly do not need a faux-fur-trimmed denim jacket with leopard-skin lapels, do you, Katie, for a night in a trekking lodge?'

'It's my favourite,' she wailed. Sasha noted the label, Christian Dior. She had never owned anything by Christian Dior, apart from a lipstick. There was a knock on the door.

'Ladies . . .' Sasha's heart stood still.

'I wonder if you are ready?' They paused, and looked at each other horrified, as if they had been caught smoking behind the bike sheds.

'Very nearly,' Katie called, and began frantically shoving things into her canvas bag. Sasha went over to the door, and opened it a few inches, as Katie was still in her knickers. Sasha had quickly dressed while she was chatting.

She peered around the edge of the door, and there he stood, a few paces back, in the pale early morning light shining through the window in the corridor. He appeared rather irritated, and was looking at his watch. It was a diver's watch, she noticed, expensive-looking and chunky, with a broad silver-coloured strap.

'Er – Miguel?'

'Yes?' He stepped forward, as she opened the door a fraction wider.

How could she have thought his beauty was a figment of her imagination, brought on by high altitude and gin? He was glorious, even at this time in the morning, a tracksuit jacket slung over a pale blue T-shirt, the same trousers as last night. His thick black hair was slightly wet, as if he had just stepped out of the shower. Sasha tried very hard not to conjure up a mental image of him in the shower, as she slid round the door, holding it ajar with one hand behind her.

'I'm sorry we're late,' she said. It suddenly occurred to her she hadn't said it like that since she was at school. He looked at her, standing just a foot away, and his proximity made her heart beat faster, a heat rise in her. She lifted her eyes to his and it was there again, that look in his eyes, powerful, hot, sexual attraction, which made everything around them stop. He was staring at her, taking everything in, her newly washed hair, her skin, the trace of lipstick. He saw her. She stared at his mouth, the way his lips stretched over his perfect teeth, and longed to . . . what? Kiss him? Oh get a grip, she said, mentally shaking herself. The moment in time was gone, and she was practical and herself once more. Only he stood, poised, immobile, waiting. His hand had made a tiny movement towards her, as if . . . She stepped backwards, the door hard against her.

'It's Katie,' she said, in a voice which sounded much higher than usual. She coughed, and made her voice normal. 'I'm afraid she's not quite ready yet. Give us two minutes, and we'll be down. Is Nic ready?'

'She has been in reception since half past five,' Miguel said. Again he had a smile playing around his lips, as if he was enjoying her discomfiture.

'I'll make her hurry up,' Sasha promised.

'May I at least have your bags? The porters are waiting.'

'Yes. Fine. Just hang on a sec.' She slid back round the door, and then leant against it, breathing hard. Katie looked at her quizzically.

'That was Miguel.'

'So I see,' Katie said. She was sitting cross-legged on the bed in bra and knickers, surrounded by stuff.

'He said . . .'

'Yes?' Katie said, encouragingly. 'Get your breath back, dear. Would you like to sit down?'

'Bog off. He said we have to get our bags out now,' she said, hissing, aware suddenly that he might be able to hear through the door.

'Now?' Katie looked alarmed, and Sasha realized that in the few minutes she had been talking to Miguel

Katie had been touching up the varnish on her toenails.

'Now,' Sasha said firmly. She walked towards the bed, and started folding things, pushing them into Katie's bag. 'They're the wrong things!' Katie hissed, trying to wrench clothes out of Sasha's hands.

'Who cares,' Sasha said. 'We're late. They might go without us. Anyway Nic's waiting. She's been up and ready for ages.'

'How surprising. Ouch, no, I need those,' Katie squealed, as Sasha tried to take the pile of pashminas out of Katie's hands.

'No you don't. There will be no pashmina moments on the trail. Go in the bathroom and brush your teeth. I'll finish this.' Swiftly she began sorting clothes out, and jammed them into the bag. At least Katie had put the essential stuff like sleeping bag, head-torch and clean trekking clothes at the bottom. There was far too much beauty stuff though, and she hoicked the various pots and jars out. Why was she going to need three different types of night cream? They wouldn't even have a mirror, for God's sake. Hurriedly, she pulled the zipper shut and lugged it over to the door. When she wrenched it open Miguel was still standing there, by now definitely irritated.

'Sorry,' she said. 'Here they are.' He reached down, and swung the bags onto alternate shoulders as if they weighed nothing. 'See you in reception,' he said, without looking back. Sasha allowed herself the luxury of watching him walk down the long corridor. She knew he knew she was watching. He walked like a model, with long, easy strides. Just as he reached the bottom, a small child ran out into the corridor, the child, presumably, of a cleaner, as no-one else seemed to be awake, or perhaps the child of the hotel manager. Easily, he moved out of the way, and then said something in Spanish to the boy. The boy looked up at him and laughed, and Miguel touched him lightly on the head. The boy looked back up at him and then ran towards Sasha, a bright smile on his face.

The road, as it approached Chilca, became increasingly bumpy. At first they had driven out of Cusco on smooth, tarmacadam roads, but these faded into pot-holed dusty tracks which were part dirt, part tarmac and a lot of holes, and the minibus bounced along. At the sides of the roads walked men herding cattle with large, low horns, tapping their flanks with pointed sticks. Women in traditional dress walked with heavy bundles balanced on their heads or tied around their shoulders, and children ran along, skipping and calling to each other. When they reached the outskirts of Chilca, Miguel suddenly said something in Quechua to the driver. He turned off the main road into a wide square, thronged with people.

It was market day. Women squatted on the ground in front of rugs covered in the familiar alpaca sweaters and hats, and also, laid out on turquoise tarpaulins, were vegetables, corncobs still wearing their green jackets of leaves, sacks of potatoes, maize and a small type of grain. It was a local market, not destined for the tourists, and people browsed, picking up fruit and vegetables, smelling them, squeezing them. Most had a thin blue plastic bag over their arm, their shopping basket. The men wore wide-brimmed hats, to keep off the sun, and the women also wore either the curious large bowler hats held on with brightly coloured ribbon, or trilbies also.

One woman caught Sasha's eye, sitting immobile under a makeshift tarpaulin roof held up by two wooden poles, shading her wares from the sun. She had an impassive, Indian face, her eyes mere slits. Her thick dark hair was divided into bunches, smoothed behind her ears, and around her shoulders was a warm, pale pink blanket. Under it she wore a stained cream shirt, and over her crossed legs was another blanket, red, pink and blue. She was young, perhaps no more than sixteen. There was no active selling, they either bought from her, or they did not. There were none of the thrusting hands of Cusco, the urgent voices in pidgin English entreating them to come into their stall, their goods so much finer, better quality, cheaper than the next. This seemed to be something she had done so many, wearying, times before, carrying the vegetables she and her family had grown to the village for market day. In her face was a calm acceptance, that this was her life and she should expect nothing more.

A woman bent over her from behind, to examine the corn, wearing a thick multicoloured jumper, the colours of the rainbow. Ernesto had told them that the word Inca symbolized rainbow. Behind them, at the far corner of the square, a man in a dark blue shirt and grubby jeans stood, his arms folded, taking in the scene. He was framed in a doorway, an elaborately carved wooden door, a symbol of perhaps more prosperous times. On the door were a pair of ripped fly-posters. The wall of the house was whitewashed, but in parts the paint had flaked away, leaving exposed dull brown plaster, and in place of a window was what looked like another door, marooned high up in the wall. Looking more closely, Sasha realized what appeared to be a door was a pair of shutters. Painted onto the wall was a mural, rainbow-coloured, mirroring the people, the stalls and the animals of the market scene beneath. It was as if they were enacting the painting below, a century on.

'We need some water,' Miguel said, following her gaze. 'You can wait here, or perhaps you would like to visit the lavatory before we begin the trail?'

On the far side of the square was a café, a few rickety-looking tables and white plastic garden chairs placed outside.

'Not sure I want a drink here,' Katie said, as they walked into the dim exterior. A single bare bulb hung from the ceiling, and behind the counter stood a woman in Andean dress, her face passive, expressionless, her arms folded. Behind her was a makeshift shelf with a few bottles of lemonade, Coca-Cola, and bottled water.

'Do you have a toilet?' Nic said, politely. The woman motioned with her head through an open door, which led out into a yard.

The yard was the family garden, too, and a child played with a puppy, lifting it into a grubby blue washing-up bowl. In the centre of the square someone had tried to make a garden, piling stones up to make a wall, and in the middle of this makeshift flowerbed stood a gnarled walnut tree, and a stunning red flower, an orchid. 'Who wants to go first?' Nic said.

'I will,' Sasha said, and pulled open the wooden door to what appeared to be the loo. Outside washing hung from a top-floor balcony, and a young girl, in a floating white nightdress, was looking down at them. In a pen on the far side, a goat bleated. The bowl of the toilet was tarnished with age, the black plastic seat had come away from its hinges and she had to hold it still to sit on it. The toilet paper was hard – paper she hadn't seen for years, not since the days of her grandfather, who thought soft toilet paper a dangerous modern invention.

'What's it like?' Katie said, as she came out.

'I wouldn't linger.'

In the square, Sasha heard the blaring of a horn, and came out hastily, in case it was Miguel calling to them to hurry up. He was not in the minibus, only the driver sat, hunched over the wheel, smoking a cheroot. She went quickly over and climbed in, looking for him. Miguel was standing, his arms full of bottled water, at the far side of the square. He looked of these people, and yet not – his Western clothes set him apart, and he was taller and slimmer than the small Peruvian men and women around him, in their thick shawls and trilbies. They hunched themselves over, even when they were not carrying anything heavy, while he stood tall, his head high. He was chatting to a man standing next to him, a man in dusty-looking trousers with a sack tied around his neck, to carry his vegetables home from market. He appeared to be complaining about something to Miguel, who patted him on the arm. The man looked up at him, smiled, and then gave an odd kind of salute as Miguel walked away. As he crossed the square several people called to him, and he nodded his head in greeting, smiling, calling back in Quechua. He was like a favourite son, she thought. It was strange, in a way, how many people seemed to know him.

Nic and Katie walked back across the square after him, and Sasha noticed how every man's head turned as Katie went past, impeccable and slim in her matching beige trekking trousers and shirt, knotted at the waist. Around her neck was a blue and white scarf, the kind of cotton scarf a gypsy might wear, but on Katie it looked chic, fitting. Her thick blond hair was piled up into a bun, casually, with bits sticking out in the style that Abbie often used, a scruffy, she called it, sunglasses resting in her hair. She looked like an advert for a trekking holiday, and Sasha could imagine her on a poster, framed on the hill above Machu Picchu. It was a good job Katie was her friend because otherwise she would have had to kill her for being so effortlessly beautiful. She and Miguel would make a striking couple, she thought suddenly. And felt a flash of jealousy.

Nic strode purposefully, without noticing the glances they were attracting. Much taller than Katie, she had smooth dark hair which hung in a bob to her shoulders. She had clear, perfect skin and slightly hooded dark eyes, and her strong jaw made her face handsome, rather than pretty. When she was not smiling, she could look rather forbidding, but her smile lightened her face. Sasha wouldn't like to be late for one of her tutorials, though. Nic could be very cutting and a bit scary, she would imagine.

* * *

Just outside the village the minibus bumped into a walled parking area, where other minibuses were parked. This would be where they were to start the walk, which after lunch would meet up with their start point of the Inca Trail. Throughout the journey Sasha had had a nervous feeling at the pit of her stomach, and once the minibus pulled up she thought she might actually be sick. It was either the altitude or anxiety, or a mixture of both. The trek was such a long one, the trail was so steep, what if she could not do it and the altitude became too much? People had died on the trail, overcome by the altitude, their lungs collapsed. Her heart beat faster, and she glanced at Nic.

'Nervous?'

'A bit. It's such a bloody long way. I just don't know if I am up to it. I've been looking forward to it for so long but now it's actually here I'm terrified.'

'God, you girls,' Katie said, breezily. 'It'll be fine. It's only a bit of a walk.'

'A bit of a walk? Dead Woman's Pass is a bit of a walk? Are you mad? It's like climbing into the sky. People have died, you know.'

'You worry too much. Has anyone ever told you that?'

Milling about in the square were other trekkers also about to start off. Sasha noticed they were all much younger – students mostly, carrying huge backpacks from which sleeping bags and pots dangled. They were all smiling, excited at the thought of setting off, and Sasha thanked God they did not have to carry all that – how did they manage? It would be hell to have to carry everything with you, including your tent.

Most, she noted though, did have guides, local men with dark, wizened faces, their arms and legs sinewy and knotted with muscle.

Outside the minibus Miguel took out his mobile phone, punched in a number and then bent his head closer as it was answered. He smiled as he talked, and Sasha felt consumed with an absurd feeling of jealousy – who was he talking to? His girlfriend, to say good-bye? She took hold of herself firmly. He was obviously simply a flirt who enjoyed seeing the effect he had on women.

'Ciao,' she heard him say, as he pressed the 'end call' button. He put it back into the pocket of his trousers, and then turned to them.

'Come,' he said. 'Come and meet your porters. The most important men on the trail.'

They stood in a group, their heads down, embarrassed by the attention from women. They ranged in age from late teens to forties, wearing an odd mix of clothing – red football shirts stained with sweat, emblazoned with 'Cusco' on the back, a Nike sweatshirt, jeans, Western zip-up fleece jackets. On their heads were either baseball caps bearing the logo 'Inca Cola' or curious straw boaters, tied round with thick red ribbon, tassels falling at the side of their head. They looked rather like the alpacas – doomed to wear silly national dress to please the tourists. The boaters were fastened under their chin with a broad strap of white crocheted lace, incongruously feminine against the dark masculinity of their faces.

While Miguel introduced them, seven porters and their cook, they smiled to the ground but would not look the women directly in the eye. Miguel clearly knew them well, and as he introduced them he chatted to them, joking, judging by their smiles. They obviously liked him. As he introduced their cook, another Ernesto, he put his arm casually around his shoulders while the older man grinned sheepishly at Miguel's description of him as the best cook on the trail.

Greetings over, the porters reached down and began to haul the mound of duffle bags, sleeping bags, folded tents and an assortment of pots and pans and a stove, packed in a blue tarpaulin sheet, onto their backs. There were a few groans as they adjusted their bodies to the immense weight, and then they were off, at a jogtrot, around the corner, out of sight. Sasha, Nic and Katie looked at them in wonder. 'Do they ever fall over?' Katie said. Miguel laughed. 'No, never,' he said, shaking his head. He obviously thought Katie was a bit of a case.

'And now we go. Ready, ladies?' Miguel ushered them on ahead of him, and as they rounded the corner, Sasha realized this was it. No turning back. They were about to begin to walk the Inca Trail. It seemed too fantastic to be true, and she felt as if she were dreaming. After only a few steps her legs felt heavy and stiff, her boots uncomfortable and chafing. They walked together slowly down a dusty track, beside a wide, brown river, running swiftly, high against its banks. On either side of them rose high, tree-covered mountains. 'This is the Urubamba,' Miguel said. 'The river which winds through the Sacred Valley. We will see it many times on the trail,' he said.

Ahead of them was a rope bridge, swaying gently in the breeze. A man was leading a reluctant horse across, its back slung with bags. It was Arabian-looking and thin. 'I didn't know you could take horses on the trail,' Nic said. 'Only on the first day,' Miguel replied. 'After that the trail becomes too steep for them, too treacherous. Only llama can be trusted on the trail, as they are so sure-footed. But then they will not carry so much, and can be stubborn.' On cue another porter walked past, leading a pale brown llama. With its swaying, delicate walk and high aristocratic head, it seemed an unlikely pack animal, too intelligent, too beautiful to undertake such a menial task. With its thick, fluffy coat, large behind and supercilious gaze, it looked to Sasha like an Edwardian lady with a bustle, out for a genteel stroll along the promenade.

Miguel walked on ahead, with Nic, Sasha and Katie behind. Just before the bridge there was a wooden shack, and ahead of them a queue of backpackers.

'We must show our trekking papers and your passports,' Miguel explained. 'The Government likes to know who is walking the trail, and from which country. Don't worry, I will pay.' The cost of their holiday had included the actual cost of walking the trail, around seventeen dollars each.

After he had sorted out the paperwork, he called them forward. 'You must sign your name and your address in this book,' he said. Leaning over Nic's shoulder, Sasha saw there was also a column requesting age and occupation. Nic carefully wrote in '50', and then 'lecturer'. Sasha was interested to see what

Katie would put. She tried to pretend she wasn't looking, but positioning herself at the side, she saw out of
the corner of her eye Katie leave the occupations
section blank, and under age she put '34'. Yeah, right,
Sasha thought, trying not to laugh out loud. As she
started to write, she was aware of Miguel having
moved forward, to stand close behind her. No point in
lying, she thought, and wrote '42' and 'housewife'.
God, she thought. How depressing. To be walking the
trail as a housewife. She should have written 'artist'. It
was true in part – you didn't just stop being an artist
because you didn't actually do it any more. It was how
she thought of herself, in the times when she thought
of the person she had once been.

Miguel was blatantly staring over her shoulder. 'Do
you not work?' he asked, curiously. He did not react
when he saw her age – he must have guessed she was
over forty. Who in their right mind would pursue a
woman over forty when he must escort twenty-year-
olds on the trail? Anyway, the phone call proved he
had a girlfriend, so she should be quite safe.

'I used to,' she replied. 'I used to be an artist – well,
I trained in art, and had a few small exhibitions. But
then I got married and had children . . . you know.'

'An artist,' he said, and smiled. 'How fascinating.
You look like an artist.' Then, turning, he led them
over the bridge. Sasha stared after his retreating back.
Smarmy bugger. She didn't look like an artist at all.
Did she?

The morning's walk took them through relatively
flat terrain, along the south side of the Rio Urubamba.
Miguel strode on ahead, and the three of them

followed more slowly behind, getting used to walking at altitude, chatting about home in a desultory fashion. Nic was a keen gardener, and she stopped to look at plants they passed. Nic and Sasha compared notes about living with a teenager – Nic said boys were quite different, less confrontational than girls but just as mad in their own way. Sasha noticed that Katie had stalked on ahead, a bored look on her face. She was feeling left out, and it struck Sasha that the trek would not only be physically arduous, but tricky in terms of keeping everyone happy. Three was a difficult number, and already she realized that Nic found her and Katie a bit silly together, while she was finding Nic had the occasional tendency to be a bit holier than thou.

After an hour they came into a clearing, where a group of four Indian women sat. In front of them was a makeshift stall, piles of stone on which black plastic bags had been laid. On top of the bags were bottles of water, Coke, lemonade and Fanta orange. There were also crisps, packets of biscuits and Peruvian chocolate. All four women wore thick woollen cardigans, and one was knitting a long red scarf. Behind them lay a fawn-coloured mongrel, sleeping.

'What an interesting life they must lead,' Katie said, and Sasha flashed a 'hush' look at her, as Miguel turned to them, frowning. 'They can make many dollars in the season,' he said, 'from the tourists on the trail. It is a lot of money compared with growing your own crops and selling them at market. We have much to thank the trail for.' Bending down, he paid one of the women for a bottle of water, although Sasha knew he had at least four in his backpack. The woman's formerly impassive face creased into a smile as he said something to her, and she raised her hand to him, as if in blessing. 'Well, that's me told,' Katie said.

Sasha was getting used to the rhythm of walking constantly. It wasn't tiring, exactly, more soothing, to meander along, looking at the trees and the flowers, catching a glimpse of the beautiful little humming-birds as they flashed and darted through the trees. Miguel stopped frequently to tell them to have a drink of water, and pointed out every bird, every unusual flower they passed along the way. At first it was charming, but then Sasha felt like telling him to just get on with it because she badly wanted to get to where they were having lunch and sit down. There were many orchids, a glorious and exotic splash of red at the side of the trail. After another hour, they came to a small clearing at the side of the track. There were odd rings of stones, and then a mound, clearly a grave, on which had been placed a wreath of paper flowers, incongruously festive. Looking more closely, Sasha could see the other graves had similar tributes.

'These aren't people who have died on the trail?' she asked.

Miguel laughed. 'No, of course not,' he said. 'These are local people, many people still live and farm in these hills. We will be coming to the settlement in a minute.'

'Why do they use paper flowers?' Katie asked, bending down to examine one.

'They last longer. Flowers die far more quickly than

the memories. Anyway, death for us is not the end. It is the beginning.'

'Why?' Sasha said.

'Death is the beginning of the greatest adventure,' Miguel said. 'We will be reunited not only with the souls of our loved ones, we will also be taken back to the mother Earth on the wings of a condor, to meet our gods.'

'Do you believe that?' Nic said. 'I thought ninety per cent of the population were Catholic?'

'But I am Catholic,' Miguel said, holding his hands up in front of him in protest. 'Here,' he said, tapping his head, 'I am Catholic, I pray in the church. Here,' he tapped his chest, 'I say my prayers in my heart to the ancient gods, to the sun, the water, the mother Earth. It is to the land, the earth, the water, that we owe our existence. It is Darwin's theory, is it not, that we evolved from water? So we should worship the water, Unu Raymi. My God.' He shrugged. 'It is a free country, Peru,' he said. 'We do not have to worship in fear. One man can have many gods.'

'Did they really have sacrifices?' Katie asked.

'In the time of the Inca, and before? Of course. They would sacrifice the best llama, the best goat, the best chicken to Inti Raymi, the God of the sun, to say thank you for the harvest.'

'No virgins?' Katie said.

'No virgins, as far as I am aware,' Miguel said. 'Our people gave what they would miss most, they chose the best for the sacrifice. It was an honour for the animal to die that way to offer thanks to the gods, and its soul would immediately go to a much better place.

Our virgins were kept for more practical purposes,' he said, grinning. 'At the time of the Incas we had the *acclas*, the virgins of the sun, who would be kept in a house near to the Inca Lord, sewing his ceremonial cloth of gold.'

'How boring,' Katie said. 'I think I'd rather be sacrificed. At least you got your fifteen minutes of fame.'

'You had to be a virgin too,' Nic pointed out, and Katie shot her a look.

'I heard they sacrificed children,' Sasha said.

'Never!' Miguel stopped short and turned, genuinely angry. Sasha was taken aback. 'I didn't mean . . .'

'My people would not have sacrificed children,' he said, firmly. 'Come,' he added. 'We must walk a little more quickly, our porters will be waiting with lunch at the ruins of Llactapata, where we join the trail proper.'

'That hit a raw nerve,' Katie whispered to Sasha. 'I wonder why he's so defensive? It's not as if they still exist, or anything. These are quite weird people.'

A hundred metres on from the small graveyard, they came into the little village, or 'community', as Miguel called it. On one side was a field, neatly divided into plots and planted with maize and corn. A woman was tilling the soil, using what looked like an ancient hoe. On the other side were houses, one-storeyed. Children played in the dirt, and a boy stood holding a pony by a makeshift rope bridle.

'These houses,' Miguel said, pausing and hitching a foot onto a pile of stones, 'are made of adobe bricks, clay and mud mixed with straw and water. They are put into moulds, and then left to dry in the sun. They dry very hard, like brick, and they will last many years. The thatched roofs are made from lachu, a very strong type of grass only found in the Andes. We feed it to our llamas, too.'

Sasha peered in through one of the windows. There was nothing inside but a few cardboard boxes and a couple of wooden pallets covered in rugs. The cooking seemed to be done outside, over a wood fire. What a life, she thought, and felt grateful for the luxuries of her own.

'What do they do for money?' Nic asked.

'They grow their crops, they sell them at the market, and some of the men from here will work on the trail as porters or cooks. There is a primary school for this community, the children learn to read and write, and they are taught Spanish. Most will be bilingual.'

'Where do they go to secondary school?'

'Not all will go,' Miguel said. 'There is a bus, from here, to take them to the secondary school in Chilca but many families need them here to work on the land, to carry food and cloth to sell at the market.'

'University?'

Miguel grimaced. 'Very few go to university. It costs many dollars, and few people who live out here in the mountains could afford it.'

'What about you?' Katie said.

'Me? I am not from here. My family lives a hundred miles from here, higher up in the mountains.'

'What do your parents do?'

'My father is a teacher, and a musician. He is a little involved in politics too. He is a very clever man. My mother, too, went to university but now she raises my brothers and sisters. We have a farm, high in the hills.' He was silent for a moment.

'What do they do for fun, here?' Katie said.

Miguel looked at her as if he did not understand the question. 'What do you mean, for fun?'

'For parties, celebrations.'

'Oh,' he said, smiling. 'There are many parties, celebrations. There are feast days to celebrate the end of harvest, the summer solstice – many days of celebrations. This community is a big family, there will be three or four generations living in the same house and there is very strong family loyalty.'

'Do they drink alcohol?'

Miguel looked amused by the question. 'The men drink chica. It is a form of fermented maize, a bit like beer. It is very strong.'

'Do you drink it?' Sasha asked.

'No,' he laughed. 'I do not drink chicha. I do not need chicha to make me happy.'

After six kilometres, Sasha was beginning to feel the strain. Her new walking boots had rubbed a blister on her toe, and she longed to take them off. She was walking on her own, with Nic and Katie chatting behind her. Sasha didn't like them excluding her, but there was only room to walk two abreast. Oh grow up, she told herself. It's like being sucked back into the politics of the playground. They aren't talking about me. Miguel walked ahead, and Sasha, screwing up her courage, quickened her pace to catch up with him.

'Where did you study?' she said, panting a little.

'At the university in Cusco, where I learned English, and I spent a year at Harvard, in America.'

'Harvard!'

'Yes, I won a scholarship to study languages. But I was not happy there. It was too materialistic for me. And I missed my home.' He sighed. 'If I am away too long my soul begins to die,' he said. He smiled. 'Dramatic, no? But it is true.' He looked sideways at her. 'And you?'

'What?'

'Where did you study?'

'Oh, at an art college, in London,' she said. 'But it was a long time ago.'

'Why did you give it up? If you had a talent?'

She laughed, embarrassed. 'You have to be really good to get anywhere and I was just average, I guess. I loved it – well, I still do, but I don't have the time any more. There's no money in art – only a very few artists in Britain make any money at all, and I had to do another job I didn't like much just to survive. Then I met my husband and, well, with the children and running a home, it seemed to slip down my list of priorities.'

'Your husband must be proud of you, though, to be married to an artist,' he said.

Sasha stared at him. Should Alistair be proud of her?

'I don't think he's ever really thought of that, to be honest. He's never really seen me paint, I'd given it up several years before I met him, and I was teaching in a school.'

'And your husband. What does he do?' Miguel

increased his pace, and Sasha had to almost run to keep up.

'He has a business, making television programmes. He used to work for a big organization and then he set up his own company which makes leisure programmes for the cable channels.'

'Does he like his job? It sounds very interesting.'

'It's a bit stressful at the moment. He's had to invest in lots of technology like cameras and editing equipment and he isn't quite seeing the money come in yet. He really needs some sponsorship.'

'That must be hard for you.'

Sasha looked at him quickly. He was very sharp at picking things up. 'It is, sometimes,' she said. 'I hate to see him worry.'

'He is a lucky man,' Miguel said, smoothly. 'To have you worry about him.'

Sasha said nothing, thinking that the last thing Alistair would call her was sympathetic.

'I'm not sure he thinks he is very lucky,' she said, slowly.

Miguel stopped, and turned to look at her. 'You have children?'

'Two. Two girls, one's a teenager, the other is nine.'

'I have a sister of nine,' he said. 'She is my princess.'

'Does she look like you?'

'Oh no,' he said. 'She is beautiful. So you stay at home and look after the house? You are happy, looking after your home and your children?'

'Yes,' she said quickly. 'I think so. Content with my lot, anyway. That's a rather personal question.'

'Contentment does not feed a restless mind, and you

have a restless mind, I think. I will fill it up,' he said, teasing her, 'with all the things I can show you.' Sasha glanced at him swiftly. It was a rather creepy thing to say, and she felt almost as if she was being preyed on. She looked back at the others. They were at least fifteen metres behind. She didn't feel quite safe with him.

'How do you know so much about the history of your country?' she said, changing the subject.

He shrugged. 'Some of it I learn at the university. Most is inside me, I hear it from my father. We grow up being taught to be proud of our culture and remember the old legends. He told me so much,' he smiled to himself. 'When I was a child he used to sit by my bed and tell me fantastic stories and legends about the condor, and the great llama in the sky that guides us. Remind me to tell you,' he said, looking at her. 'When we have time. When we are alone.' A shiver ran through her. 'I would like to teach you what my father has taught me.'

The path took them over a bridge, and then through some trees, before they came to a clearing. The porters had set up the tents, and smoke rose from a campfire. 'Here we have lunch,' Miguel said. When they had set off on the trail there had been sunshine, but now it was dull, overcast, with the threat of rain, and they squeezed thankfully into one of the tents, inside which the porters had set up a wobbly folding table and chairs.

'Tea,' Miguel said, lifting the flap, two cups in his hand. 'I hope it's not coca tea,' Katie whispered. 'It isn't,' he said. 'It is PG Tips for the English ladies.' They all laughed, and Nic got up to help him. Miguel motioned her to sit down. 'You will be tired. Do not worry, it is our job to serve you.'

Lunch was an odd mixture of Peruvian and Western food – boiled potatoes with a strange sauce, full of unidentifiable lumps. There was also bread, butter and tomatoes, for which Sasha and Katie were very thankful. As they ate, the rain drummed on the roof of the tent. 'You bring the rain,' Miguel said. 'It should be only a shower, we are out of the rainy season.'

'Does anyone walk the trail in the rainy season?' Sasha asked.

'A few, but it is very muddy and slippery. There are points on the trail when you will be walking down very steep steps, and it can be dangerous. This is the best time to come, in May. In the summer, the trail is very busy – there is a constant stream of people. I do not like it then. This is my favourite time.'

'Don't you get bored of it?' Katie asked, biting into a pear.

He looked at her incredulously. 'Bored of the mountains? To be bored here you must be dead inside. Every day they feed me and fill me with gratitude that this – ' he waved his hands around – 'is my office. Now. On to Llactapata, our first ruins.'

Before leaving the tent, they pulled on their waterproofs. No-one, not even Katie, could look glamorous in a full-length waterproof with a hood, but it was either that or get very wet, and there would be nowhere to dry their clothes. They trudged on for over two hours, the hoods of the capes making them unable to look about them, and Sasha felt very damp and miserable. Her feet hurt, and the mist hung low over the mountains, blanking out the view. It wasn't what she had expected at all, and she hoped the rain would not last.

Llactapata was a small ruin, little more than individual piles of stones, on a hillside at the side of the trail. 'It means literally the city above,' Miguel said, taking hold of Sasha's hand to pull her into a circle where they could all shelter, surrounded by the ancient stones. His hand felt warm and dry. He was very quick to touch her, and it made her feel edgy, as if her personal space was being invaded. Being near him made her feel jolted and uneasy, and she didn't know if it was because she found him attractive – which he obviously was – or because the way he stared at her made her nervous. I don't quite trust him, she thought. He's an adventurer, and I'm not going to be another of his little conquests on the trail. She watched to see if he tried to touch Nic or Katie in the same way, and he didn't. I'm not going to look at him, she thought. I most certainly am not going to give him the idea that I fancy him. How embarrassing, when nothing could be further from the truth.

'Interesting chat?' Katie murmured as she squatted down next to her inside the ruins.

'Boring history stuff,' she hissed back.

'I should watch Mr Gropey,' Katie said, quietly.

'What?' Sasha said, and then realized Miguel was staring at her again.

'Now I tell you something about the Inca trail,' he

159

said, motioning to them to crouch down against the walls, out of the wind. 'This is an administration point, very useful for communications. The trail was built by the Incas around 1400 AD and it took over a hundred years to build. Many thousands of men were involved in its construction, and it covers 28,000 miles in all, stretching from Quito, in Ecuador, through Peru to Bolivia. Its use was as a route for communication, with couriers, *chaskis*, situated in huts, *tampa*, at three-mile points along the trail – every two miles in the most mountainous regions. These *chaskis* were the most nimble young men, and they could run a mile easily in under four minutes – three minutes twelve seconds was the record. That way the nobles could send messages very quickly to the king, the Inca Lord, about invasions, uprisings, financial problems – anything. It was a most efficient way of transmitting information, like a relay race. The trail is laid with tiny paving stones, the steps each made by hand.'

He paused, to make sure they were all paying attention, and Sasha had to snap out of her daydream about lying in a long, hot bath. It was so pleasant here, out of the wind and the rain, and it made her feel sleepy. 'We think we can create so much,' he said wistfully. 'But it is nothing compared to the achievements of our past. They achieved so much with so little, just their bare hands and the breadth of their thoughts.' Sasha shifted awkwardly. Her knees were going to sleep, and, fascinating as it was, she was going to have to stand up in a minute to stretch her legs. Being bent over like a paper clip was not her most comfortable position.

'This small town,' he waved his hand at the stone ruins, 'would have been a place where grain and produce was stored, and administration of the land was handled. Most of the Inca tribes lived in these small settlements or the larger cities such as Cusco, because it would have been dangerous to live on their own, and people derived much pleasure, comfort and support from their community. When men were at war, or away building the trail, their wives and children would be given produce to help them. There was no monetary system, simply bartering. There was no written language, either,' he said, and then reached into his pocket. 'Instead they would use this, the *khipu*.' It was a row of different-coloured wool threads, like a wool necklace. 'This way they could keep track of the number in the population, each knot in the string representing a hundred, or a thousand people. They could record how many had paid their taxes with produce, and it was also a way of recording the passage of time. Clever, no?'

'Very,' Nic said, and held out her hand to feel the *khipu*. Miguel passed it to her, and then, taking it back, handed it to Sasha. He let his fingers rest against hers, so lightly the others would not have noticed. His fingers felt warm, and it was pleasant to be touched. But it would be so easy to give him the wrong idea, because he was obviously very practised at this rather cheesy seduction routine of staring and touching. There's nothing very subtle about him, she thought, as he showed the *khipu* to Katie, flashing her a smile which showed his very white teeth. Then he felt her eyes on him, and looked up. Sasha's heart missed a

161

beat – he really means it, she thought. Staring into his eyes was like drowning. It was, she had to admit, immensely seductive to be stared at like that with such blatant intent. Flattering, too. But he probably did it to everyone, or at least one woman each trip. She really must get a grip. She was acting like a teenager. But it was, she admitted to herself, rather fun. Harmless fun, she added, hurriedly. She hadn't been looked at like that in a very long time. Behave yourself, woman, she said, sternly. What would Katie and Nic think?

'We will leave now,' he said, noting how they were shifting from foot to foot trying to keep the circulation going in their thighs. 'I had hoped to tell you more about the Incas but I will tell you tonight, when we are dry and comfortable in our tents.' He flashed a look at Sasha. 'And who is sleeping alone tonight?'

'Me again,' Nic said.

Was Sasha imagining it, or did a look of disappointment cross his face?

'And you,' Katie said, boldly. 'Will you be sleeping alone?'

'Of course,' he said, laughing. 'Unless one of you wants to share with me?' They all laughed apart from Sasha, who looked down at her muddy boots, and felt a blush rising to the roots of her hair.

'I told you,' Katie said, as they slogged behind him up the next hill towards the evening campsite. 'He's shameless. You had better watch yourself.'

'What about you?'

'Oh, he doesn't fancy me. You, for some reason, are the chosen one.'

'Well, I wish he'd choose someone else. He's giving me the creeps.'

'*Vraiment?*' Katie said, raising her eyebrows at her. 'Are you sure you don't fancy him the teensiest weensiest little bit?'

'Absolutely not. Oh come on, he's young enough to be my son, sort of.'

'Oedipal. Even more fun.'

'You have one sick mind.'

'I know. It may be small, but it's gratifyingly sick.'

'And crammed with idiotic notions.'

'We'll see,' Katie said, laughing, shaking the droplets out of her hair. 'We'll see. I should keep the zip done up on your sleeping bag anyway, just in case he comes a-creeping round in the night.'

By the end of the day, they were exhausted. Soon after they had joined the trail proper, they started the long climb into the mountains. At one point Sasha had been directly behind Miguel, and stopped to look back at Katie and Nic. They were walking, heads bowed, leaning on their walking sticks, knees rising and falling in the rhythm of the trail. Behind them the land fell steeply away, into a deep gorge, the trail they had already climbed snaking away beneath, winding around the curves to the foot of the mountain. In the valley floor, no more than a brown thread, weaved the Urubamba river. Had they really walked so far? The hills around them were rocky, with patches of green grass, but mostly they were dark brown in colour, covered in rough, high bracken-like growth. Away behind them another mountain rose, its peak shrouded in cloud. It was as if they were climbing into heaven, the trail their footpath to the clouds.

They camped the night at a place called Huayllabamba, above another small settlement of houses. This village had a school, and as they approached Sasha heard a roar, and screams. She looked enquiringly at Miguel. 'It sounds as if the football match has started,' he smiled. The rain had eased a little, and as they got nearer they could see a rough playing field, really just a flat area of grass flanked by goalposts. Small groups of trekkers and other porters stood watching, with little children from the village running in and out of their legs. The game, between the porters, was unbelievably fierce and competitive, played at a speed Sasha had never seen close up. It was brutal too, with hard tackles. They seemed incredibly skilful and swift.

'Football,' Miguel shrugged. 'Our country's passion.'

'Do you play?'

'A little,' he replied. A couple of the backpackers had joined in, fit young Australians, but they were being crucified, the fleet Peruvians running rings around them. They did not seem to notice the altitude, although the sweat, despite the rain, poured from them. And they had no change of clothes, Sasha thought. Ew. Nice.

Their tents were pitched slightly to one side of most of the others, but the ground was still damp, and had been churned into a thick mud. Sasha thought wistfully of the Hotel Monasterio, and their marble bathroom. It seemed a very long way away. Was it only last night? This was another world entirely.

The porters had put all their bags onto a blue tarpaulin, to keep them out of the mud, and Sasha collected hers and hauled it onto her shoulder. Miguel was behind her in an instant. 'Let me,' he said. He took her bag, and carried it over to one of the tents. Katie laughed behind her. 'Favouritism,' she said, loudly. Sasha turned and made a face at her. Miguel reached down and unzipped the tent, kneeling carefully on the groundsheet as he slid the duffle bag inside. Then he leant back. 'After you,' he said. His eyes were teasing. There was barely room to squeeze past him to get into the tent. Sasha looked back, and saw Katie had stopped to chat to Nic.

His eyes held hers. She leant forward, almost bent double, and then placed one hand on the ground just inside the tent to steady herself. He was so close, she could feel his breath on her neck, his body only inches from hers. She slid forward, while he held the flap of the tent open, and she could feel him against her. She felt the long, hard muscle of his thigh against her side, his chest against her arm. She could not look up, but knew his lips were almost touching her neck. She closed her eyes. How could she fall for this? But it was so exciting, so immoral, to let even the smallest thing happen, the merest touch. She would stay in control, though, and not let it go too far.

'I hope you're not going to take up all the space.' Katie's voice made her start, and Miguel jumped away from her. 'I don't think there would be room for me in there,' he said smoothly. 'Too right,' Katie said. Sasha, who had quickly pulled herself right inside the tent, out of harm's way, sat up and hugged her knees. She assumed the most innocent expression she could, while Katie looked at her accusingly. At her feet were her sleeping bag, rolled-up sleeping mat and her duffle bag.

'I saw you,' Katie said, once Miguel was out of earshot. 'He was practically biting your neck.'

'He was just helping me with the zip.'

'Yeah, right. Trying to help you out of your knickers more like.'

'Katie!'

'Well, he's hardly subtle, is he?'

'He seems a very good guide and I think you are imagining it,' Sasha said primly, rooting about for her book. 'It's all in your mind.'

'Let's just hope so. Christ, I am knackered. My knees hurt, my feet hurt, I am soaking wet and I cannot do anything with my hair. Look at me.' Sasha looked at her and snorted. Katie's hair, normally so immaculate, was hanging around her face in soaking rat's tails. Her mascara had run, and she looked pale and shivery. 'I have seen you look better,' Sasha admitted.

'I feel like shit. I would give anything for a bath, anything.'

'There is a shower in the campsite,' Sasha suggested, trying to ease her soaking trousers down over her hips without taking off her knickers at the same time.

'Fantastic, if you want to shower in freezing cold water surrounded by twenty-year-old Australian backpackers.'

'Sounds like fun.'

'Female backpackers. Honestly, Sasha, I'm worried

about you. At home you are Miss Goody Two-shoes and here, well . . .'

'Hardly fair,' Sasha said. 'I haven't done anything.'

'Yet,' Katie said, darkly.

'How am I going to dry these trousers?' Sasha said, holding them up, dripping onto the ground sheet.

'Stick them in a plastic bag. You've got another pair.'

Sasha levered herself into clean, dry trousers and felt much better. Sliding into her sleeping bag to keep warm, she said, 'I could almost go to sleep now.'

'Well if lunch is anything to go by,' Katie said, smoothing baby wipes over her face, 'I don't think you'd miss much by not having dinner.'

Katie settled down to read her romantic novel. After half an hour, Sasha was bored with reading.

'I'm going to go and have a look about.'

'Mm. Call me when it's dinner, will you? Yum, yum. I can't wait. What will it be tonight? Hairballs in tomato sauce?'

Outside, the rain had eased, but there was still a leaden mist in the air. She could hear shouts from the football pitch, and around her the porters were setting up the meal tent. The cook was crouched over a small Calor gas stove, and Sasha tried not to look too closely at what he was cooking, because it seemed as if camp hygiene left a lot to be desired. She set off through the campsite to the far side, where there was a clear view of the mountains beyond. They were relatively low here, at almost three thousand metres – on the third day they would rise to the highest point, the Warmiwanuscca Pass, or Dead Woman's Pass, at over four thousand metres above sea level, which Sasha was dreading. To be that high you needed to have cloven hooves.

Stretching away ahead of her were the distant peaks, the peaks of the mountains they would climb. From here, it looked impossible. Behind her rose the sounds of the campsite, the clanking of pots, the unzipping of tents and the murmur of conversation. In front of her there was nothing but the sight and sounds of the mountains. They rose away from her, majestic, clad in deep green vegetation in the fading light, a trace of cloud hanging suspended in the air between two peaks ahead. It was like looking at the roof of the world, she thought. The peace she had felt in Cusco settled on her again, and, to her astonishment, a tear slid down her cheek. She reached up to brush it away. It wasn't a tear of sadness, but a tear of happiness. Not content-ment. Happiness.

'Beautiful, isn't it?' She started. It was an Australian voice. She turned and saw one of the young men from the football game. She remembered him because he'd been playing in a woolly hat with earflaps, and she'd thought at the time what a nice face he had. 'It is like standing on top of the world, isn't it?' he said.

'It's incredible,' she sighed.

'Is this your first time out here?'

'Oh yes. I've never been to South America before. You?'

'First time on the trail,' he said. 'I'm Mike, by the way.'

'Sasha.'

'Nice name.'

'Are you travelling with a group?'

168

'Just me and my mate,' he said.

'No porters?'

'No way. We're roughing it, doing it properly. None of this namby-pamby porter lark.' She felt she was being teased.

'You mean we aren't really experiencing the trail because we don't have to carry everything with us?'

'Too right,' he said.

'So you wouldn't want to use our chemical loo, then?'

'You're kidding! You have your own loo?'

'Yup.'

'I gotta stay in with you. That's the worst thing about the trail. Crapping in the great outdoors.'

'How long have you been in Peru?'

'Three weeks now. I've taken a sabbatical from work, I'm spending two months in South America and then I'm heading north for a month, and then home.'

'That's really brave,' Sasha said, wistfully.

'Brave? Stupid, more like. I don't know if they'll hold my job open for me. But hey, you only live once. Australia's a small place for such a big country.'

He was tall, much taller than Sasha, and he still wore his woolly hat. Remarkably, it suited him. He had an open, handsome face and Sasha judged him to be in his late twenties, maybe early thirties.

'You want to come to a party tonight?' he asked. Wow, thought Sasha. Two propositions in one day from handsome men. This was seeing life. 'We're going to have some beers around the old campfire. It might be fun. Bring your friends.'

'I will,' she said. 'Thanks.'

'No worries. See you.'

Sasha stood for a moment, drinking in the view. I can be anyone I want, she thought. She wrapped her arms around herself and stood, immobile, as a huge bird – was it a condor? – soared up from the base of the valley and then glided, without apparent effort, over the summit of the mountain. For the first time in her life she felt perfect, perfect peace.

That night in the meal tent they were all in a good mood, with Katie complaining loudly about the lack of alcohol. They had relatively normal spaghetti bolognaise, for which they were profoundly grateful. Miguel said he would make sure they tried ceviche before the week was out, a type of fish marinated in lime and coriander, a traditional dish. At the Sanctuary Lodge, he said. The food was very good there. 'Are you staying there too?' Katie asked.

'I don't think so,' he said, looking directly at Sasha. 'I will stay further down the mountain at Machu Picchu Pueblo,' he said. 'I know my place.'

After dinner, they set off to find Mike, Katie moaning that she hadn't had time to put on any make-up. Miguel had seemed rather huffy about their desire to go off, because he was obviously working up to one of his lectures, but they all felt they'd had enough history for one day. They left him looking rather forlorn, alone in the meal tent.

'He could have come with us,' Katie said. 'I think he's jealous.'

'This is descending to the level of school disco.'

'Just because you've got two blokes after you,' Katie laughed.

'I have not. Don't be so silly.' Across the campsite they could see the glow of a fire, and hear the murmur of conversation. Someone had a battery-powered CD player, and the dull thump of the bass drifted over to them.

Mike jumped up when he saw them. 'Hey, glad you could make it. Take a seat.' He'd found some canvas folding chairs, and, looking around, Sasha saw twenty or so people, mostly young men and women in their twenties. Quite a few of the girls were astonishingly pretty, and Sasha wondered if the three of them looked very old by comparison. But then she stopped herself. What did it matter? Why did she even think about it, what difference did it make how old she was, it didn't make her any less interesting or give her any less right to be there. She had to stop doing this, writing herself off.

'Tinny?' Mike said.

'Thanks.' They all took a beer, and sat down. Mike, who'd obviously been in the middle of a story, started talking again. 'And then, fuck me, there was this huge shark swimming towards me.'

'So what did you do?'

'What do you think I did? I swam off as fast as buggery.'

Beyond the glow of the fire lay the dark, steady bulk of the mountains. They were really there, in this extraordinary place, sitting drinking beer on the top of the world. She wanted to freeze the moment, hold it in time.

*　*　*

At two in the morning Sasha woke, her bladder full. She was desperate for a pee, but going to the chemical toilet meant sliding herself out of the worm-like sleeping bag, pulling on her trekking trousers, putting on her jacket over the jumper she'd kept on in bed, finding her head-torch and putting it on, all without waking Katie, who lay snoring gently beside her. Then she would have to unzip the tent, and tiptoe in the darkness, with only the head-torch's meagre beam, past the tent containing all the porters, and somehow pee without waking up the entire camp. And it would be cold. If she lay there and thought about something else, not beer, the feeling might go away. She felt simultaneously cold and clammy, her face and hands sticky, because the only thing they had to wash themselves with were baby wipes. They'd cleaned their teeth in a basin of water provided by one of the cooks, and once she'd spat in that, there was no way she was going to use that water on her face.

She lay there and found her thoughts drifting to Miguel. She was finding it hard to weigh him up. He was an odd mixture of the mature and immature – mature in that he knew so much, seemed so responsible, but immature in that he appeared to think she would consider it remotely feasible to fancy him, and his seduction routine was more teenage than mature. He was so attractive, though. He took the history of his country so seriously, as if he was personally responsible for what happened to the people – what had he kept saying? – 'his birthright'. It was an odd phrase, and she wondered what he meant by it. Mike was really nice too. How wonderful to have your whole life ahead of you, with the freedom just to take off and do what you wanted. She'd talked to him at length about his travel plans, or rather lack of them – he just seemed to drift about, waiting for opportunities to come up, and seemed supremely unworried about not knowing where he was going to stay after the trail and not having any money.

Sasha was so used to making plans. If she looked at her life, it seemed so small, so hemmed in by comparison. Of course with children you had to have a structure, you had to know what was going to happen day after day and there were endless deadlines to be met. But maybe once Emily was at university, she could take off. There was so much she wanted to do and for the first time, it felt possible. Nic was talking about climbing Everest next year, and at first Sasha had thought she was joking, but then she said you could trek to base camp. That would be fantastic.

Suddenly, all these opportunities were opening up in front of her. But Alistair. Thinking about him was like bringing down a lid on her happiness. He'd never let her go off again. If only he would want to join her and try something like this. But he'd look at her as if she was mad, and say did she really think that at this stage in his career he'd be able to just take off on such a pointless escapade? Only it wasn't an escapade, she thought. It was living. It was making the most of your threescore years and ten. As Mike had said tonight, you were a long time dead.

Katie had been very flirtatious with Mike, but he hadn't responded, had paid them all an equal amount of attention. He was just a lovely guy. She'd forgotten what fun men could be. She'd never been the flirty type, and being married to Alistair, who in the early years had been very jealous, meant that she didn't let herself get close to other men, or talk to them intimately.

Her thoughts went back to Miguel. There was something odd about him, she thought. Something very mysterious. There's something he's not telling us. His clothes were too expensive – what teacher's son could afford cashmere sweaters, no matter how much money he made on the trail? And how could he have travelled to Harvard, and Britain and France when it was apparently hard for Peruvians to obtain passports, never mind afford the cost of air fares?

'Sasha, are you awake?' Katie's whispered voice made her jump.

'I am. I cannot sleep in this thing, I keep sliding off the end of the sleeping mat, and then my legs get twizzled up in it and I have to untwizzle them. I don't think I am a natural camper. Do people really choose to do this for a holiday?'

'Didn't you camp as a child?'

'God, no, my mother would have died at the thought of taking a holiday on a camping site. That was what the common people did.' Sasha laughed, rather bitterly.

'Did you love her?'

'Wow, that's a question for the middle of the night. Did I love my mother? Um, no, not really. I was more frightened of her than anything, both Daddy and I

174

were. She had such a powerful presence, she had – has – such definite views on everything that we spent most of our lives hiding from her. There was no give in her. Daddy plunged himself into his work, and I, well, I suppose I escaped into art. I spent most of my childhood in my bedroom, drawing or reading. I think marrying Alistair was a form of escape. He was the first boyfriend I ever had who could stand up to her. That should have been a warning, shouldn't it, really, that I was simply exchanging one dictator for another.'

'Our only holidays were camping when I was a child.'

'Really?' Sasha could not keep the astonishment out of her voice. This did not fit in with her idea of Katie's background at all. She had always been reluctant to talk about her past, and Sasha had assumed that she'd had a middle-class background like her own, been to a private school, that kind of thing. Katie's voice, for a start, was far more plummy than her own. She had always visualized Katie growing up in London, her father something in the City, her mother an older glamorous version of Katie. It was one of the things she'd always taken for granted about Katie, that she was posher than Sasha herself was, although it had occurred to her that it was odd she didn't talk about her parents.

'You have got the wrong idea,' Katie said, her voice so quiet Sasha could barely hear her. 'I was brought up in a one-horse northern town beneath the old mill chimneys. In a high-rise block. My father worked for the council. Our holidays were camping by the coast in Skegness.'

175

'No!' Sasha said, and had to stop herself laughing. There was something in Katie's voice which told her it wasn't funny at all.

'It's not something I boast about, obviously,' Katie said, and there was a smile in her voice. 'So don't you dare go around telling anyone, Lydia especially.' Lydia was what Katie called a pretend friend, a mwah, mwah friend who lived in the same village and often went to the same parties, a ruthless snob and one who would simply adore this little nugget of information because she deeply resented Katie's bigger house, more expensive clothes and exotic foreign holidays.

'So how did you meet Harvey?'

'That, as they say, is a long story. I'd been through a tough time, and he – well, he helped me. You could say he saved my life.'

'A bad time?'

'Oh, yes, a very bad time. You see . . . I had a baby, a girl, who died when she was just ten days old. I was only seventeen, and my parents had thrown me out. It was hardly the Dark Ages, but they wanted me to have an abortion, and I wouldn't.'

'God, Katie!'

'The baby's father, you see, was in prison. Not very socially acceptable, is it? He lived on our estate and was always very wild, always in trouble with the police. Of course, he's out of prison now and I'm terrified of bumping into him – irony of ironies, he was jailed near where we live now, and I have a horror that he's settled around us somewhere.' Her voice broke, and Sasha thought about reaching out to touch her shoulder, but decided against it. Whatever she

176

could say would sound trite. Katie was lying on her back, talking to the roof of the tent in a calm, matter-of-fact voice.

'So, there I was, pregnant by this bloke my parents couldn't stand. They said I had ruined their name and that everyone on the estate would think serve them right, thinking they're better than everybody else. I was working then, but just as a temp, and I couldn't earn enough money to keep me and a baby, and rent a flat. I could have gone to the council, but that was not in my life plan. I was going to escape and have a very different life. Ending up in another council flat would have been admitting defeat. My midwife said I could give her up for adoption, but then there was no need.' There was a pause, as Katie drew her breath in slowly.

'There was no need because she was born with the cord around her neck, and she was starved of oxygen. They said later her death was a blessing, really, because she would have had severe brain damage.' Katie was crying now. 'I'm sorry.'

'Don't be silly.' Sasha rolled over, and reached out to touch her arm. 'Hang on,' she said, and shuffled forward to pull some tissues out of her sponge bag.

'Thanks.' Katie took them, and wiped her eyes. 'Crazy, isn't it, after all these years. I was all alone at the birth, but then as soon as she was born they took her from me, and I didn't know what was happening. I didn't see her until the next day, when she was on a ventilator. I never held her, Sasha. I never got to hold my baby, not even in the moments before she died.' Sasha held her hand tightly. 'The doctor said the risk of infection was too great – they didn't know she was

177

about to die – but I wished I'd just pushed them all aside, opened it up and held her, and then at least she would have died knowing what it felt like to be held by a person who loves you.' Both she and Sasha were crying. 'She died in that sterile little unit, and the closest I got to her was holding her finger. I don't know if she ever even saw me, or had any understanding that she wasn't totally alone in the world.'

'I never knew – why didn't you tell me?'

'No-one knows,' Katie said, blowing her nose. 'Apart from Harvey, and you, now. I don't keep up with any of my old friends from school, and my parents are dead. They didn't even come to the funeral. It was me and the vicar, standing by that tiny grave, and as they threw the earth on her I couldn't bear to think of her body, so alone and cold. I could do nothing for her, she didn't even know she had ever had a mother. I can never make it up to her, or make it better. Do you know what it's like, to feel that you have failed someone so fundamentally?'

'You didn't fail her,' Sasha said. 'There was nothing you could have done. It wasn't your fault.'

'Do you think that makes it any better? A child was born into a world of strangers and not one person really touched her, or held her, or told her they loved her. What kind of torment do you think she is in?'

'I'm sure . . .' Sasha didn't know what to say. She couldn't bring herself to say, 'She's in heaven,' because it sounded so trite. 'I'm sure she did know you were there.'

'After she was buried,' Katie went on, 'I used to go and sit by the grave, for hours. I used to imagine what the worms were doing to her little body and it was all I could do to stop myself ripping her out of the earth and trying to hold her.' There was a long pause.

'You can't blame yourself,' Sasha told her again.

'I know,' Katie said. 'But it's very hard not to.'

Chapter Eleven

'There, do you see it?'

'Miguel, you are making this up. There's nothing there.'

'There is – look, look. Halfway up the mountain, just by that fallen tree.' A group of fellow trekkers paused behind them, to see what they were staring at.

'I've got some binoculars,' Nic said. 'Hang on.' She took the binoculars out of her backpack.

'I think he's right. It's a bear all right. And wow – it's got a cub with it.'

'Let me see.' Katie took the binoculars Nic had lifted from her neck. 'It is too. That is so cute. Here, Sasha, have a look.'

They stood four abreast on the narrow trail, gazing at the side of the mountain opposite them. All morning they had walked, climbing steadily, and there had been little conversation as they needed all their breath just to keep going. The terrain had grown steadily more bleak as they climbed from the lush valleys where the llamas grazed and smoke rose from the chimneys of the small settlements, to this higher, rocky place, the paving stones of the trail giving way to steep steps cut into the rock. Ahead of them the trail snaked upwards, winding its way to the next summit, and far in front of them fellow trekkers moved slowly, like small ants.

Sasha could only motivate herself by setting points ahead of her – 'I will walk to that rock, and then I will rest.' And when she stopped, she had to lean on her walking stick, fighting for breath. Her thighs were burning, and this was nothing compared to Dead Woman's Pass, the pass they would be climbing to-morrow. Fear rose inside her – already she was struggling, her breath coming in thin, high gasps, and sweat trickled down her back. Miguel had told them that once altitude sickness had really taken a hold, the only sure remedy was to drop back down to lower levels where there was more oxygen. And that would ruin their journey.

'You see,' Miguel said. He took the binoculars from Katie, and then stood directly behind Sasha, holding them up in front of her eyes. She could barely con-centrate, as he stood so close behind her. His voice was very close to her ear. 'There – do you see them?' She reached up with one hand to steady the binoculars, and her fingers touched his. His hand curled around hers, and for one split second, she let herself rest against him. His hand tightened on hers.

'It is the spectacled bear,' he said to the others. His other hand reached up and rested gently on her waist. Now she could feel all of him, in this apparently innocent pose. It was reckless, but she did not move away from him, and she could feel his breath on her neck, the warmth of his body. Katie's confidences the night before had emboldened her in a strange way.

'I want to see the cub again,' Katie said, pointedly. Miguel reluctantly lifted the binoculars away from Sasha's face. 'Here,' he said, stepping back. Sasha turned to glance at him, and met his eyes. He gave her a wicked, blatant look. No-one had looked at her like that for years. She was twenty again. What had Katie said? You never knew what life would bring. At that moment he was all she saw, this man who was so much a part of this country, this country which was enchanting her. In a strange way, it felt quite right to transfer her passion for Peru to this man.

Last night she and Katie had slept curled in towards each other in their sleeping bags, protectively. At six, when she woke, she looked over at Katie, who was already awake.

'Are you OK?'

'I'm fine. I feel – I feel kind of free. You have no idea what it's like lugging something like that about with you. It's as if I have two lives. The person I am, the person I'm ashamed of, and the person everyone else thinks I am. You were brilliant,' she added.

'I didn't do anything.'

'You listened. You didn't pass judgement. You weren't shocked.'

'I was a bit,' Sasha admitted. 'I'd like . . .'

'What?'

'I'd like to see the grave, if I may. Is that too weird? Tell me if that's intrusive.'

'It will be such a relief,' Katie said, 'to be able to take someone with me. Someone who understands. Maybe I've been silly. No. Correct that. I've been too feeble, too stupidly fearful what other people will think of me if they know. I have been denying, in a way, that she existed. It's very shallow of me, isn't it?'

'No. It's understandable.'

'But she did exist, and the more people who know, the more of a life, a real life, she had. Do you see that? I can't just airbrush a child – a *child* – out of my life, and pretend she never existed.'

'I do see.'

'Otherwise she was just a mistake, and people aren't mistakes, are they?'

'No. You can still love someone after they're dead, you know,' Sasha said. 'It doesn't just end. Love doesn't die.'

'Do you think so?' Katie's voice held a note of hope. 'Do you think she knows, somewhere? That I still love her, and think about her all the time?'

Sasha turned over onto her stomach. 'I do. I think that love can be as strong, and as purposeful, as when people are alive. It sounds mad, but that love can be often even more of a support after death. It doesn't just have to be a negative emotion, such a powerful sense of loss. My father – well, since my father died I have felt much stronger as a person. It's as if you finally have to grow up. Does that sound stupid? I loved him so very much and he was always there for me, but since he died I have felt differently about myself, I've felt that I have to make something of my life and not waste it, because I need to do it for him. I can't just rely on him to make things better any more. He's there, I know, watching me. There has to be a use, doesn't there, to so much love? It can't just die, when they die. This sounds crazy but when things get really bad I can feel him with me, and all I need to do is reach out my hand and I can feel his hand in mine, and we are together. He guides me even more now that he is no longer here, in body. He is with me very powerfully in spirit. There. You must think me a complete loon.'

'Not at all. It makes sense to me. I can't just mourn Jessica, I have to do something positive with all that emotion. Just making myself feel bad about it is so pointless, isn't it?'

'Yes, it is. I know it's none of my business but I think you should have a child. Or adopt. If that's what you really want. Otherwise, you'll spend your whole life looking back. Not that another child would replace Jessica, but it would give you, I don't know, a reason. A reason to appreciate what you have.'

Katie looked long and hard at Sasha, as if making a decision. 'There's something else,' she said, very quietly.

'What?'

'How I met Harvey. Look Sasha, you must never tell anyone else this, not even Nic and especially not Alistair. Harvey would never forgive me. But now I've started I have to tell you everything. God, it must be this place. I've never dared before.' She took a deep breath. 'I stole a child. A baby. It was in the months after Jessica's death and I was just basically mad with grief. I was shopping, just wandering around town and there was this beautiful baby in a pushchair in Marks and Spencers and I went up to her, just to look at her, and she was just the same age as Jessica would have been. She was so beautiful, and as I looked at her, she opened her eyes and smiled at me. And it wasn't a baby I didn't know, it was her, and I reached down and picked her up. She was so warm, and she smelled just as I imagined Jessica would smell and I wrapped her up in the blanket and just walked out with her.'

'God.'

'I ran home with her in my arms and then when I shut the door I realized what I had done. She started to cry, and I had no milk, nothing to feed her with, and there was this great gap inside me that she filled, and I held her and held her, just trying to make her stop crying, but she wouldn't. I looked at her face, and it wasn't Jessica at all, but a stranger, a baby that was afraid of me.'

'So what did you do?'

'I rang the police, and told them what I had done, and they came for me. The woman, the mother,' she was crying hard now, 'the mother was completely hysterical, they said, and I had caused all this grief. Could I imagine what I had done? But I had this mad justification.'

'So Harvey was your lawyer? That's how you met?'

'Oh no,' she said. 'Harvey was the baby's father.'

Sasha sat bolt upright, banging her head against one of the tent posts. 'What?'

'Crazy, isn't it?' she said. 'I saw him in court, and right from the start I could see he was fascinated by me. It all came out, you see, all the details about Jessica, and his face was so kind. He took an interest in me, wanted to make me have some counselling and said he knew some people who could help and it went on from there.'

'But his children were older when he and his wife split, they were almost teenagers.'

'I was his mistress for years,' she said. 'We just carried on until, well, until we both realized we loved each other too much to be apart and he told his wife. I didn't ruin one child's life, I ruined three. His wife was such a bitch in the early years, she would hardly let him see the children.'

'How have you kept all this quiet?' Sasha asked in wonder.

'I'm very good at putting a brave face on things, keeping up appearances. Basically, I have reinvented myself,' she said. 'It was a long time ago. How long have you known me? Four years? That's four years after we were married, since I became who I am today. Of course we moved away, moved down south where nobody knew us. You see, don't you? That no-one can ever judge you.'

'Is that why you didn't have children of your own?'

'I didn't think I deserved them,' Katie said, simply. 'I was too scared as well that it might happen again, my baby might die, and Harvey wasn't keen – he had had his family, and he felt it would be even more of a betrayal to them to start a new one. But I see children, like you with Abbie and Emily, and it hurts so much. I would give anything to have what you have. When I hear you and Nic complaining about your teenagers, you have no idea what it does to me. You take for granted what I long for most in the world.'

'I know what you mean,' Sasha said. 'A tiny bit, about taking life for granted. When I worked in the school, one of the mums had an older child, a teenage girl who was so profoundly disabled she could not move, or see. She just lay in bed, and had to be fed through a drip and have twenty-four-hour care. Yet her brain was perfectly active. And you know what the mother said to me? She said, "Every day, I hear teenagers on our estate, moaning that there is nothing to do, how bored they are. And it is all I can do not to walk up to them and say, 'My daughter would give anything to have what you have, even just for an hour. To see, to walk around, to be a human being. To have the incredible gifts that you have.'" That's always brought me up short when I think I have a problem. Do you ever go back up there? To Jessica's grave?'

'Occasionally. On my own. But it's a long way . . . I've carved a life, and to be honest I'm a bit scared. It makes me feel out of control. People think my life is perfect,' she said, brushing away her tears. 'Don't they? It's so very hard to have something like this in your past, so enormous, and not have the courage to tell people. Sometimes I get angry with myself, but then why should I foist it on other people? And there's a big bit of me that is really ashamed, even now.'

'You never know,' Sasha said, slowly, 'what there is in other people's lives.'

'Christ, no. There's no such thing as the perfect life. You have to grab what you can. But I can't make it go away, airbrush it out of my life, because it's just too big. And there is a part of me which thinks that by hiding it, denying it ever happened, I'm twisting a

187

knife within myself and one day it will all come out and I won't be able to control it. It will bring me down. Does that sound too dramatic? You have no idea what it does to Harvey, the fear of people finding out. And I scare him, I know I do, when I drink too much and he looks at me and thinks . . . well, he must think of what happened, that I might blurt it all out. In many ways, he treats me more like a father would treat his daughter, and I must be this big responsibility to him. Like a case always around his neck.' She laughed bitterly. 'I'm like a project. And my life is to be beautiful and make his life run smoothly and his home look wonderful and create this fantasy of the perfect middle-class couple and entertain and flirt with his colleagues and make them think what a lucky old dog he is to have such a stunning young wife. I think that's why he was pleased I was going away, it must be a strain for him sometimes, never knowing when my past might pop out. What do you think of me now?' She turned onto her stomach, and looked searchingly into Sasha's face.

'I'm not sure,' Sasha said, slowly. 'I am shocked. I would never have thought . . . but you were so young, and none of it was really your fault. I admire you, I guess, for turning your life around and not letting it destroy you. Anyway, none of us have so much to be proud of. I think you should be proud of yourself for coping, for surviving and making a proper life.'

'I don't know if it is a proper life,' she said. 'A life without children.'

Sasha said nothing, as she knew Katie was right.

'I don't know why I've told you all this,' Katie said.

'It must be being here. Do you feel it? There's a kind of spirituality about it, in the mountains. As if you can't lie any more. Have you got any dark secrets in your past, to make me feel less of a lunatic?'

'Sorry, no,' Sasha said, staring at the roof of the tent. 'I have led a very blameless, dull little life. You mustn't envy me. But I do think –' She hesitated, not sure how to express herself. 'It isn't so healthy to have such a father–daughter relationship with Harvey. You aren't his child, to be looked after, you are his equal. You can't spend your whole life being grateful to him for rescuing you.'

Katie looked at her, astonished. Then she smiled, understanding. 'For a dim person you're quite clever,' she said.

'Thanks. I'm not clever, though. I'm really crap about lots of things.'

'Like what?'

Sasha sighed. She could no longer pretend. 'Like being married. Like being a wife. Like being a mother. I'm – I'm, well, kind of useless, sometimes. I know I need to make decisions but I'm scared to. I'm too scared of making the wrong one. It terrifies me that . . .'

'What do you mean?' Katie's voice was shocked, but hesitant, as if Sasha should only go on if she wanted to. 'You're the last person I would call useless. You always seem so organized to me. And so happy.'

Sasha stared at the tent wall. 'Alistair and I don't love each other,' she said, finally. 'We put on a good act in front of other people but we haven't loved each other for years. We just exist, in this kind of madness, and I'm terrified of our marriage turning into my

189

parents, but then by the same token I'm so scared of letting it all go. My parents seemed to live to make each other miserable, at least that's how my mum seemed to regard her role in life. It was so destructive, and it had a lasting effect on me. When I look back on my childhood, it seems to me that I lived in my head, in a fantasy world, because I was trying to escape the tension of home. I just don't know what is the best thing to do for the children. Should we stay together, and row endlessly, or should we split up and stop being a family? It's got to the point where we can't see the good things about each other. Sometimes I look at him and all I can see is bitterness and resentment that I'm not someone else. It sounds awful, but I just don't think he likes me very much as a person, and I don't like him. Maybe we've made each other that way, I don't know. We did love each other once, but I don't know where those two people went. I look at Alistair, but I can't see the man I married. I'm sorry. It's one of the reasons why I was so desperate to get away, and just be myself again. I feel that with him I have become someone I don't like, and I don't know if I can live like that any longer. The children do know – Abbie especially. I can't decide what is best – to make them live with two people who tear each other apart or make them go through the trauma of divorce and all that that entails.'

Katie reached out to her, as she had to Katie last night. 'You never do know, do you? And there was me thinking you lived this blissful, cheery little life. I envied you so much because you had everything I wanted. What will you do?'

'I don't know. I don't honestly know. The thing is – the thing is that both the children adore him, and he is a good father, so how can I take that away from them? It's the worst thing, the worst possible thing you can do to a child, and I don't think I have that right. And if I managed to make such a wrong decision about the person I married, how can I trust myself to make any other decisions? My judgement must be so crap. I've lived a half-life for a long time now, so I don't suppose there's any reason to think I can't carry on. Anyway,' she said, 'I have the kids, you, and Nic, and my other friends. Life isn't that bad. I'm very lucky in so many ways. Living without love is not the end of the world, is it? Most of all I have the children, and their love makes up for everything. I can cope.'

'Well,' Katie laughed. 'Look on the bright side. You can always run off with Miguel.'

'And live in a mud hut?'

'Adobe bricks,' Katie said, reprovingly. 'Anyway, think of the sex,' she added. 'Whoof.'

'You,' Sasha said, rolling over to hug her, 'should be minted. I love you.'

'Too right. Now should we mad dysfunctional bats get out of sleeping bags and greet the day?'

'Why not? Why not indeed?'

Chapter Twelve

That night Sasha slept alone in the single tent, exhausted by the day's climb. She had been looking forward to having some privacy, but now she found she did not want to be alone. She heard Nic and Katie chatting to each other as they got into their sleeping bags, and envied them. Having talked openly about Alistair made her think about her marriage so much more. She felt raw, exposed, and she needed Katie's support and reassurance. She lay still, wondering what they were talking about. Just feet away, Miguel slept. The single tent was the nearest to his, and she could feel his presence. What harm would it do, was her second to last thought before she fell asleep. The last was, quite a lot.

She woke early the next morning, the pale light brightening the dull green of the tent ceiling. She heard the murmuring of the porters as they chatted to each other in Quechua, the clanking of pots, the sound of plastic bowls being rinsed out before being packed into the tarpaulin sheets, the rudimentary but effective way of keeping the dust and grass out of everything. Miguel was awake, and she could hear him chatting and joking with the cook and the porters, short bursts of incomprehensible conversation, punctuated with gales of laughter. Today they would climb Dead Woman's Pass, and she was scared.

The porters all slept in one tent, and Nic said she had seen them, on a late night visit to the loo, innocently curled around each other, sleeping like puppies. They did not appear to have any changes of clothes among them, and now, on the third day, they were rather pungent. But their energy and stamina was incredible – their little group would be toiling along at a snail's pace, and Miguel would cry, 'Porters,' and they would stand back to let a team of them through, borne down by backpacks as big as themselves, always at a jogtrot, not pausing or watching their steps. They were so sure-footed, and Nic had asked Miguel if they ever collapsed under the weight. He told them a porter had had a heart attack last year, here, at Dead Woman's Pass, and as a result there was now a weight restriction on how much they could carry. 'They can push themselves too hard,' he said. 'But then this is how they make their living.'

Stretching, she pushed her feet against the warm interior of the sleeping bag, feeling the edge of the mat beneath. She still felt tired, not ready for the day. She had slept for ten hours, but ten hours of tent sleep, which meant waking every hour – it wasn't like waking, exactly, but had rather a dawning consciousness, an awareness of her surroundings, a moment to get her bearings surrounded by the breathing of many other campers, before falling back to sleep. Last night there had been something else that woke her – what was it? Oh yes, the sudden explosion as a bird took flight. Miguel had pointed it out the evening before, crouched low in the grass near to their tent, before they'd had their meal. The chuchico bird, a big brown bird, a member of the owl family. It made its nest in the high grass near the top of the mountain, and when it took flight it made a startling whirring noise before it shot off across the valley, as if wound up and fired from a gun.

Her eyes felt heavy, and full of sleep, and she was aware of a musty smell, the smell of a person who had not washed for two days. Yuk. Reluctantly, she unzipped the sleeping bag. It was like pulling herself out of a comforting warm womb. Automatically, her hand searched for her head-torch, but it wasn't needed, as the dawn had come and all around her the campsite was waking too. She pulled on yesterday's trousers, and reached for the boots which had become her friends. Unzipping the tent, the sound was so loud in the still morning air. She heaved herself up and out of the tent, breathing in the fresh mountain air, and the smell of breakfast cooking over the kerosene stove. The sun was shining, and she was glad – it would be warmer than yesterday.

Two steps from the tent, she turned away from the campsite, and looked out over the mountains. The panoramic view had become so familiar, as natural as breathing. But it still filled her with awe, and some-thing else – a sense of belonging. Of knowing your place in the world. The mountain closest to her was thrown up in sharp relief, pale green with shrubs at the base, darkening as the trees became thicker towards the summit. Behind it lay peak after peak, grey and pale brown in the early morning light. Much further beyond, at the limit of the horizon, stood snow-covered mountains, so high the snow never left. This is what privilege means, she thought. To stand here and see all this, a view timeless in its majesty which has not changed in thousands upon thousands of years. No wonder the Incas worshipped the mountains, the sun, the water, and built structures in their image. She understood what Miguel meant when he said that even though he travelled, the mountains were always inside him.

From where she stood, the trail rose almost vertically in front of her. No more than four feet wide, the little mosaic of paving stones which made up the trail lower down had given way to endless steep, jagged steps cut into the mountainside, a stairway to heaven. These steps rose, and turned, and rose again to the summit of the mountain. Dead Woman's Pass, the highest point of the trail. Where the porter had had a heart attack. God, no, she mustn't think of that. They'd all managed so far, although it was incredibly hard work and all of them had rubbed, sore feet, and aching legs. They tortured each other as they walked by talking about long, hot baths, Radox, a massage. Nic said her back was really beginning to play up and she'd need some physiotherapy when she got home.

As Sasha stared at the mountains, she gathered her courage for the day ahead. She couldn't bottle out, it just wasn't possible, even though she still felt tired, and as if she was coming down with flu.

After breakfast, they hitched their light backpacks containing water and cereal bars onto their backs, tied waterproofs around their waists, picked up their walking sticks and watched gratefully as the porters carried their heavy duffle bags.

'Are you up for this?' Katie said to Sasha, quietly. Her unmade-up face was worried. 'I'm not sure I am.'

Miguel turned to smile at them. 'Of course you can do this, ladies! It is quite possible.'

'Are we the oldest people you have taken up here?' Nic said, quizzically. Miguel looked shocked.

'You are not old! No, I have taken a gentleman of seventy-five up this pass.'

'Did he live?' Katie asked.

'Of course he lived! Just keep pace with me and you will be fine. You have your snacks with you? We will rest at the top, but you must take stop to rest all the time, whenever you are tired. I give you an incentive. Tonight we will have wine.' They all whooped. 'To celebrate your success,' he said. 'I would not have brought you so far if I did not think you could make it. I am impressed by how fit you are.'

Katie and Sasha looked at each other dubiously. They didn't feel fit. They felt knackered. Only Nic, apart from her bad back, seemed to be coping well, but then she had such long beanpole legs and no weight on her at all.

'You mean you've had wine with you all the time and you haven't told us?' Katie stared at him beadily. 'I may have to kill you.' He reached forward and ruffled her hair. It was an intimate gesture, and Sasha felt a sudden stab of jealousy. Stop flirting with him, she thought. He's mine, not yours.

As they set off, a familiar voice called to them.

'Hey! I'll race you to the top.' They turned to see Mike and his friend Nicko, loaded down with their backpacks. They had thought he must have been staying at different campsites, because they hadn't seen him. He must have just arrived later than they did, and Nic had surprised Sasha and Katie by saying she hoped they'd bump into him, he was so cute. Today, though, he didn't look so cute. He was very pale, and though they hadn't even started the climb, a bead of sweat ran down his face.

'Are you OK?' Nic asked him. 'Bit of a gippy tummy,' he said, grimacing. 'I was up and down like a wallaby last night.' They smiled sympathetically at him. Nic looked really concerned. 'Are you sure you shouldn't just rest up here for the day?'

'No worries,' he said, shifting his shoulders to balance his load. 'I'll be fine. We'll have a rave tonight, hey? Only one more day to Machu Picchu.'

They set off walking together, but then Mike and Nicko moved off, their pace quicker. Miguel frowned.

'They go too fast,' he said. 'I think they are trying to impress you.'

'Don't be silly,' Nic said.

Just put one foot in front of the other, Sasha told herself. Do not look up, because then you will scare yourself, by the height you are climbing and the length you still have to go. There was no conversation, because they simply didn't have the breath to talk, and Sasha could hear Katie, who was walking closest to her, breathing heavily. This was no fun, she thought. Her lungs felt like they were being squeezed by two powerful hands, and her legs were like lead. She had to think about every step. Miguel had chosen to walk behind the three of them, and Sasha felt as if he was chivvying them up the mountain like a sheepdog. 'At least he can catch us if we fall backwards,' Katie said, dryly, when she still had enough breath.

The path climbed steadily and there was no respite, just footstep after footstep. Sasha could not even lift her head to take in the scenery, she could only focus on the thought of keeping going. I cannot believe, she thought, that anyone has actually run this trail. Miguel had told them a man, an Iranian, had run the entire length of the part of the trail they were covering in just over a day. It seemed impossible, when achievement to Sasha meant walking ten yards without having to stop, lean on her walking stick, and pant like a dog. The only good thing about it was how much weight she was losing – she'd noticed last night, pulling off her trousers, that her thighs were much slimmer and firmer. All she needed now was the trots and she'd go home a new woman. Although getting the trots on the trail would be the ultimate torture, not to mention embarrassment.

It took them two hours even to reach the base of steps which signalled the final climb over Dead Woman's Pass. Each time Sasha looked up at the summit, it seemed no nearer. But slowly, slowly, they ascended, and at one point she stopped and looked back, and could not believe how far they had come. The campsite was a tiny dot in the distance. Through her agony, she felt a real sense of achievement. I've climbed this far, she thought. To arrive at Machu Picchu on foot was the only way to do it, she thought. You need pain and privation to give you that sense of achievement. At least, I will think that if I don't die today.

'Water,' Katie gasped behind her. 'Water stop.'

'Yes.' Sasha unzipped her backpack and handed Katie a bottle of San Antonio. She seized it and drank, gratefully. 'I've finished all mine,' she admitted. 'Thanks,' she added, wiping her mouth. 'How long will it take us to get to the top?'

'Just another half an hour,' Miguel called from behind. 'Keep going, but slowly. No summit, no wine.'

'Imagine a bath,' Katie said, leaning on her stick, her breath coming in short gasps. 'Imagine a big, foaming hot bath surrounded by candles, with a long glass of champagne at the side, within reach. Imagine being able to take these horrible dirty clothes off, and be clean and shiny, and normal.'

'I don't think I'll ever be normal again,' Sasha said.

'Keep going,' Katie said. 'Keep going. We can do it. We are woman. We are strong.'

'I am blancmange,' Sasha said. 'Oh fuck, off again.'

Each step was torture. She planted her stick above her, leant on it, and heaved her body upwards. It never got any easier, and she tried to sing a song in her head, to stop thinking about the pain, anything to take her mind off the vertiginous climb. The wind was howling about them, making her sway, and occasionally she had to lean against the rocky side of the mountain to keep her balance. To her right, at the side of the trail, was a sheer drop which tumbled thousands of feet to the valley below. It was terrifying. Nic was the first of their group, and Sasha only realized she had reached the top when she walked into her. She hadn't been able to lift her eyes from the steps, hadn't dared to, and suddenly she banged into Nic's back.

'Watch it,' Nic said, reaching out to steady her. The wind whipped the words out of her mouth, and Sasha grabbed her arm. Taking two deep breaths she said, 'We've done it!' Katie stepped up behind her, and the three of them threw their arms around each other, rocking in the wind at the top of the mountain.

'Not dead women!' Katie whooped. 'It hasn't got us!'

Sasha, her arm round Katie, giddily looked down. Before her, the world fell away. They were standing, as high as a condor, afloat upon a sea of green peaks, which undulated away as far as the eye could see, and etched against the clear blue sky, in the distance, were the snow-capped mountains, their sharp summits piercing the horizon.

'I will take your picture,' Miguel said. 'Turn now, the light is behind me.' They linked arms and stood, their walking sticks in front of them, fighting to stay upright in the wind, their hair whipped against their faces, and grinned with sheer elation into the camera. I'll remember this for ever, Sasha thought. I've finally done something I can be proud of.

'Hang on,' Katie said, turning.

'What?' Sasha called into the wind.

'I can hear something.' Just over the summit was a

200

small flat area, with a huge pile of stones. Sasha stepped forward so she could see over the edge, just as Nicko ran up the steps towards her.

'Thank Christ!' he said. His face was pale and panic-stricken. 'I didn't know what to do. It's Mike, he's collapsed. Jeez, man, I think he's dying. He can't seem to breathe.' His own breath was coming in short sobs. Nic who hadn't heard this stepped forward and grabbed his arm. 'What's the matter?' He turned to her. 'We've got to get help.'

'Miguel!' Miguel, who'd been chatting to Katie, ran forward at the panic in Sasha's voice. He took in the scene in an instant, and ran to where Mike lay, slumped over, his head down. He knelt by him, and took his pulse, then took his coat out from his back-pack, swiftly rolled it into a ball and put it behind Mike's head, raising his chin. 'It is the altitude,' he said, his face alarmed. 'I fear his lungs may have collapsed. His pulse is racing.'

'Oh my God.' Sasha's hand flew to her mouth. 'What can we do?' But already Miguel was in charge. Mike's breathing was laboured, and his eyes were closed, as if he was unconscious. Miguel took out his mobile phone.

'Can you get a helicopter up here?' Nic asked. Miguel motioned her to be quiet, and then spoke in rapid Quechua into his phone. He paused, listened, and then snapped his mobile shut. 'The porters at the next camp are coming,' he said. 'With a stretcher. It is the quickest way, and then we can land a helicopter at the next site, where the land is flat.'

'Is there anything we can do?' Katie said.

'Just keep him still,' Miguel said. 'I have some medicine in my bag which will help his breathing, but we must get him down. That is so important.'

'What will happen to him?'

'We must get him oxygen,' Miguel said. 'It may be a pulmonary oedema – fluid in the lungs. The porters will bring a tank.' As he spoke Mike coughed, and water ran from his mouth. His head lolled forward. Miguel turned to Nicko. 'Has he been sick?'

'He was sick last night,' he said, 'at the camp. But we just thought it was Peruvian trots, something he'd eaten.'

'That is the problem of trekking alone,' Miguel said. 'Altitude sickness can strike anyone.' Sasha looked in horror at Mike's face, which was so white, his lips blue.

'All the way up he said he felt weird.' Nicko's voice was trembling. 'I said we ought to go back but Mike said he'd be fine, we'd be able to get to the next camp. And then when we got to the summit he just,' he faltered, 'he just collapsed. Oh my God. Could he die?' He looked at Miguel in fear. Miguel took his arm. 'I am sure we can save him. This happens often, I just hope we can get him back to the hospital in Cusco quickly enough. They may have an altitude chamber at the camp – I will call to see.' He took out his mobile again.

'Yes,' he said, after a rapid conversation. 'We are lucky. They have a hyperbaric chamber there, a temporary chamber which will stabilize him.' Nic knelt down next to Mike, and gently put her arm round him. 'Keep him warm,' Miguel said, and Sasha and Katie took out their spare jumpers, and put them

202

over Mike's chest. He looked so young, so vulnerable, and Sasha suddenly thought how she'd feel if this was one of her children. She'd been toying with the idea of bringing the girls up here, as it had been such a fantastic experience, but now she realized it was too dangerous. If Mike, a fit, young man could be struck, then it would be foolish in the extreme to bring children so high.

'Should we give him water?' Nic asked.

'No, he is not conscious and cannot swallow,' Miguel said. The five of them crouched down, out of the wind. The waiting seemed endless, and Sasha could not take her eyes off Mike's face, willing him to hang on, to live. With each moment, his breathing seemed to get worse, despite the injection Miguel had given him. Perhaps it was too late, perhaps he would die there, in front of them. The thought was surreal, and Sasha felt so helpless – if only there was some-thing they could do but wait for help. She put her arm around Nicko, who was shaking and looked as if he was about to be sick. 'It's OK,' she said. 'The porters will be here soon.'

'His parents,' Nicko said, his words coming out in sobs, 'they didn't want him to come. They said he ought to stay and build up his career, and he shouldn't take such a long time off. But it was me who said he should go, because I wanted to come here so badly. Oh shit.' He rocked backwards and forwards, and Sasha held him tightly. 'It's all my fault.'

'No it isn't,' she said. 'You couldn't have known, it isn't anyone's fault.'

'But if he dies . . .' The words hung in the air.

'He won't,' Sasha said definitely. 'Miguel won't let that happen. He knows just what to do.' Miguel had spent the last twenty minutes on the phone, fluctuating between Quechua and Spanish.

After three quarters of an hour, they heard the voices of the porters further down the mountain. 'Thank God,' Nicko said. Mike had not regained consciousness, and looked as if he had slipped into a coma, but he was still breathing.

Gently, the four porters lifted Mike onto the rudimentary stretcher, covering him in warm brightly coloured Peruvian woollen blankets and strapping him on with worn leather straps. 'How the hell are they going to get him down all those steps?' Nic said.

'Carefully, I hope,' Sasha said.

Miguel spoke rapidly to them, a string of instructions, and they nodded, before setting off. It was extraordinary how swiftly they could move, balancing the stretcher between them as they jogged down the steep steps to the valley and the campsite way below.

'Is there anything more we can do?' Sasha asked.

'No. He will be taken care of.'

'Can I use your mobile?' Nicko asked Miguel. He looked at Nicko, consideringly. 'You want to phone his family?'

'Sure.'

'I would wait. I would wait until he has been stabilized,' Miguel said. Sasha flashed a look at him. He was quite right, and how well he was handling this. He was really impressive, so calm and authoritative. Now he put his arm around Nicko's shoulders.

'Your friend, I am sure he will be fine. You come with us.'

The five of them slowly made their way down the punishingly steep steps in silence. How close we are to death, Sasha thought. We take our lives for granted, but anything, anything can wipe us out. She kept seeing Mike's cheerful face in the light of the campfire, listening to his plans for the next part of their trip, so full of enthusiasm and energy. All that could not just be snuffed out.

A fine rain began to fall on them as they headed down towards the camp, past two deep lakes. It was a well-organized campsite, with showers, changing rooms and a small building with a cross on the top, a rudimentary medical centre. As soon as they arrived, Miguel disappeared to check Mike's progress. Their porters and cook had already arrived, and they gave Nicko a cup of tea and some food.

'You're so kind, man,' he kept saying.

'Don't be silly,' Nic said. 'You must eat. How do you feel?'

'I'm fine,' he said. 'That's what I can't understand – Mike's much fitter than me.'

'It's quite random,' Sasha said. 'No-one could have known.'

When Miguel returned it was mid-afternoon. They were sitting chatting around the fire, and looked up at his approach. He was smiling, and Sasha felt a wave of relief.

'He seems to be fine,' he said. 'They have stabilized him and the helicopter will be here soon. Do you want to go with him?' he asked Nicko.

'Sure,' Nicko said. 'I must.'

'You could carry on with us,' Katie suggested. 'He may not be conscious for a while, and you can get the train back to Cusco with us.'

'Nah, I want to be with him.'

'You're a good friend,' Miguel said, and Sasha smiled at him. He held her gaze and she just let it happen, a connection, a bond. He had taken charge without any fuss, or posturing. Mike owed him his life, and Sasha realized, in that moment, how much she liked him. Not just found him attractive, sexy, but really admired him. He has great qualities, she thought. There's something very special, indefinable, about him. Everyone seemed to defer to him, not just the porters but also the other guides they passed on the trail, even if they were older than he was. Maybe it was because he was well educated, well spoken, she presumed, but it was also simply the way he carried himself, his natural air of authority and well, breeding. She didn't know if Peru had a class structure, but he was obviously pretty near the top of the pecking order, having been to Harvard.

After the helicopter had departed with Nicko and Mike on board, Miguel said, 'I had planned to show you some ruins beyond the campsite. Do you still want to go on, or do you want to rest?' They looked at each other consideringly. Sasha's legs were aching and her feet were sore from the climb, but, now that Mike appeared to be safe, she also felt a restless energy, a kind of exhilaration. 'I'd like to,' she said. Nic and Katie nodded. 'Why not?'

* * *

They walked slowly to the ruins of Runturacay, and once inside the walls, sat in a ring at Miguel's feet. He explained that this was an important staging point along the trail, with a watch tower, temple and lodges offering provisions for travellers. Sasha noticed how a lot of their fellow walkers would sidle up when Miguel was talking, to listen to what he was saying. Many had their own tour guides with them, but they seemed to know far less than he did. His voice was very seductive, mesmerizing, as the facts flowed effortlessly out of him.

As they climbed back down towards their campsite, Katie walked alongside him, just in front of Nic and Sasha. 'How long will you be a tour guide? Don't you want to do anything else?' she asked him. He looked at her in surprise. 'Why? Do you not think this is a good job? In your country, would this not be considered a prestigious career?' Katie realized he was teasing her.

'No, not really,' she said, honestly. He rubbed his nose thoughtfully. 'Well,' he said, slowly, 'this is what I choose to do for the moment. I enjoy it. I meet people, like you, and I learn about other cultures. I am very proud of my country and its history, and I like to tell people about it. That is all,' he shrugged.

'But you don't make much money,' Katie persisted.

'Why should that be the most important thing?' he asked.

'Well, because it gives you a standing in society, it helps you buy things.'

'Standing in society?' He laughed. 'I have enough standing in society, thank you very much. As for buying things, I have everything I need.' He pointed to his body. 'I have a strong, healthy body.' He pointed to his head. 'I have a quick mind, I like to learn things.' He held up his hands in front of him. 'I have two strong hands. What more do I need?'

'Do you have a car?' Nic said. He looked at her as if that was a very odd thing to ask.

'Yes,' he said, smiling. 'I have a car. But I do not drive it in Cusco, it is impractical. I cycle around the city. We should not drive cars when we do not need to.'

'What type of car do you have?' Nic pressed him.

'How very curious you are,' he said. 'I have a Mercedes. There, are you happy?'

'But how,' Katie said, hurrying after him as he turned and walked off, 'do you afford a Mercedes?' He stopped and turned to her, his face unsmiling. 'Enough questions,' he said, 'for one day.' Then he marched on ahead, back to the campsite.

'Maybe he deals in cocaine,' Katie said, as they all three crammed into the double tent before dinner for a chat.

'Oh, don't be silly, he's far too intelligent for that,' Sasha said. 'Maybe his family are much more wealthy than he's letting on.'

'I don't want him to be rich,' Katie said, dreamily. 'I like to think of him as a son of the soil.'

'Labouring with his shirt off?' Sasha suggested.

'God, yes. I don't know how we could ever have thought him creepy. He was magnificent today. All that striding about, fixing things. Yum. What do you think, Nic? Don't you think he is the hunkiest thing on two legs?'

'Not my type,' she said, dismissively.

'Then who is?'

'Oh.' Nic paused, and a cloud seemed to move over her face. She hesitated, as if about to say something, and then thought better of it. 'I'm too old for fancying people,' she said.

'I don't believe you,' Katie said, flashing a look at Sasha. 'I think you've got some kind of guilty secret you're not telling us . . .' Her voice was teasing, and she was quite unprepared for the reaction.

'Not everyone is as shallow as you are,' Nic said, sharply. 'We don't all live in a romantic bubble. Can you pass me my sponge bag? I'm going for a shower.' Reaching over, she quickly unzipped the tent and was gone. Katie looked hurt.

'I wasn't prying,' she said, close to tears. 'I was only teasing . . .'

'I know,' Sasha said. 'It's not your fault. I've never seen her like that. I wonder what on earth could be up? She really liked Mike, maybe it's just that, worry about him.'

'No,' Katie said, slowly. 'I know her pretty well and I haven't seen her like this before either. It was like I touched a really raw nerve. You don't think . . .'

'God, no, Nic? Don't be daft. She and Johnny are about the most secure couple I've ever met.'

'She doesn't open up much, though. I see a lot of her and she's always the same, you know, calm, organized, making me feel daffy. Am I shallow?' she said, suddenly changing tack.

'Of course not. I mean, people who don't know you might think you're a bit fluffy but you do that on

209

purpose, don't you? It's quite calculated. And God knows I know you're not shallow now, not after all you've been through. Maybe you should tell Nic?'

'I don't know. In all honesty, I'm a bit frightened of her. I'm sure she thinks I am a bit of an airhead, and she keeps me around for light entertainment. I'm kind of a one-woman circus, a bit of light relief.' She laughed, but without conviction. 'I'm scared of telling her because she'd be so shocked. I knew— I kind of knew you wouldn't be judgemental,' she said. 'She might be, and I don't think I could cope with that. I've a hard enough job constantly judging myself and telling me I'm crap. I don't need Nic to do it as well.'

'The more time I spend with Nic, the more I think she's a real dark horse,' Sasha said. 'But it's none of my business. If she wants to open up to us, she will.'

'I'm kind of fascinated though now, aren't you?' Katie said.

'Riveted,' admitted Sasha.

As promised, Miguel cracked open some barely drinkable local wine at dinner, and after two glasses each they were garrulous, and overly sentimental. Katie started crying about Mike, and Sasha could see Miguel looking at her as if she was a bit mad. They made him tell them all about Machu Picchu, and the thought that they would see it for the first time the next day made Sasha's stomach turn over. Well, it could have been that, or it could have been the fact that Miguel did not miss an opportunity to catch her eye, or brush his fingers against her hand. The wine made her bolder, and she caught herself stealing glances at him out of the corner of her eye, then swiftly looking away, and flicking back her hair. Flirtation techniques she had not used for years. God, she just hoped she didn't look grotesque in the process. But Miguel's eyes were clearly admiring, although it was now three days since she had washed her hair because the showers were so disgusting, and she couldn't swear she hadn't missed her mouth with lipstick, because all she had was a tiny compact mirror, and putting on make-up with a head-torch was pretty difficult in a dimly lit tent. For all she knew, she might look like a clown. Once they'd polished off two bottles between the four of them – Miguel only had half a glass – they reluctantly agreed they ought to go to bed because tomorrow was such a big day.

Sasha, who was sharing a tent with Nic, could not sleep, and lay awake listening to the murmurings of the porters as they washed the plates and chatted. They often sat up late around a fire, talking and telling stories. It was hard work on the trail, but they obviously enjoyed the camaraderie. At first the voices were indistinguishable, but then she realized Miguel was still up. She lay still for a moment, full of indecision, and then slowly started to slide herself out of her sleeping bag. Nic was asleep, her head resting on the guidebook she had been reading. The moon was high, and there was just enough light inside the tent to pull on her trousers and lace up her boots without the torch. She pulled the puffa jacket out of her bag, and put it on. Slowly, crouching down, she gently unzipped the tent, trying to make as little noise as possible. She slid out, and looked around.

He was sitting with the porters, his face lit by the fire. He saw her at once, and stood up. His face registered surprise, and some alarm.

'Are you OK?' he said quietly, walking towards her. Sasha saw all the porters were staring at her, and she felt embarrassed. What did they think she was up to?

'Yes, fine,' she said, quickly. 'I just needed to go to the toilet.'

'You are cold.'

She realized she was shivering, and pulled her jacket more tightly around herself.

'Would you like my jacket as well?' He started to unzip his thick fleece, which had the name of the travel company emblazoned on the back.

'No, really, I'm fine. I won't be a minute.'

He smiled. 'I'll wait.'

She hurried off to the toilet, trying not to trip over guide ropes. God, she must be acting like such a gauche girl in front of him, he'd think she was an idiot. She concentrated very hard on not tipping over the chemical loo – it was a very rickety thing and you had to get your balance just right or the whole lot would go over. Now that would be embarrassing, because it was quite likely the whole tent would go with it. Balancing on a tiny toilet was easier said than done with almost a full bottle of wine inside her, and she found herself giggling as she lowered her posterior, and then tried to pee as quietly as she could.

She wished she'd brought her head-torch, because it was somehow darker when she came out. The porters had stamped on the fire, and were moving about, getting ready for bed. She couldn't see Miguel, maybe he'd gone to bed too. Head down, she watched her feet as she walked back, stepping over tent pegs and trying not to crash into the side of tents. She hit him full on as she went round the side of a tent. 'Oof. God, I'm sorry, I didn't see you.' In the dim light he reached out and put both hands around her waist, steadying her. It was a quite wonderful feeling. 'You have had a little too much to drink,' he said, his voice low and soft, by her ear. 'Nonsense,' she said. 'It's just too dark.'

'But the moon is high,' he said. 'Come. I want to show you something.' Holding her firmly by the elbow, he led her through the campsite to a watch point, where they could look out over the ruins of Runturacay, the site they had visited that afternoon. In the moonlight, the stones looked eerie. 'It is very beautiful, isn't it?' he said. 'At night, whenever I come here, I like to sit and watch the mountains.' There was a flat stone near the edge, and he led her towards it. They sat on the cold stone, side by side, and gazed out over the peaks beyond.

'When I sit here,' he said slowly, 'I feel the souls of my ancestors. I feel the spirit of the mountain inside me, and it feeds my soul. These mountains fill me with positive energy. I feel very light and full of joy.' He glanced at her. 'You think me very romantic, or foolish?' he said. She glanced at him, smiling. God, he was cute.

'Neither,' she said. 'I think you are very lucky.'

'In what way?'

'To have such an understanding of yourself, and to have such a strong belief.'

'This is not just mine,' he said, gesturing around the

mountains. 'It should touch us all. If this does not fill you with awe then your soul is dead.'

'You don't understand,' Sasha said. 'At home, in Britain, we don't have this connection, like you do, with nature. It's just there to be looked at occasionally, and admired, like a painting, not like a living thing. We are not a part of it. I suppose, in a way, it isn't so important to us. We don't rely on it, like you do, for food, or worship it in any way. I mean, of course we need the land for food, but we buy that in a super-market, we don't grow it ourselves. I guess in a way we've lost our connection with the land, with nature, it's just something we live in. A lot of our food is grown artificially, in greenhouses – we can buy pretty much anything all year round.'

'All of my people used to depend on the land for everything,' he said. 'We grow our crops in the earth, we live with our animals who give us clothing and meat. People laugh at us for worshipping the sun and the gods of the water and the mountains, but they give us life, we could not live without them. Is your God a better god? Does he give you life and energy, as the sun gives us?'

Sasha laughed. 'We don't really worship anything any more,' she said. 'We're all too busy making money, buying things, surrounding ourselves with gadgets and machines that save time.'

'And do these things make you happy inside, as the mountains make me happy?' He reached out, and gently took a lock of Sasha's hair. She felt his fingers play with it, twisting it between them. She hardly dared breathe.

'No,' she said. 'Not happy like this. We always want more, you see, and we judge each other by how much we have and what we choose to spend our money on.'

'You cannot buy this,' he said, and slowly drew her to him, so that she rested against his shoulder.

'This is my wealth,' he said, his arm moving around her shoulder. 'Everything you see before you is mine.'

'Your people's,' she corrected him.

'Yes,' he said, 'it is my birthright, but sadly no longer truly mine. This is a national park, protected. It belongs to the Government in Lima. I can no longer call it my own. But in my heart, yes, it is mine.' He was silent, and she let her head rest on his shoulder. She had never felt so safe, nor so full of joy.

'Why do you like to drink?' he said, suddenly.

'What?'

'Why do you all want to drink wine so much?'

'I suppose it makes us feel better. It's an escape, really.'

'Surely that happiness should be there? Why do you need to put it inside you? Is that not a false happiness?'

'I don't think you really understand how we live,' she said. He brought his hand up to smooth her hair and she leant into his touch, like a cat being stroked. She reached up with her other hand, and caught his wrist. 'Where did you get this?'

'My watch?'

'Yes.'

'It was a present.'

Sasha felt a flash of jealousy. 'From who?'

'A girlfriend.'

'Where did you meet her?'

'On the trail. She was a client, like you.'

A dawning realization stole over her, and she moved away from him. 'Oh.'

He sensed her change of mood, and looked at her challengingly. 'What is wrong with that?'

'What was she like?'

'Do you really want to know?'

'Yes, I do.'

'OK. She was French, she worked as a journalist, and she was writing a story about the trail. We . . . she . . . we got on well, and the next year I went to visit her in France.'

'And what happened?'

He shrugged. 'It ended. I could not stay away from Peru, she did not want to come here. It is hard to keep a relationship going like that.'

'Did you love her?' He stared out over the mountains, a quizzical look lifting one eyebrow.

'I am not sure I know what love is, beyond the love of my family.'

'Desire?'

'Desire? Oh, yes. I can feel desire to look at the mountains, desire for food, desire to drink when I am thirsty, desire for you . . .' He turned to look at her. It was a direct statement of intent. No going back. The words hung in the air, spoken.

'I must go.' Hurriedly, she got to her feet, scrambling, breaking the spell.

'Sasha . . .' He called her name as she walked swiftly away, her cheeks flaming. What was she so scared of? What did she have to lose? When would she ever get such an opportunity again, and what did it matter if all he wanted was sex? So what – after all, what else did she have to offer him? Why was she such a coward? Outside the tent, she stopped, trying to compose herself. She had been seconds away from kissing him, was that so very bad? What was holding her back? She thought hard. Oh, yes. It was fear. Fear of letting go of something she held very tight inside. Fear of being hurt. Again.

Chapter Thirteen

From the campsite near to the ruins of Runturacay, they had to climb a pass which took them close to four thousand metres once more. 'I thought that was it,' Katie said, gasping. 'Once we'd done Dead Woman's Pass.'

'I lied,' Miguel said, smiling.

Sasha had been dreading seeing him this morning as she felt such a spineless fool, but he acted as if nothing had happened. He could hardly be used to being rejected, she thought. Sleep had not come easily, as she played and replayed the scene over and over in her mind, each time imagining what would have happened if she had leaned forward to him, and put her hand to his face, drawing it down to hers. She lay there rigidly, imagining what his lips would taste like, how he would kiss ... He's a child, she told herself. You must be mad. Get a grip. You're just in this unreal situation in which anything seems possible, but this is neither fitting, nor possible. It is potentially highly dangerous and embarrassing and anyway, God, anyway. Imagine taking your clothes off in front of him. She shrank in horror at the thought. Her body was not too bad, much better for losing this weight, but still her thighs were dimpled and her stomach was not as flat as it ought to be and he would be used to young women, with smooth, tight skin, and no – the idea was too impossible to be borne. And, in the back of her mind, was the fear. That it was all too easy to be hurt, and rendered ridiculous.

After they had climbed the pass, each saying a silent prayer that it was the last, they headed down the mountain, towards the ruined fortress of Sayamarca, and then up again to Phuyupatamarca, literally the city in the clouds. Miguel set off at a brisk pace, and Nic and Katie followed, grumbling that even that small amount of wine had left them with a hangover, and it was inhuman to be expected to get up at seven every morning.

'Not far to Machu Picchu,' Katie said, falling into step with Sasha. 'You're a bit quiet this morning. Is anything the matter?'

'No, I'm fine. Just didn't sleep awfully well, that's all.'

The countryside they were moving into gradually became much more lush, and the steep steps of the trail gave way to a wider path, bordered on both sides by huge clumps of pampas grass, bamboo and the sudden flash of a beautiful red orchid. They had entered the rainforest, and either side of them rose fantastical trees, with lichen overhanging the path. Hummingbirds darted to and fro, their wings a blur. It was, effectively, the jungle, and Miguel warned them that there could be snakes.

219

After a couple of hours they came to two small lakes, and from there they could see the distant snow-capped mountain range of Cordillera Vilcabamba, the last place where the Incas had retreated. Sasha remembered Miguel telling her that when Machu Picchu was first discovered by Hiram Bingham in 1911, he had thought he had found Vilcabamba. But now it was accepted that Vilcabamba was a town called Espiritu Pampa, much deeper into the jungle.

Miguel fell into step beside Sasha. 'Did you sleep well?' he asked, politely. She glanced back at Nic and Katie.

'Not really,' she said.

'Nor I. I want to tell you a tale my father told me,' he said. 'At the time of Pacahcutec, the transformer of the world, there was a strong and very skilful warrior. His name was Ouantatampu. He was very close to his Inca Lord, and once he got to meet his daughter. Her name was Cusiccoyllur, or Happy Star. He went often to her house, the Inca palace, before she was moved to the *accllauasi*, the house in which the virgins of the sun lived, and the place where the women of the nobility were closeted. There she learnt religion, how to weave beautiful textiles, and all that was required of her to become a cloistered woman. She was rarely allowed out, and when she did come out for ceremonial occasions, like the summer solstice, she had to keep her face covered. The women were guarded at all times by eunuchs. But she had seen the warrior, and they fell in love. They had to keep their love a secret, until he managed to convince the transformer of the world that he was a fit person to marry his beautiful daughter. But the Inca Lord was very strict, and he wanted her for another noble. Somehow, they managed to meet in secret, and she became pregnant. The Inca Lord was furious, and he decided to cloister her against her will – she was shut into a dark room, with no light. She was shut behind a partition wall, away from all her friends. She was left in this room for ten years. Her baby was born, and she was named Sweet Soul, or Imasumac. The Inca Lord loved this baby, and brought her up as his own. He told her her parents were dead, and she grew up with her grandfather. Ouantatampu became a great fighter, and he believed that his love was dead. He came back to Cusco, and he discovered that she was not dead. In the meantime, Sweet Soul had managed to find the lady in the cloister, her mother. By now she was blind, and she never saw her daughter. But the Inca Lord gave in, when he saw how much the warrior and his daughter loved each other. They were allowed to marry, and they were happy.'

'What a sad tale. Are all your legends so sad?'

'I do not think it is sad,' he said. 'It shows that in love, you must be patient.' Then he walked on ahead. Love? Sasha looked at his retreating back cynically. He had told her he didn't know what love was. What he was saying was that he would not give up. She quizzed herself. Flattered, or alarmed? Hm. Flattered, and full of a tingling sensation of anticipation.

Phuyupatamarca was a beautifully restored town, the stones reassembled to show the walls and the houses, and it contained a series of ceremonial baths, through which the water still flowed. 'The irrigation systems built by the Incas,' Miguel said, stooping to scoop up a handful of the clear water, 'still work perfectly today.' Sasha leant back against the stones and looked at him, leaning against a wall, and chatting with Nic. He was wearing baggy grey trousers, a sloppy jumper with the sleeves rolled up to his elbow, and big walking boots. Yet, thought Sasha. Yet, there is something not quite of our time about him. What was it? Was it his height, the breadth of his shoulders, the way he carried his head? There was something – she laughed at herself for thinking this – something noble about him, an unconscious aristocracy in his bearing, something that set him apart, even when he was surrounded by his own people. He would have been a great warrior, she thought. A leader of men.

They camped that night just beyond Phuyupatamarca, and Miguel opened another bottle of wine. He poured himself a glass, but Sasha noticed he did not drink it. During their afternoon walk he had several phone calls on his mobile, and Sasha heard him talking in rapid Spanish, and Quechua. He moved fluently between the two, and into English, without a pause. Katie had made him list the languages he could speak, because she said she still didn't believe him. 'English, Spanish, Quechua, German, French, Italian, Dutch, and a little Japanese. Once you have the key to languages, it is not so difficult,' he said.

He told them that Mike seemed to be doing well, although he was not out of the woods yet, and breathing on his own. His parents were flying out to see him, and they would take him home. Sasha felt so sad. The end of his extraordinary adventure.

'What will you do after you leave us?' Katie said.

He smiled. 'Will you miss me?'

'Of course!' they said.

'I exist only for you,' he said, teasingly.

'Really what will you do?' Katie said.

'Really?' he said, mimicking her accent. 'Really I return to Cusco with you, then I spend a few days sorting out paperwork before I bring my next group up here.'

'And who are they?' Katie asked.

'How very curious you are tonight,' Miguel said. Sasha noticed that Katie was flirting with him much more this evening, possibly because she had some wine, and possibly because she had undertaken the Herculean task of washing her hair in a bowl of cold water, as there were no showers at this site. Both Nic and Sasha had decided to wait until they reached Machu Picchu, and regarded Katie's act as something of a betrayal of the sisterhood. If one had greasy hair, they should all have greasy hair. Now her hair was gleaming clean, and she'd let it fall to her shoulders instead of pulling it back into a bun as she had on the trail. She looked devastatingly pretty, and Sasha felt dowdy by comparison. Why was she beating herself up about Miguel, when he wasn't even looking at her tonight, and they only had two more days together? The thought made her heart sink. Two days. It was as if a cloud had passed in front of the sun.

'They are a party of Germans,' he said. 'Eight people, including two children.'

'Do you like children?' Sasha said.

He grinned at her. 'Of course I like children. I have told you, family is very important to me. I have two younger brothers and two younger sisters, my youngest, Jessica, I told you, is nine. She is my little princess – she texts me often on my phone. She misses me a lot when I am on the trail.'

'Jessica?' Katie said, her voice faltering.

'It is a Spanish name, yes. My name, too is Spanish, and yet I am an Indian. My parents wanted us to blend in, they did not want any prejudice to come our way.'

'What is your surname?' asked Sasha, out of interest.

'What a lot of questions about me. No, I want to know about you. Tell me about your children. Katie, do you have children?'

Sasha shot a look at her. Katie raised her chin. 'I had a child,' she said. 'She died, as a baby.' Nic was staring at her, astonished.

'I had no idea,' she said. 'When? How old were you?' Miguel was looking between them, aware that this was a bombshell. Katie looked straight at Nic, and whirled the cheap wine around in her glass. 'This isn't the ideal place,' she said, slowly. Sasha, sitting next to her, put her hand on her arm, and Katie smiled at her. 'It's OK, Miguel, it's just I don't talk about it much. But there isn't any point in hiding it any more. I had a child, Nic, when I was a teenager. I got pregnant accidentally, and then she died, days after she was born. I don't talk about it because . . . because I'm kind of ashamed of it and also because it's still pretty raw.' She looked at Sasha, wondering whether to go on. Sasha gave a minute shake of her head. This was not the place to tell such secrets. Later, when they were alone. Katie took a drink of wine. 'I lived up north then, that's where I'm from, and the father wasn't exactly the kind of man I'd choose to father my child.' Nic watched her, her mouth open, realization dawning. 'Is that why you haven't had any more children?'

'Kind of. And also Harvey doesn't really want them. He says I'm enough of a handful.' She gave a bitter laugh, and Sasha squeezed her arm.

'You poor thing,' Nic said. 'I had no idea.'

'And you,' Katie said to Miguel. 'Will you have children?' He leant back on his chair, one arm draped over the back. He smiled. 'I hope so, eventually. I am still young, and there is much I want to achieve first.'

Sasha bit her lip. Perhaps it was the wine, but she felt on the point of tears. He had a future which of course had absolutely nothing to do with her and soon, very soon, she would have to say goodbye to him, and all the happiness and hope she was feeling would be gone and she would have to go back to her life with Alistair. Or make a decision not to go back to her life with Alistair. Oh God. She had only borrowed these feelings, they were not hers to own. She was fantasizing about something which would be, at best, a night of sex. And after the night, like gorging on wine, would come the hangover, the remorse. 'Would you marry someone who wasn't Peruvian?' Katie asked.

'I do not think so,' he said. 'She would need to understand how I feel about my country. And anyway . . .' He seemed on the point of saying something, and then thought better of it.

'Come. Tomorrow is our big day, we arrive in Machu Picchu. To bed.'

On their way back to the tent, Katie said, 'I'm longing to be there, but at the same time I don't want any of this to end.'

'Nor do I,' Sasha said. 'Can you imagine, going home?' She just stopped herself from saying, 'Leaving Miguel.'

Instead she said, 'I'm looking forward to seeing the girls, but . . .'

'I know,' Katie said. 'Let's not think about it now.'

The next morning the trail took them down through the rainforest, towards the settlement of Initpata, and then on to Winaywayna, a city almost as remarkable as Machu Picchu itself. The sun was high in the sky, and by nine in the morning it was hot. Sasha had never seen a sun so high – it seemed directly overhead and by midday the heat was intense. They had smothered themselves with sun cream, and, because they were now in the rainforest, they liberally applied mosquito repellent. Before they had been too high, the air too thin for mosquitoes, but now there was a real danger of malaria.

They drifted along, enjoying the warmth of the sun. Sasha felt dreamlike, as if her body was moving without any apparent effort. After three full days on the trail, she was so used to walking, she hardly noticed what she was doing. It was stranger to stop, or sit down – walking was what you did, you put your boots on in the morning, and you put one foot in front of the other. She felt much more fit, and lean, and pleasingly her trousers were now too big around the waist. She liked that – she could let them fall onto her hips, and there was a gap between the bottom of her T-shirt and the low waistband of her trousers. Her stomach did not bulge, but was flat, and smooth, apart from the little bit of crinkled skin around her tummy button, the stamp of pregnancy. She had noticed Miguel glancing at her as she emerged from the tent that morning. She stretched sensuously, and rolled her neck around, while he watched her. If only her bloody hair was clean she would feel pretty foxy.

'Now I want you to be serious,' Miguel said, as they walked down the steps towards Winaywayna. They giggled, and he gave them a stern look. 'Ladies, concentrate.' The morning's walk had given his face a deeper tan, bringing out the whiteness of his teeth. Sasha noticed how very white his eyeballs were – how clean, which was an odd way of describing them. But they had no red veins at all. He really had the most extraordinary eyes. They were almond-shaped, and slanting, so the corners tilted slightly upwards, and she had never seen such a deep chocolate-brown colour.

'Sasha, are you listening?'

'What?'

'You were staring,' Katie whispered into her ear. 'With your mouth open. Do try and concentrate, darling. This is very interesting. It's all about astronomy and agricultural science.'

'Oh, right.'

'As I was saying,' Miguel said, patiently. He flashed a smile at her. Today he was wearing a tight white T-shirt. How did he keep his clothes so clean?

'As you can see, the land all around the town is

227

divided into terraces. This was part of the micro-climate they discovered, as different crops would grow better at different levels, as the sun shone on them at different times of the day. The astronomers were the priests, and they would watch the skies, to map the seasons of the year and determine at what time of year the seeds should be planted. It was not a blind worship of the stars, but a serious scientific investigation. On a full moon, the seeds would germinate much faster.' They were sitting on a grassy bank, looking down over the ruins. It really was very warm. Sasha lay back, and felt the soft grass beneath her. She stared up at the sky. I'd like to paint the sun today, she thought, and frame it. It was the first time she had wanted to paint for a long time. When I get home, she thought, I will paint again. Why had she left it so long?

Miguel's voice drifted over her, like a warm blanket, and she closed her eyes. 'Planting on the hillsides, on these terraces, increased the chances of the plants transferring the sunlight into glucose by photo-synthesis. They also studied the wind, and worked out how it acted as a natural refrigerator, and that is why they built the granary stores at the edge of the hillside.' I could die quite happily here, she thought. Here, in this warm place, listening to his voice. 'The terraces also had their own natural irrigation, so that the crops never became too wet. The name of the city means Forever Young. Are you nearly asleep?'

His voice was closer, and Sasha opened one eye. He was kneeling above her, blocking out the sun. 'Almost,' she smiled.

'I hope you were listening. It was one of my best lectures. What did I say?'

'Forever young,' she said.

'And the rest?'

'Not absolutely sure.' She smiled up at him. 'Something about plants?'

'You are a very bad girl,' he said. 'You must be punished.' He gave her a sharp push, and to her amazement she started rolling, over and over. It was an extraordinary feeling, one she hadn't had since she was a child, and she shrieked with laughter, before throwing out her arms and bringing herself to a stop, just before she fell off one of the terraces. Nic and Katie were leaning forward, laughing.

'I'll get you . . .' she said, jumping up, running towards him. 'I don't think so,' he said, and took off like an athlete, running down the terraces, leaping off the edges. Nic and Katie jumped up and sped after him, and the four of them ran, and ran, shrieking like children, until they collapsed in a heap at the bottom, panting, hysterical. A group of backpackers stood way above them, looking down at them in astonishment. Walking back up behind Nic and Katie, Miguel took her hand, and it felt the most natural thing in the world. Today, anything could happen.

It took them two hours to climb from Winaywayna to Intipunku, the gate of the sun. As they approached their first sight of Machu Picchu, Sasha felt her heart beating faster. Yards away from the huge stone entrance, Katie and Nic stopped, and turned towards them. Miguel dropped her hand – the hand he had

229

held on and off for the entire climb, pretending, whenever Nic and Katie glanced back at them, that he was helping her up steps, or across a small stream. 'Come here,' Katie said to Sasha. 'We are going through together.' The three of them held hands tightly. Sasha, on the end, stretched out her left hand, and felt, as she did so, the strong grasp of a man's hand. Her father's. He was with her. 'Now,' Katie said, and they stepped forward, through the stone archway.

'My . . . God,' Nic gasped. A shaft of sunlight pierced the clouds and fell onto a vast majestic city laid out beneath them, its white granite walls vividly defined against the dark green of the steep mountain standing guard behind it, Huayna Picchu. It was perfect, far more so than they could ever have imagined. They stood, speechless, gazing down at this city which had been lost for hundreds and hundreds of years, now restored to its full magnificence. Sasha had never believed it could be so perfect, each house, each building virtually intact, missing only its roof. She could make out the streets, the wide central square, the temples and the sentry posts. It was the most remarkable thing she had ever seen in her life, and her soul sang at the sight.

'Look, oh, look,' Katie breathed, pointing into the sky. Above them soared a vast black bird, the unmistakable shape of a condor, its enormous black wings with their feathered tips outstretched, gliding high above them, effortlessly. Sasha realized she was crying, and turned to Katie. Tears were streaming down her friend's face. Thousands of people must have looked down upon Machu Picchu, Sasha thought. And everyone must have felt as she did, that they were witnessing one of the great wonders of the world. And there was more than that, much more. It hung in space, timeless, not just a city of granite, but a place of such intense spiritualism it filled every part of her with peace.

Miguel was standing behind her, very close. 'What do you think?' he asked. She turned to him, the tears wet on her face. 'I am glad,' he said. 'I am so glad you feel the spirit of this city and my people.' Then he kissed her gently on the mouth. Katie saw what was happening and caught his arm, spinning him around to her, and he kissed her on the cheek.

Nic brought her camera out of her bag. 'Stand close together,' she said. 'Now.' And they beamed into the camera, ecstatic, with the lost city behind them.

'Tonight,' he said, 'I will not take you into Machu Picchu itself, but you can see it close up, from the sentry's tower. Tomorrow, we will rise very early – at five, and come here to watch the sun rise over Machu Picchu, and then I will take you into the city.'

'I want to see it now,' Katie said, excitedly.

'It is too late,' Miguel said, looking at his watch. 'The gate closes at half past four. It will be better tomorrow, and more quiet.'

Sasha walked up to the sentry's tower in a daze. She felt drained, as if the elation she had experienced had taken everything out of her. She also felt tremendously peaceful, and as if nothing could ever hurt her again. The city's grandeur put everything into perspective.

At the tower, a small group of tourists stood taking

photographs. They had obviously come up on the train, with their clean clothes and their training shoes, not walking boots. 'Tourists,' Katie said, dismissively. 'Not real people of the trail.' They were all so glad they had made the trek – it had been, Sasha now realized, a type of pilgrimage. Only by experiencing the privations of the trail could they really be justified in appreciating the wonder of the city. They had approached in the footsteps of the Incas, and this was their reward for hardship.

Lying down on the grass, looking over the city, was a large white llama. 'This is one of the four llamas who live among the ruins,' Miguel said. 'The parents have recently had a new baby – you will see it tomorrow. This is the father,' he said, giving the old llama a pat. The animal regarded him coolly. 'He is an aristocrat, this one.' He smiled at it. The jaws of the llama moved methodically, quite unperturbed by the people around him and their flashing cameras. This was his city. 'They are the only inhabitants now,' Miguel said. The llama turned to look at him with an unblinking stare, its large ears flicking backwards and forwards.

'Will you have a drink with us?' Katie said, as they made their way down towards the Sanctuary Lodge. To get to the hotel, they had to pass through another lodge where Miguel had their papers stamped and signed.

'No, I cannot,' he said. 'I have some things I have to do.' Sasha felt a sharp stab of disappointment. 'I must hurry to get the last coach down to my hotel.'

'What will you do tonight?' Katie called after him. But he had gone, caught up in the crowd of holidaymakers heading down to the railway station.

'Well, that was a bit sudden, wasn't it?' Nic said. 'He could have stayed for a drink. Very mysterious.'

'We have to let him go!' The words came out far more loudly than Sasha had intended. 'What on earth do you mean?' Katie said, looking at her curiously. She had been watching, and it made her fearful. No good could come of this. Sasha was too vulnerable, and she could see that Miguel, no matter how charming and intelligent, was an adventurer. If she had pulled out all the stops, she was sure she could have attracted him, but she had seen at once that he had trouble written all over him. How had Sasha, who was always so rational, fallen for it? He must try it on with every attractive woman on the trail. It didn't make him a bad person in her eyes, and he was devastating-looking, she was just wise enough to steer clear. It was a good job they'd say goodbye to him tomorrow, and she could get Sasha out of his clutches before she did anything, well, anything she might regret.

'I mean . . .' Sasha was embarrassed as Katie was looking at her so intently. As if she was concerned for her. What did she mean? Why had she said that? 'I mean,' she said, trying to make a joke, 'he isn't some little pet of ours, there to entertain us. He's got to start thinking about the next group, and stuff . . .' she ended, lamely.

'What this girl needs is a drink,' Katie said firmly, steering them towards the bar. The hotel was smart, with a cool marble reception area and Spanish-looking staff. Sasha realized she had now started to make instant judgements about people – Andean, not

Andean. Why did the Spanish-looking Peruvians have the jobs like this, the work in the hotels, better paid, cleaner? But then this hotel was part of an exclusive chain, probably owned by a company in Lima. Of course they would bring in their own staff, rather than recruit locally, from the mountain people.

'Drink first, or a shower?' Nic said.

'Drink,' Katie and Sasha said firmly. The bar was part of the restaurant, and they flopped gratefully into huge squashy sofas. It felt odd to be in such a luxurious setting, and Sasha was acutely aware of their travel-stained trousers, muddy boots and unwashed hair. The barman brought them some nuts, and gave them each a cocktail list. 'Pisco Sours?' Katie said, looking around. Sasha groaned. 'Oh, go on then,' she said.

The cocktails seemed much nicer than the ones she'd had before, in Lima, and they all felt it would be politic to have another.

'These,' Katie said, 'have been the happiest four days of my life. The most exhausting, of course, but the best. What about you, Nic?'

'Not bad,' she said, grinning. 'Not bad.'

'Do you ever get excited about anything?' Katie said, teasingly, to her. Nic reached forward and took a handful of nuts, which she stuffed into her mouth. 'I guess I'm too old for surprises,' she said.

'What about you, Sasha?' She shook her head, not trusting herself to speak. She felt tearful, over-whelmed. The sights, the sounds, the sense of freedom would never leave her. Was she the only one who felt like this, that everything they had seen and done was a life-changing experience? She was so terrified of leaving it behind. The other two seemed much less affected, as excited about the luxury of the hotel as they had been by the trek itself. It was done now, finished, a pleasant memory to be neatly parcelled and put away. Maybe she was letting herself be too emotional, and was placing too much significance on the effect being here was having on her. Her feelings for Machu Picchu, and Miguel, were intertwined, and she could not separate them. She felt profoundly disturbed, nervous, elated, reckless. She had to calm down, get back to normal. She was exaggerating her own emotions. Stop it. But she knew this had been more than a holiday. It was an awakening.

Katie bought a bottle of champagne from the bar, and they took it to their rooms. Their duffle bags had already been taken up, and Katie and Sasha looked at each other, unzipped their bags, upended them and let everything fall to the floor, muddy, sweaty, damp and creased. It was chaos. 'Fuck it,' said Katie, pouring herself a glass of champagne. 'I'm going to have a bath.' Sasha lay down on the bed. It was so comfortable, the room so clean, so luxurious. If she closed her eyes . . . within minutes, she was asleep.

Katie had to gently shake her awake, and when she woke, she felt jolted, as if she had no idea where she was.

They had another drink before they even sat down to dinner, and after three Pisco Sours plus a glass of champagne in the room, they were all exceedingly tight. Sasha and Nic had done their best with their cleanest T-shirts and least stained trousers, whereas Katie had pulled out the stops with a black silk shirt and crumpled mauve floor-length skirt she'd saved from Sasha's military packing. Their newly washed hair hung glossily to their shoulders, and, with make-up, they felt exceptionally glamorous. Sasha, standing naked in the bathroom after the most blissful shower of her life as the dirt streamed out of her hair, surveyed her body and was pleased by what she saw. The revolting food on the trail and the constant walking had streamlined her waist and her thighs. Turning this way and that in front of the steamy full-length mirror, she held a hand against her flatter stomach and sucked it in further. Her face, the only thing exposed to the sun apart from her arms, was deeply tanned.

Heads turned when the three of them walked into the bar. Katie's blond hair was fluffy from washing, and she'd caught it up in a loose bun at the back of her neck. Her wide blue eyes outlined, her skin unlined, she looked little more than a teenager.

'Yo foxy chicks,' Katie said, raising her glass to the other two. 'Go us.' They clinked glasses obediently. 'Christ, look at this menu. Real food! So delicious. I'm never going to take any luxury for granted again, ever.'

'Yeah, right,' Sasha said.

'This has just been fantastic, though, hasn't it? Apart from Mike, of course, but Miguel said today he'd had a call saying he was flying home tomorrow, so he must be OK. God, he was so cute.'

'Have you ever been unfaithful to Harvey?'

Katie thought for a moment. 'No. I can't say I haven't been tempted, but no. I owe him too much.'

'You're going to have to tell her,' Sasha said, as Nic looked at them enquiringly.

'You mean there's more?' she asked, shocked.

So Katie recounted the story. When she had finished, Nic stood up from the table, walked round and gave her a big hug. 'You are so brave,' she said. 'And I feel a complete shit for calling you shallow.'

'Doesn't matter,' Katie said, wiping her eyes. 'I am still a bit shallow.'

'That's fine,' Sasha said. She knew she was getting pretty drunk. 'There's nothing wrong with shallow. I'm going to work on being a bit more shallow myself.'

'Quite right. You need to lighten up.'

'It's very hard though, when, oh God, Nic, I have to tell you too. I'm not sure I want to stay married to Alistair. Or if he wants to stay married to me.'

'I know.'

'What?'

'I said, I know. I know that you and Alistair are unhappy.'

'How?'

'Because someone told me.' Sasha was aware she was holding her breath. All the conversation in the restaurant around them seemed to have stopped.

'Who?' She hardly dared ask the question, and in an instant she realized why she was so frightened. Not Nic. Not Nic and Alistair. No. It was not possible. Her whole body was rigid with disbelief.

'Tim,' Nic said. Sasha felt all the air was escaping from her body in a long sigh. Would she have minded, that much? Really, really, honestly? The answer surprised her intensely. Yes. Yes, she would have minded. A lot.

'You met him through us . . .' Sasha said, realization dawning. No wonder Nic hadn't wanted Carol to come on the holiday.

'Through Alistair. I bumped into him by accident in town – this is five years ago – and we went for a drink because we both had to wait for the train and Tim was there too. And . . .'

Both Sasha and Katie leant forward, unable to believe what they were hearing.

'And I fell in love with him,' she said.

'This is April Fool,' Katie said. 'Impossible.' Sasha stared at Nic, at her calm, serene face, and thought about all the times she had envied Nic and Johnny for the way they had got marriage just right.

'Not straight away, of course. But he was like me. He had everything you could want in life except joy and passion.'

'But Carol . . .' Sasha said. 'And the children. She's so possessive of him . . .' She realized that she felt very shocked indeed, and not a little judgemental. What right did Nic have to jeopardize a family? No-one's family was perfect, but did anyone have the right to take someone who wasn't theirs? But then . . . if this holiday had taught her anything it was that you didn't own people, and no-one could afford to be smug about falling in love. It could strike anywhere, at any time, and no-one was safe. Marriage, at best, always remained a choice, and it never stopped being fluid and vulnerable to outside attack. 'You can't be having an affair with Tim. I would have known,' she blurted out.

Nic regarded her sardonically. 'It's easy to hide,' she said, coolly.

'But how – how have you hidden it?' Katie said. 'God, all the times you could have told me . . .'

'We both promised we wouldn't tell anyone. It isn't difficult, when you both work in London. He has a company flat, and at lunchtimes, we . . .'

'Make love?' Sasha was so astonished she could hardly speak. 'You don't go to Pret A Manger and buy a sandwich and mooch about the shops . . . you go to a flat and take all your clothes off and have sex?'

'Thank you for putting it so graphically,' Nic said, dryly. 'That's about it.'

'Why?' Katie gasped.

'Because otherwise I would die,' Nic said.

'But Johnny, he's so . . .'

'Dependable? I still make love to him, too,' she said. 'He has everything he wants. A home, me, the children.'

'Only he doesn't have you,' Sasha said, quietly. 'Not all of you.'

'He's so sweet,' Katie said. She realized she felt profoundly sorry for Johnny. 'He doesn't deserve . . .'

'Does he know?' Sasha cut in.

'Oh, no. I keep the two sides of my life quite separate. You get used to it, after a while.'

'But it isn't going anywhere,' Sasha said. 'There needs to be an outcome to love, a conclusion.'

'Does there? Why? Why can't you just accept love for what it is?'

'But how can it mean anything when you're hurting two other people?'

Nic regarded her calmly. 'How can it be hurting them, when they don't know? We're very clever. They will never find out.'

'But you're betraying them,' Sasha said. 'You're taking him away from his wife.'

'He hasn't left her,' Nic said, draining her glass. 'She has everything she wants too.'

'I would be so terrified,' Sasha said, 'of someone finding out and losing everything.'

'That's part of the attraction,' Nic said. 'The danger. Everything else in my life is so predictable.' Sasha looked at her serene, handsome face, and thought, I don't know you at all. She wondered if Alistair had ever suspected what was happening and, if so, why hadn't he mentioned it to her? But then, she realized sadly, they were well past the confiding stage.

'I don't think either of you have the right to criticize me,' Nic said. 'Come on. You took Harvey away from his first wife, didn't you?' Katie looked down at the table, as if she was about to cry. 'And you've been flirting like mad with Miguel.'

'But I'm not actually living a lie!' Sasha said, defensively.

'You're living with a man you say you don't love, who is, as I know, profoundly unhappy, yet I'm the one who's supposed to be living a lie. I do still love Johnny, in my way, and it would hurt him far more, and the boys, to break up both my relationship and Tim's.'

'But don't you want more?' Katie asked, fascinated.

'I used to.' Nic looked at her glass. 'But I'm used to it now. I can see that it would cause far more harm than good to smash up both of our relationships and try to start again. It isn't worth it. I have enough of him, and the excitement of fantastic sex. Sex can never be boring if there's that element of danger.'

'And what will happen?'

'Who knows? One day maybe we'll get fed up of sneaking around and we'll say "enough". And he will go back to his life, and I will go back to mine, and no-one will be any the wiser, or hurt. I wish,' she said, twirling the stem of her glass, 'that I hadn't told you. You don't understand, either of you. It must be this place.'

'So you've got what you want,' Sasha said. She felt absurdly angry, cheated that Nic did not have the life she wanted her to have. And that she knew so much about Alistair. How humiliating. How she must have pitied her, running her pretend little life of happiness. Katie saw the tension between them. What a tangled web we weave, she thought. Here's me, thinking I was the sinful woman.

'I think,' she said, slowly. 'I think we should make a promise to each other.'

'What kind of promise?'

'Well, we all have a kind of mess, don't we? We're all living lives which are one thing on the outside, quite another inside. I'm in a mad relationship with Harvey in which I'm never allowed to grow up or be responsible for myself. Which I have fostered,' she admitted, 'and allowed to happen. I should at least try for a baby, before it is too late. Or else I'm going to end my days forever wishing I had had the courage. I owe you so much,' she said, turning to Sasha, 'for making me see that.' She paused, weighing her words. 'And you should promise to stop being unhappy. If that means splitting up, then so be it. Do you really want to spend the rest of your life feeling like a victim? There are no gold medals for putting on a brave face and grinning and bearing it. Sometimes you just have to accept the fact that you married the wrong person. You can't just endlessly sweep it under the carpet, and pretend it isn't happening. You'll end up killing each other.'

'And me?' Nic said, a trifle sardonically. 'What should I promise?'

Katie looked at her reflectively. 'You should promise to break it off with Tim because it will explode. Someone will see you, or he'll tell a friend and they'll tell a friend, and you will be pitched into chaos and I don't think – correct me if I am wrong – that you want to leave Johnny.'

'No,' she said, slowly. 'I don't. But . . .'

'Don't but me,' Katie said. 'Life is hard.'

Sasha looked at her in amazement. 'And we thought you were the fluffy one.'

'You never can tell,' Katie said. 'A toast.' They all raised their glasses, and clinked them.

'I'm not promising I'll keep my promise,' Nic said.

'Let's go and sit outside,' Katie said, when they had drunk the last drop of the next bottle of wine.

'Coffee?' said the waiter, hopefully.

'I don't think so, do you, girls? Another bottle of champagne, I think.'

'Very well,' he said, with some alarm. 'And three champagne glasses,' Katie called after him.

'It's a bit cold,' Sasha said, as they tried to work out how to open the front door of the hotel, watched coolly by the receptionist who obviously did not approve of drunken women. 'Is it pull, or push, oh fuck,' Katie said, as they all fell out onto the drive. 'This way.' She waved the champagne bottle towards the grassy slope at the front of the hotel.

'We have to get up at five,' Nic pointed out.

'Oh, sod that,' Sasha said. 'Stop being boring. I won't allow you to be boring.' She weaved forward. 'You're still lovely,' she added, consolingly. Nic looked at her beadily. 'We're all lovely. I love you.' She tried to put her arms around Nic and Katie simultaneously. 'You're really pissed,' Nic said, but there was fondness in her voice. 'And we love you too, even if you have— What's that in your hair?' Katie said. Sasha felt her head.

'It's a flower,' she said, proudly. 'I picked it in reception.'

'It's an orchid,' Nic said. 'Oh dear, oh dear.'

'Another toast,' Katie said, as they flopped down onto the damp grass. 'This is an easy one,' she said, as Nic groaned. 'This is not the end, and we will do this again. Himalayas next year. Everest, here we come!'

'And no shagging the sherpa,' Nic said.

Sasha lay flat on her back, looking at the stars. 'I haven't,' she said. 'It is all in your mind.'

Then she raised herself up on one elbow and lifted her glass to the silent valley. 'To the mountains!' she cried. And the words drifted out, over the ancient sleeping city. The sky was filled with stars, huge, glinting stars, somehow much nearer, more vivid, in

243

this land of dreams. 'I can see the llama in the sky!'

'She's much more drunk than we are,' Katie said, confidingly, to Nic.

'No, really, Miguel told me about it. There's its nose, its eyes … it's looking down on us.'

'Perhaps it is time we went home,' Nic said. 'I'm not sure there's a cure for this one.'

'I don't want to be cured,' Sasha said, to the sky. 'I've only just started to live. I AM NOT BORING!' she yelled. 'OR USELESS!'

'Quite mad,' Katie said. 'Come on. Let's get her to bed.'

Chapter Fourteen

'Katie, wake up! Oh arse, it's five to five!'

'It can't be.' She raised herself on one elbow, mascara smudged beneath one eye, hair a bird's nest. 'Oh bollocks, so it is.'

'He's going to kill us,' Sasha said.

'Ouch, oh God. Why did we drink so much?' Katie said. 'This is your fault. I feel like an alien.'

'No it isn't. You kept buying champagne.'

'Oh God,' Katie said, slumping back on the pillow. 'We're about to witness one of the greatest sights in the modern world and I feel like someone has hit me over the head with a brick. I may be sick. Actually, I want to be sick.'

'Well, go and puke in private,' Sasha said. 'You'll set me off. Come on.' She levered herself from her bed, and began trying to find wearable damp clothes from the chaos on the floor.

'I wanted to be all sleek and beautiful this morning,' she added, sorrowfully. 'Thank God I washed my hair last night.' She dragged herself into the bathroom, and staring in the mirror, she stuck out her tongue. 'Gah. If I was Chinese they'd have me put down.'

'Why Chinese?' Katie said, putting her head around the door.

'They hold great store by the state of your tongue. It depicts your general health.'

Katie peered at Sasha's tongue. 'In that case, you're already dead,' she said.

'Thanks. Can I borrow your halter-neck shirt?' Sasha asked.

'It'll be a bit chilly at this time in the morning.'

'I can put a jumper over it. It'll be hot soon.'

'Not trying to impress anyone, are we?'

'Nope. Just sick of looking like a tramp, that's all.'

'It is now exactly five o'clock,' Katie said. Sasha ran a brush through her hair, tried to fluff it up, and splashed cold water on her face. Yuk. Furry teeth. She brushed them vigorously, using a bottle of water by the sink, and then, after drying her mouth, put on some lipstick and outlined her eyes, borrowing Katie's make-up. A few flicks of mascara and she didn't look too bad. Thank God for a tan. Even the bags under her eyes looked less pronounced with a tan. Brushing her hair again, she found remnants of the orchid. They were not going to win guest of the year prize, were they?

'Just come on!' Katie grabbed her, and, after banging on Nic's door, they ran down the corridor.

Miguel was standing with his back to them, his tall frame outlined in the doorway. He turned, and Sasha was relieved to see he was smiling, amused.

'It was a good night, last night?' he said.

'Very,' they chorused, as Nic ran panting up behind them.

'And none of you had anything to do with this?' He indicated a disgruntled-looking waiter who was sweeping up leaves and bits of soil from the large flower arrangement, which looked as if it had been charged by a particularly heavy wild animal. Did she, had she? Sasha thought hard. The orchid yes, but surely she'd just picked it, or had she maybe tripped . . . oops. Oh yes. She had a dim memory of losing her balance, twirling about, reaching out to grab something, and then getting stuck between something prickly and the wall . . . It might well have been her.

'Nic did it,' Katie and Sasha said, as one.

'I do not believe that,' Miguel said. 'Come. We will miss the sunrise.'

Outside, a pale light was just beginning to rise from the foot of the valley. The shingle of the path crackled underfoot, and along the path, each flower, each leaf was hung with dew. The air was cool, and fresh, and there was a stillness, a sense of intense calm before the day began to wake. A bird called, far away, down the valley, echoing into the silence.

In a subdued line they followed him down the steep steps leading to the gate into the city, and then they climbed, puffing and panting, up to the top of the hill, which Miguel said would give them the best vantage point, by the sentry's tower where they had stood yesterday.

Already a small group of tourists had gathered, some trekkers like themselves, in crumpled, dishevelled clothing, and other tourists who had caught the train and then stayed the night in the lodge. Sasha wondered if they had been in the restaurant, because the three of them seemed to be attracting a lot of black looks.

'Sit here,' Miguel said, spreading his waterproof coat out on the ground. They all sat, thankfully, after the steep climb, which had made Sasha's head throb. The city beneath them was still shrouded in mist, and the sky was cloudy and grey.

'I hope the sky clears,' Katie said. 'Otherwise we won't see anything.'

Miguel was sitting between Katie and Sasha, and Sasha could feel the warmth of his leg through her trousers. He turned his face to her, smiling, and dropped his chin, his eyes staring into hers. Sasha tried very hard not to breathe on him. 'Did you have fun, last night?' he said.

'It was a bit wild,' Sasha said, trying to breathe out of the corner of her mouth, away from him.

'You did not get to bed early?'

'Not exactly.'

'You should follow my orders,' he said, sensuously, and Sasha's stomach disappeared. 'I told you to be in bed early.'

'What about you?' she said. 'Did you sleep well?'

'I finished my paperwork and was tucked up in bed by nine o'clock.'

'What did you do last night?' Katie said, eavesdropping.

'I ate, met some of my friends who are also guides, played a game of pool, did some work and then went to bed. All alone. I was very lonely without you all around me,' he said, laughing.

Being near him was so luxurious. But she only had today, the train ride back to Cusco, and then they would say goodbye. The thought was devastating. No, she would not ruin today by dwelling on it. She had to seize the day and stop obsessing. This was part of the new her, the promise, to be true to herself and her feelings. How, though, when her true feelings were telling her to throw herself into his arms?

'Look,' he said, pointing at the sky. She felt the muscle in his thigh move. That didn't help at all. 'The skies are clearing.'

And they were – high above the peak of Huayna Picchu, the dull grey of the cloud began to part, and behind was a pale, white sky, rising into the palest of blue. And beneath, a golden light. Slowly, slowly this golden light rose behind the crest of Huayna Picchu, and then, breathtakingly, the sun appeared above the tip and the whole of Machu Picchu was illuminated, bathed in its iridescent glow. Miguel became very still beside her, and, glancing aside, she saw his lips move, as if he was praying. She leant slightly closer, and she could just hear what he was saying, a stream of ancient words, the language of Quechua. She wanted to memorize every detail of his profile, the black wavy hair standing up from his forehead, the high, clear brow, his thick dark eyebrows, and long, curling black eyelashes. Sensing her gaze, he turned to her, but his eyes were far away, in another time. He seemed to shake himself. 'What do you think?' he said. 'Is it not an incredible sight?'

'Incredible. I can't . . .' and suddenly she felt herself

249

close to tears. 'I can't express how I feel.' He smiled. It was only a matter of time.

They all had breakfast together at the hotel, Miguel tucking heartily into eggs, sausage and bacon. There were also salads and ceviche, but none of them could face fish. It could well swim back up again. Sasha drank coffee after coffee, trying to clear her head. Her headache was receding a bit, but she still had the curious, alien feeling, as if she was not quite of this world. Before they set out for the city, she excused herself and went back to the room, ostensibly to get her backpack, but really because she wanted to put on some more make-up. Katie followed her departure with knowing eyes. They should have talked through the Miguel thing last night, but Nic had taken the wind out of her sails. Still, not much could happen now.

Back in the room, Sasha closed the door and leant heavily against it. Then, to her horror, she burst into tears. Moving blindly forward, she fell onto the bed, and sobbed, and sobbed. All the emotions she had been suppressing for years came flooding out, all the tears she should have shed, all the anger she had restrained, anger at herself for not being the person she should have been, for endlessly apologizing. And mixed with it was fear, a dark, horrible fear of losing Miguel, never seeing him again, never being able to feel like this. And it wasn't just him, and Alistair, it was anger at her own lack of guts, for being so feeble in putting up with a life which was so second best, so timid, so apologetic, so lacking in balls.

Why had she stopped painting? Why hadn't she had

the courage to stand up to Alistair and have a proper, independent life with a career which meant the world to her? She thought she'd been so clever, living her life through everyone else, but in fact all she'd done was make herself into a martyr, endlessly sacrificing what she wanted to do at the altar of everyone else's needs. It hadn't helped anyone – Abbie despised her nearly as much as Alistair did, and Emily was overly reliant on her. All that self-pitying sacrifice, for nothing. No wonder he despised her. No wonder he thought she was useless and no longer desired her. I have failed, she thought. I have failed not only the children but Alistair too, taking out the resentment I now realize I felt on him, turning him inwards on himself, draining the life and joy out of him. You cannot live without love, she thought, her face pressed into her arms. Just to feel, now, what she felt for Miguel, made her realize what a gaping void lay inside her. And it must lie inside Alistair, too. There had to be a dynamic relationship at the heart of a family. Not the death of one.

'Sash, are you all right?' Katie's voice whispered through the door.

'Fine,' she lied, lifting herself up, wiping her eyes.

'We'll wait for you in reception,' Katie said.

'Sure. I'll be down in a minute.'

She went into the bathroom and switched on the light. Staring at herself, she saw a blotchy face, puffy eyes and a pink nose. She splashed water on her face, smudging her mascara, and then looked at herself sternly. Enough. Enough self-pity. Nothing was too late. It was not too late to make huge great bloody changes. She had to get out there and stop waiting for everyone else to make the decisions. She leant forward and looked herself directly in the eye. You have to grow up. Daddy will not make it better. He is dead. Alistair is not your father and your unhappiness is not his fault. You have to stop blaming him. Only you can be responsible for your own life, you helpless little wimp. Galvanized, she put on eye make-up and brushed her hair. It would be very warm outside now, and she pulled her jumper over her head, and knotted it around her waist. Her arms were burned brown from walking, and the halter-neck shirt looked great.

'You'll do,' she said to her reflection. 'I quite like you.'

'Bingham's search,' Miguel said, ushering them through the gate and saying something swiftly in Spanish to the guard, 'was actually for the lost city of Vilcabamba, which was the last stronghold of the Incas, fleeing from the Spanish conquistadors. They were forced back into the mountains, into the jungle and away from their birthright of Cusco.' His voice hardened. 'They sacked our temples, melted down our gold and sent it back to Spain to support the war against England, they raped our women and they killed our children. For the majority of people, there was no choice but to comply with the new regime, to save themselves. But some were prepared to fight, and fled to the hills. The last major uprising was in 1780, when Tupac Amaru II, a noble descendant of the Inca Lord, led his people against the Spaniards. But they were clever, and tried to entice him to Cusco saying they would make him part of the Government. They fought for two years, until he was betrayed by his right-hand man, who told the Spaniards where to find him. He was captured at night, with his wife and two eldest sons. They hanged him, and they kicked his wife to death. They cut out the tongue of one of his sons, and both sons were finally pulled apart by horses after they had been tortured. Finally, in 1821, our country was given independence. But our history is written in the blood of our people, and we have not forgotten.'

'Were all the descendants of Tupac Amaru killed?' Katie asked.

'Not all,' he said, and smiled to himself. 'The blood of the Incas lives on. Not far from here, about five kilometres north, a new city has been discovered recently by local and American archaeologists who have named it Maranpampa. The Spaniards never discovered Machu Picchu because it is thought that at the time of the conquistadors it was already a forgotten city, perhaps because it was too far from Cusco, the heart of the Inca nation. You must walk where I walk,' he said. 'The guards are very strict here, and we must not damage the stones.' He was leading them down a narrow path at the side of the city, and Sasha thought how beautiful it was in the morning light, many of the walls topped by the deep red of orchids. 'They have been planted here,' Miguel said, following her gaze. 'And these trees, they too have been planted.' She followed his arm and saw two small trees with curving branches, planted in the middle of a wide grassy square.

The city was built on a row of terraces, and outside the walls were layer after layer of wider terraces, circular, cut into the mountain as they had been at Winaywayna. 'It is thought,' he said, pausing to lean against a wall, 'that the city was built as a residence for the nobles, as it is so perfect in its architecture and stonework, moulded by the geography of the land.' It did look moulded into the land, Sasha thought, the buildings, streets and terraces following the curve of the mountain. Unlike modern cities it was in perfect harmony with the natural surroundings, with the dark green mountains forming the ideal backdrop. When it was alive and full of people, it must have been even more of a breathtaking sight when approached from the trail. No wonder Machu Picchu was regarded as a deeply religious city, quite literally awe-inspiring and worshipped as a god itself.

'It was built,' Miguel continued, 'around 1430, by the ninth Inca Lord. Around five hundred people, many of them servants, would have lived inside the walls, and at least a thousand men would have lived outside, guarding the city and tending the land. Hey – get down!' he called to two young men, who were balancing on top of the walls, shouting and laughing, larking about. They looked at him uncomprehendingly, and he repeated the order in rapid German. They looked mockingly at him, and carried on walking. 'Excuse me,' Miguel said politely. Then he turned, and walked swiftly up to the youths. They heard more rapid, furious German, then saw the youths jump down off the wall, chastened.

'Apologies,' Miguel said. 'It is all too easy to damage

the stones. Now, where were we? Of course, Machu Picchu would not have looked like this when Bingham discovered it – it would have been heavily overgrown, with plants and lichen.'

'How did he find it?' Sasha asked.

'For many hundreds of years people around the world had known there was a lost city of the Incas, full of fabulous gold treasures. It was called El Dorado – you have heard of that?' They nodded. 'Bingham and his team knew it must be somewhere near Cusco, as that of course was the centre of the Inca nation. There would have been some Quechua farmers who knew of its existence, as they still farmed the area. With their help, he stumbled across these ruins. At that time, he could only map them out, because he did not have enough men with him to begin clearing the stones.'

He coughed, and then continued. 'He returned a year later, and then again in 1915, to begin the difficult task of clearing the thick forest away from the ruins. Since then, the work has continued to resurrect the houses, and one has even had its thatched roof replaced. Over fifty burial sites were discovered, and many important remains. Follow me.'

Obediently, they followed him in a line over a dry moat, to a large, semicircular, walled, tower-like temple. 'This is the Temple of the Sun,' he said, as they stepped into its cool interior. 'You see the stonework, how each stone fits perfectly into the other? The people here had their own small quarry on site, or the stones were transported many, many miles along the Inca Trail. Each stone would be smoothed, and polished and cut to exactly the right shape before it was manoeuvred into place. You see this boulder here? This would have been some kind of altar, and it is also the entrance to a small cave. Through this window here the sun will shine directly during the June solstice, and it also frames the Pleiades, the constellation of stars which were – and are – an important signpost in our agricultural calendar. You remember, how important astronomy was? We had no watches or calendars to record the time, the days and the months, but we watched the sky. It told us all we needed to know.'

They walked back down the same path, and came to a series of interlinked, cascading ceremonial baths. They were built of grey granite, with tunnels and small waterfalls through which water still ran. 'It works perfectly today,' Miguel said. 'We can learn much about engineering as well as science from the Incas.' From there he took them up to another large stone building, which looked out over the biggest area of grass, the Sacred Plaza. 'The priest would have preached his sermons from here,' Miguel said, 'and all important orders would have been given by the nobles to the people.' Sasha stood behind him, and tried to imagine the vast square beneath full of people, in tunics of woven cloth, shoes of llama skin on their feet, children playing and dogs wandering about. As if on cue, two little llamas appeared. 'Oh, cute,' Katie said.

'These are the babies of the llama you saw yesterday,' Miguel said. 'This white one with the black face was born last year, the little black one this year.' The smallest of the llamas flopped down onto the grass, and the white one gambolled around it on stiff legs, trying to make it play. 'Emily would love them,' Sasha said, reaching for her camera. 'They make good pets,' Miguel said. 'But you must always buy a pair. These ones are very tame.'

On the top of the hill above the square, they all sat down, thankfully, and Miguel took out his bottle of water to drink. The sun was already very hot. Sasha lay back on the grass. She closed her eyes, and looked up at the sun. It filled her vision, even with her eyelids closed she could see a vivid yellow ball, surrounded by its aureola of gold. She relaxed her hands against the grass, still damp with dew. An intense feeling of peace came over her, yet all her senses were on the alert. She felt sensuous, her skin tingling. 'Many people who come here feel it,' she heard Miguel saying. 'It is said that the spirits have never left Machu Picchu, and anyone who comes here is aware of a higher being, a spirituality.'

'Do you feel it?' she heard Katie asking him.

'It never leaves me,' he said, simply.

'Enough rest,' he said, after a few minutes of silence. 'We have much to see.'

From the square he led them up to a huge carved pillar of rock. 'This,' he said, 'is Intihuatana, or the hitching post of the sun. You see it overlooks the Sacred Plaza, the Rio Urubamba and the peak of Huayna Picchu? You see these carvings at the base?' They all bent forward to look. 'At first it was thought this was a map of the Inca Empire, but in fact it is a clock, a clock which maps the interrelations between the stars and the constellations. Using the angles of the pillar, the astronomers could predict the solstices, and so know when to plant different crops. This is one of the few that have survived – the Spanish smashed the other Intihuatanas because they wanted to wipe out what they saw as the blasphemy of sun worship.' He let his hand rest gently on the stone. 'Thank goodness they did not succeed in destroying all of our cultural heritage.'

At the back of Intihuatana, another staircase led them down to the Central Plaza, at the end of which was a labyrinthian maze of interconnecting cells, niches and passageways, both under and above the ground. Sasha tried to imagine being entombed under the cold stone, and shivered. At the entrance to the cells was a large stone carving. 'What does this look like?' Miguel asked. They all peered at it. 'The wings of a condor?' Sasha ventured. 'Correct,' he said smiling. 'The bird that takes us back to the mother earth when we die. Why did we worship the sun?' he said, suddenly.

'Because it brings light and energy to the crops?' Katie ventured.

'And because he creates the earthly paradise for us, as well as giving us his son as our ruler,' Miguel said. 'All things on earth come from the sun.'

'Wow,' Katie said to Sasha, as they followed him through a narrow doorway. 'He's getting a bit religious on us, isn't he?'

'I suppose he just believes it, that's all,' Sasha whispered back.

'He'll be offering us up as sacrifices next,' she murmured. 'Although God knows where he's going to find a virgin. Hey, I wonder if his wife has to be a virgin?'

'Ask him.'

'No, you.'

'Oh, stop being so childish.'

In the Temple of the Sun, he showed them five niches set into the elaborate white granite wall. Inside three of them had been placed a handful of maize, coca leaves and tobacco. 'Who put them there?' Nic asked, curiously. 'Local people,' Miguel said. 'There are many who still believe in the old deities. You remember when we walked past the houses in the settlements? Did you notice that on some of the thatched roofs there were two small bottles?' They shook their heads. 'I should have pointed it out at the time. They are a form of offerings, of worship,' he said. 'One bottle would be full of oil, representing the fat of the land, an offering to the sun which gives us health and vitality. The other would contain water, the fountain of life.'

'Interesting idea,' Katie said to Sasha as they followed him back towards the Sacred Plaza. 'We could have a carrier bag on our roof, to represent the sacred god of Waitrose.' Sasha laughed. Nic was bombarding Miguel with questions about everything they had seen that morning.

'Wonderful history,' Katie said. 'Now it is time to feed the inner soul with a nice glass of wine, don't you think? I think I need a hair of the llama that bit me.'

'What?' Miguel said, confused.

'Too complicated,' Katie said.

* * *

Sasha declined wine at lunchtime, on the basis that she did not want Miguel to think she was a complete lush. The hotel had laid on a marvellous buffet, with many different types of salads, ceviche and marinated meats. After the trail, it was total heaven to be confronted with so much delicious food again, and they all piled their plates. Miguel had a very healthy appetite, Sasha noticed. His phone rang constantly through the meal, and he kept having to leave the table to hold conversations.

'Why doesn't he just switch it off?' she said, crossly. 'He's supposed to be with us.'

'He's starting to leave us already,' Katie said. Sasha looked at her. She was right, of course she was right. Mentally and physically he was leaving them, getting ready for the next trip. She was so dependent on him after such a short time, she felt like a tree being torn up brutally by the roots. She had to be mature and let him go. She hardly knew him, after all. They thought they knew him, but they didn't. Not really. He had only given them as much of himself as he was prepared to show.

After lunch they sloped off to their rooms, reluctant to begin the dreary process of packing up. 'We still have a night in Cusco,' Katie said, trying to cheer them up. 'And most of a day in Lima.'

'True,' Sasha said, trying to quell the dull, leaden feeling inside her. Maybe, just maybe, he would come for a meal with them this evening, in Cusco. They had already decided they would eat in the Inca Grill in the main square, because the food looked great and was not too expensive. They didn't want to eat in the hotel – they wanted to be out in the atmosphere of the city. 'It's party night tonight,' Katie said. 'Cheer up.'

'What was last night then?' Sasha said.

'Practice,' she laughed.

'I hope the train journey to Cusco doesn't take too long,' Katie said. 'I've still got loads of stuff I want to buy.'

'I haven't bought anything yet.'

'Well, you must come with me then. I found the most fantastic shops. And we'll make Nic come with us. She looks a bit depressed to me.'

To their relief they didn't have to walk down to the station as a coach stood outside the hotel waiting to take them to Machu Picchu Pueblo, the town where Miguel had spent the night. As they got onto the bus, Sasha noticed a small boy, aged just nine or ten, wearing an Inca tunic, sandals on his bare feet, and his face painted like a mini Inca warrior. 'What is he doing?' she said. 'You'll see,' Miguel smiled. As the coach set off, the boy started running.

'Is he going to chase the coach?' she asked, twisting around to try to see where he had gone, worried about him. As the coach turned one of the sharp bends, he disappeared into a gap in the trees. Then, when they came round the next bend, there he was waving at them. They all clapped and cheered him, and, as he waved, he made a strange, high-pitched wailing sound. 'The Inca farewell,' Miguel said. It had a curiously haunting, sad quality. As the coach passed him, he darted off again.

'Does he run all the way to the bottom?'

'Yes. You see, he cuts out the bends.'

At each bend, he was there, wailing his strange cry. Once they had reached the foot of the hill, the coach slowed down to a stop and he jumped on, grinning from ear to ear.

'He is a *chaski*,' Miguel said. 'A messenger from the Inca Trail.'

They clapped him again, and then people started fumbling in their backpacks for some change. As he passed Miguel and Sasha, Miguel said something to him in Quechua, and the boy grinned at him and nodded, almost like a bow. Nic gave him some money and he said, 'Cool. Thanks.'

The path to the railway station took them past stall after stall full of hand-knitted jumpers, scarves, socks, hats and jewellery, the last chance to extract yet more dollars from the tourists. After ten minutes Miguel became impatient with their browsing, and said that unless they got a move on, the train would go without them.

When they reached the platform, the train looked like something out of the Wild West. It had a wooden verandah at the back, with a viewing platform.

'How long will the journey take?' Katie asked.

'About four hours,' he said. They groaned.

'At least we can sleep,' Katie said.

'The views are spectacular,' he said. 'It would be a shame to miss them.'

After he had loaded their bags onto the train, he disappeared down the carriage. Sasha tried not to look bothered, and slumped down in the seat opposite

Katie and Nic. Katie took out her postcards, and, balancing them on an expensive coffee-table book she had bought of pictures of Machu Picchu, she started to write. Nic made a ball out of her fleece, and, leaning against the train window, closed her eyes. The train jerked violently, and then set off. Sasha had put the book she was reading in her backpack, but couldn't summon the energy to read. She felt very tired and drained, the four days of strenuous walking finally catching up with her. Until now, she had kept going on adrenalin, with the excitement of seeing Machu Picchu and, she admitted to herself, being near Miguel. Now he was not next to her, all that adrenalin drained away. She ought to write some postcards too, but the thought of it was too boring. She rested her head against the back of the seat, and felt her eyes closing. It was warm in the train, as the sun streamed through the windows, and the rhythmic clatter of the wheels was soporific. Slowly, she felt herself drifting into a comfortable sleep.

She was lying on something soft, being rocked gently by the sea, and whatever she was lying on was warm against her cheek. She felt herself encircled by arms she could not see, and she felt totally secure. She wanted to open her eyes, but she couldn't. She could hear a voice – was it her father's? It was coming from far away, little more than a murmuring. She snuggled deeper into the warmth.

Slowly, she became aware of a voice above her. She opened one eye, and looked down. Her hand was resting on a leg which was not hers. They were Miguel's grey trousers. Gently, she lifted her hand from his thigh. Oh, God, how embarrassing. Her head was pressed against his chest, nestling under his chin. Her mouth felt damp. Slowly, imperceptibly, she lifted her head from his chest, and turned to look at him. To her immense relief he too was asleep, his head thrown back. She looked down to where her head had been, and, to her horror, there was a vivid patch of damp on his pale blue T-shirt.

She looked up to see where the voice had come from. It was a guard, selling bottled water and crisps, but he had moved away down the train. Her left arm had gone to sleep where it had been pressed against Miguel, and she leant away from him, shaking it gently. At the movement, he stirred in his sleep and his hand fell across her thigh. Instinctively he turned his hand over so it curved around her leg. Gently, he spread out his fingers and slid his hand further up her thigh. Horrified at how arousing it was, she inched her leg away, so his hand fell onto the seat. He moaned, and curling his fist into a ball, he turned away from her. She sat, hardly daring to breathe. She was terrified by how very much she wanted him.

As the train neared Cusco, he woke with a start. He rubbed his hand over his face, and turned to Sasha, who pointedly looked out of the window. He looked at his watch.

'Have I been asleep long?' he said.

'I don't know.'

'Of course. You were sleeping when I sat down. You looked very sweet,' he said. Oh really, she thought. I bet I had my mouth open and was snoring like a drain.

He leant across her to look out of the window, his arm pressing against her chest. 'If you look now, you will see Cusco. Oh, it is the other side. Come, stand up.' He stood up, and then moved back to let her slide out of the seat. Both Nic and Katie appeared fast asleep. 'You must look here,' he said. She leaned forward, and gasped. Beneath them, Cusco stretched away, thousands of street lights winking in the dark, like a city covered in fairy lights, the cathedral floodlit and clearly visible.

'It is very beautiful, isn't it?' He stood very close behind her, and she could feel every inch of him. The pressure was deliberate, she was sure. She could not take much more of this, or she would explode. He steadied himself against the rocking of the train, and gently put one arm around her waist. 'Sasha . . .' he murmured, sensuously, in her ear. 'I know you . . .'

'Are we nearly there?' Katie stood up, and, stepping out of her seat towards them, stretched. How long had she been watching? Miguel moved away from her. 'God, look at the city. Nic, wake up. This is amazing.'

As the train approached the station, Sasha saw a group of small boys playing by the line. The train slowed down, as it was passing through a small station. Miguel, catching sight of the boys, stepped forward. He wrenched down the window, and let fly with a stream of Quechua. The boys looked at him sullenly, and then moved back, away from the tracks.

His eyes flashed. 'It is so dangerous,' he said angrily. 'They must not play there.' He turned to look for the guard, and, seeing him much further up the train, he strode off.

'He's awfully masterful, isn't he?' Katie said. 'It's almost as if he owns the place.'

'I just think he has a very strong social conscience,' Nic said.

'Weird,' Katie said.

When the train stopped, Miguel jumped off ahead of them and pulled their heavy bags down off the luggage racks, one by one. Sasha stood and watched him, weak with longing. She had got to the point where she was ready to do anything. She had never wanted anyone so badly. Ever. It was like being in the grip of a powerful addiction. But why did he encourage her, and then just leave her? He could have had a meal with them last night, yet he chose not to.

Outside the station, a row of taxis stood, the drivers approaching them, gesticulating. A few curt words from Miguel sent all of them but one away. Then he turned to them. 'I leave you here,' he said. Sasha felt that the world had stopped, and an icy hand clutched her stomach. Now. He was to go now? This was it? She felt faint, and was glad Katie was standing so close to her. Katie glanced at her quickly and said, 'You will eat with us tonight, won't you? We'd love you to come.'

'I'm sorry,' he said. 'But there are too many things I have to do. Besides . . .' He looked down at Sasha. What? Did he think she would reject him? Oh God, no. She tried to tell him with her eyes that she really, really wanted him to have a meal with them, and then, maybe . . . But he looked away. I've blown it, she thought. Somehow, I haven't got the message across and it is too late.

'Besides,' he went on smoothly, 'you ladies will want to have your final night on your own.'

'No, we don't,' Katie said, sensing Sasha's panic. 'We had last night.'

'I will see you,' he said, 'tomorrow morning. You have an early start, you know, you must be away from the hotel by half past six, so you should not have such a late night. I will come to the hotel to see you off.'

Tomorrow morning. At least she would see him again. She made a pledge, there and then, that she would kiss him, even if it was in full view of Nic and Katie. She could not go home without one moment of real physical contact, no matter how brief. He motioned the taxi driver to pick up their bags, and then put his fingers to his lips. 'Ciao,' he said, and blew them a kiss. They stood motionless as he walked away, down the dark hill into the city, his own duffle bag slung easily over his shoulder.

'Let's get dressed up, go shopping and then go straight out for a meal,' Katie said firmly, as they stood in the foyer of the hotel in Cusco. They weren't staying at the Monasterio again, but at the Libertador, which was also a five-star hotel but Sasha thought was far less intimate, less welcoming. She'd been looking forward to this night so much, but now it held nothing for her, as he was not there. Nothing, without him, meant anything. How weary, stale, flat and unprofitable were to her all the uses of this world.

She couldn't be bothered to search for something nice to wear, but instead pulled on a crewneck jumper and her battered trekking trousers. It was their uniform, it meant that the holiday, their connection with the trek, still existed. Katie too was wearing her baggy trousers and a T-shirt, but was immaculately made up when she knocked on their door. Sasha took one look at her and realized she had to make an effort, if only for them. She went into the bathroom and put on some make-up, and pulled a brush through her hair. She could not kill this last night for them, just because of her misery.

As they walked out of the hotel, Katie said, 'I don't believe it.'

'Hello Katie,' said the boy.

'Do you have spies out, or what?'

'Did you enjoy the trek?' he asked, as he trotted along beside them.

'Very much,' Katie said. 'Now here is a dollar. I give you this dollar, you go home to bed, OK?'

'OK,' he said. 'But I do very bad business today.'

'Yeah, yeah,' Katie said. 'Scoot.'

Sasha tried to summon up enthusiasm for the shopping trip, but it was so hard. Try as she might, she could not quell the desperate hope that at any moment she might see him – this was, after all, his city, and they might just bump into him. And they had told him they were eating at the Inca Grill, so it would be awfully easy for him just to be near there as if by accident . . . at every corner they turned, she scanned the faces passing by. Most of the people out on the streets were European, American or Australian. At every dark head she turned, her heart beating wildly. But it was never him.

'For God's sake cheer up,' Katie said, as they sat in the restaurant.

'You're right,' she said. 'I am being stupid, aren't I?'

'Yes,' they chorused.

'Look,' Katie said. 'He was very lovely. Very lovely indeed. But there are a number of facts not in his favour. One, he is very young. Two, he lives here, in Peru, and you do not. Three, you are married. Four, you have two children, and your eldest child is just nine years younger than he is. See? It cannot be natural. And, if Abbie was here, he'd probably make a play for her as well.'

'Oh, please tiptoe around my delicate emotions,' Sasha said, but a laugh escaped. 'I suppose you're right. It's totally hopeless. Anyway, I don't really want him, of course I don't. I guess my head was just turned by someone appearing to fancy me, when it hasn't happened for ages. There. I'm OK now. Come on. I shan't think of him again. What shall we eat?'

She was lying. He filled her mind, obsessing her. Again, and again, her eyes strayed to the floodlit square outside, scanning the people walking past, the people sitting there. A couple of times she thought she saw him, sitting on a bench, or walking on the far side – both men had his long, easy stride, his height and his hair colour, but she could not be sure. It would not be him, he had far more important things to do than hang about in a square. How arrogant she was being. She didn't mean anything to him, she had just been an amusement, something to keep him occupied on the trail. He probably did it all the time, Katie was right – after all, he had met his French girlfriend on the trail. She had to brush this passion aside, and make it an amusing memory. But right now it wasn't an amusing memory. It was real, and it really hurt. He was in this city, possibly just a mile, less, from her.

They stayed in the restaurant for over two hours, and all the time she thought, it isn't too late, he could walk in at any moment. Every time the door swung open, her heart stood still, and every time it was not him. By eleven o'clock, she knew he was not coming. They were the last people in the restaurant, and the owner was beginning to put the chairs up on the tables.

On the way home they linked arms, and Sasha forced herself to sound happy. But the joy she'd experienced in the last few days was gone, replaced by a sick feeling of dread. Even the stern talking-to she'd given herself in the hotel room this morning – was that just this morning? – was not working. She felt full of chaos, the only still, certain thing, her longing for Miguel.

'You're very quiet,' Nic said.

'I'm just tired,' she said. 'I think it's all catching up with me.'

'I hope they haven't locked up,' Katie said, before she pushed open the impressively wide hotel doors, just as a liveried doorman reached them. They all concentrated on walking in a steady, dignified manner to reception. After they were given their keys, they turned. Miguel was sitting in one of the sofas, reading a newspaper.

'Bloody hell,' Katie said. He looked up, and smiled. He had come. They walked over to him, and Katie plonked herself down next to him, and put her hand on his leg. He looked bemused. 'Have you had a good night?'

'We certainly have,' Katie said. 'Come to the bar and have a nightcap. What are you doing here, anyway?'

'I came to see you got back safely. I thought,' he looked over at Sasha, 'I thought you might be celebrating and the streets are not always safe at this time of night.' He has been watching us, Sasha realized. He was in the square. He was there, after all.

'Actually,' Nic said, 'I think we've probably had enough for one night. And we should have an early night.' She shot a swift look at Katie, and Sasha realized she was to be hustled to her room, out of danger.

'Oh, all right then,' Katie said, grumbling.

The three of them stood up, and, holding their keys, they headed for the lift, together. Sasha looked back at him, and his eyes told her to be quiet. They were not to know.

'That was weird,' Katie said, in the lift. 'Why show up now?'

'Maybe he did just want to check we'd got back safely,' Sasha said. 'Maybe he was just passing.'

'Yeah, right,' Katie said. Sasha looked away, and studied the floor numbers. Her heart was a trapped bird, its wings beating inside her.

Chapter Fifteen

The door opened, just after he lifted his hand to knock. She stood back, to let him in, and as she did so, in one movement he was against her. She stepped back, and he pressed her into the wall, insistently, so she could feel every inch of his body. Then he lowered his face to hers, and kissed her. His mouth was hard against her, frighteningly hard, and as she felt his tongue, his hands fell to her waist and he pulled her, roughly, up against him. Part of her was scared, that she had no control, but she had to trust him, she knew he could not stop. His hand was in her hair, pulling her head back so forcefully it hurt, he was so frantic. I have to let this happen, she thought. She put her hands into his thick hair, and felt the hot skin on the back of his neck, breathing him in.

'Stop,' she said. She had to forcibly push him from her, he held her so tightly she was being crushed. His eyes were burning down at her, his face covered in a fine sheen of sweat. He was out of control. He held out one hand to her, and pulled her back to him, kissing her hard. Then he lifted his face just inches from hers, breathing heavily. 'Don't you dare tell me to stop. Not now. Not now I have you.' He put his fingers, burning, on her lips. 'You're mine,' he breathed. 'I can do anything I want with you.' She could not take her eyes from his, she was drowning. She had never thought he would be so passionate, so controlling, and the rational part of her brain screamed 'stop'. But if she said no now, he would rape her.

He reached down, and, with a practised gesture, pulled her jumper up over her head. His lips were on her neck, her chest. She was breathing so fast, she thought she might faint. Sex had never been like this. It was as if she was looking down at herself, unable to believe this was happening. He reached behind her neck, and pulled off her necklace, breaking the clasp. He ran his hand up her body, from her stomach, over her breasts. 'You want me?' It was not a question. How arrogant he was, and how helpless she felt. Aroused, frightened to death. He slid one arm around her, pulling her to him again. 'Feel how much I want you.' There was no way she could stop him now, and the part of her brain which was still working told her just to let go, let it happen. He would not hurt her, surely? Love-making had always been a partnership, but this was not. It was domination. Infinitely seductive, but terrifying.

He leant over her in one sinuous, controlled movement, arching above her. Staring into her eyes, he reached down with both hands and pulled his T-shirt over his head. He was hard, and muscular, with not an ounce of fat. Straddling her, he started to unbutton the waistband of his trousers.

She lay as if hypnotized while he slid her trousers down, over her hips, her knees, her feet. 'You are so beautiful,' he said, his hand moving up her stomach, and she believed him. There was no way she could stop now, consumed with desire.

It was sex as she had never known it. He took her to a dark place, a place where there was nothing but the movement of their bodies against each other, his mouth, his hands, his eyes. It was forceful, a powerful, dark ballet. After the first climax, though, he changed, and she was no longer afraid. She felt as if she knew him again, not the terrifying wild animal who had assaulted her. He held her in his arms and began to kiss her slowly, arousing her with practised movements. His body was perfect in every way, and she could tell that he loved to be touched, his skin so sensitive. He was a man who enjoyed sex for sex alone, she realized, and had no time for the emotional baggage. 'I do not know what love is,' he had said. Now she understood. This would never happen again, and she had to accept this night for what it was. But that didn't make it shameful. This was sheer, animal passion without guilt. He gave her total confidence to let go. He turned, and moved her, so she did not know where she was, one moment he was behind her, the next she was above him. A sequence of movements which didn't stop, but flowed on, and on.

He lay next to her, propped up on one elbow, lazily tracing the curve of her mouth with his finger. His hair dark with sweat, he lay, with one leg thrown over her body, in possession of her. 'Tell me your thoughts,' he said, his voice low, sensuous, full of laughter. He was triumphant, perfectly in control once more. 'I am thinking,' Sasha said, slowly, 'that I will never be the same again.'

'Good,' he said. 'Did you think you would escape me?' He moved against her. 'Did you ever doubt that I would make love to you? I would not let you go.' He leant down and felt for her hand, lifting it, and inter-linking their fingers. 'When you feel like this, there has to be a release, and you wanted me just as much. I know. You can't lie any more, Sasha.'

She woke in the night, and looked at the clock. It was three, just over two hours until they had to get up. She had only slept for half an hour. He lay next to her, his sleeping face perfect in its beauty. She lay, and stared at him. Falling in love with him would be like trying to capture the sun. No-one would ever own him. He was too self-possessed for that. He would have many women. Probably already had. She smiled into the darkness. Thank God she could be realistic. But that did not make it any less extraordinary, for all that.

Chapter Sixteen

Miguel Aljehandro Amaru. She stared at his card. Of course. It explained everything. Looking out of the window of the minibus as they headed towards the airport, she turned it over in her hand. Had the others noticed? She held it to her face, feeling the sharp edge against her cheek, smiling. Maybe she would tell them, point it out, later. But for now, it was just for her, and she wanted to laugh aloud, hug the revelation to her. No wonder he thought no woman could resist him, and no wonder he was so arrogant. He was a direct descendant of the Incas. It was faintly ridiculous, and yet quite apt. He had thousands of years of arrogance bred into him. His ancestors had been worshipped as gods. She thought for a moment. Maybe he would become a leader and change the lives of the mountain people he cared about so much.

Chapter Seventeen

She pushed the back door open tentatively. From inside the kitchen came the thump, thump of Bob's tail. From within the house she could hear the shriek of laughter from the television set, cartoons. Loaded down with bags, she felt exhausted, an alien, in a jet-lagged world with a surreal, dreamy edge. As Nic drove her towards home, she felt like she was moving underwater, nothing quite real. Everything she passed was so familiar, and yet not. The memories were there, in her mind, and nothing had changed. But she had changed, and she saw everything that she knew so well as if for the first time. Walking out of Heathrow at six in the morning, a low, cold mist hung in the air and the sky was grey, leaden. After the blinding light of Lima, this was like plunging into cold water. The clouds were pale grey, ridged, their bulging stomachs pregnant with rain, and the light behind, barely visible, was filtered down to a watery pallor. After eleven hours on the plane, trying to sleep in the dry, unnatural air had left them all dehydrated, grey beneath their tans, dark circles under their eyes. Stepping off the plane was like stepping onto another planet, a planet where the sun could not break through. All their optimism seeped away under this cold, grey reality.

They hardly spoke as they collected their bags, each one wrapped in separate thoughts. On the plane Nic and Katie had chatted in a desultory way about their plans for the week, but Sasha was silent – now it was such an imminent reality she was filled with a dark, hollow dread of returning. Miguel was gone, he could not protect her and she had to face her life alone. She longed to see the children, but she was terrified of her own decision. Was she right? Yes, the voice inside her kept saying. 'You are right. You must have courage, because this is the only thing you can do.'

In Nic's car after Katie and Harvey had driven them to their house, where they said a tearful goodbye, she closed her eyes for a moment, lulled by the movement, consoled by the warmth of the car, the murmur from the radio. Nic had said how good it was to hear Radio Four again, but to Sasha the voices were meaningless, she could not decipher the words or understand what they were saying. The issues they were discussing were quite foreign to her, they made no sense in her world. She may have slept, she wasn't sure, but too soon they were pulling into her drive, she wanted to stay in the limbo of the car, where she felt safe. Nic helped her out with her bags, and then reached forward to hug her. 'It will be fine. We're with you. Call me.' She pulled back and looked at Sasha searchingly. 'You will be fine? Do you want me to come in with you?'

'No,' she said. 'I'm better on my own.'

Harvey had been at the airport, and Katie cried when she saw him. She ran to him and he enveloped her in a great hug. Nic and Sasha hung back, embarrassed, until Katie turned and ran back to them, tears streaming down her face. She flung her arms around both of them. 'I love you so much,' she said, sobbing. 'You don't know what you've given me.'

The clock ticked. Bob lifted himself stiffly from his basket and came to greet her, his lips drawn back in a Labrador smile. The sight of him finished her off, and she sank to her knees, hugging him, her tears wet on his sleek head. He laid his face gently against her, and lifted his paw onto her arm. Then she slowly rose, and dragged her bags into the hall, shutting the kitchen door. At the noise, there was a shriek. 'Mummy!' Emily hurtled out of the TV room, her face wide-eyed, glowing. 'Mum!' She threw herself onto Sasha, almost knocking her over. 'You're back! You're back!' Sasha held her so tight, the connection so strong, the animal warmth of love, the need fulfilled. She breathed in her smell, like a tiger nosing its cub, pressing her face against her hair, imprinting herself upon her child.

'Hey, Mum.' Abbie stood in front of her, leaning coolly on the door frame. 'What are you wearing?' she said. Sasha disentangled Emily and looked down at herself. 'It's a jacket I picked up in Cusco,' she said. 'Quite cool,' Abbie said, walking around her. 'You look different.' 'Different how?' 'I don't know,' Abbie said. 'Just different.' Sasha reached forward, and pulled Abbie towards her. Awkwardly, with sharp elbows and stiff-backed, Abbie let herself be hugged, but did not surrender herself as Emily had done. 'Got me a present?' she asked, muffled, into Sasha's shoulder. 'Might have.'

Emily was already rooting about in her bags. 'Hang on,' Sasha said. 'Give me a minute. Where's Dad?'

'Here.' Alistair stood in the doorway, hesitant. 'Hi.'

'Hi.'

'Good trip?'

'Not bad. Excellent, really. I didn't ring because . . .'

'No.'

'Abbie, can you give me a hand with these bags upstairs? Then I can show you your presents.'

'Hope they're good ones.'

'Just be grateful, can you?'

'What's going to happen with you and Dad?' Abbie said, closing the bedroom door on Emily, who howled. Sasha flashed a glance at the door, meaning no, not now.

'Why? Why do you say that?' Sasha asked.

'I just have a feeling. You don't . . .'

'What?'

'Love each other any more. Do you? Is it our fault?'

'Of course not. Look, it's too soon. I'm exhausted.'

'I've talked to Dad.'

'What?'

'While you were away. Dad and I talked.'

'And?'

'And he said you don't love each other any more.

That you don't make each other happy.' She dragged out the words.

'What do you think?'

'I think that if that's the case you should split. It isn't fair.'

'Fair to whom?'

'Fair to you.'

'But don't you mind?'

'What does that matter?'

'It matters a great deal. You matter. You're the most important thing.'

From outside the door Emily's howl rose to a scream, and she rattled and rattled the doorknob. It was so loud, Sasha could hardly hear what Abbie was saying.

'We don't matter,' she said. 'We don't matter to you and Dad.' Then, slowly, she walked to the window.

'What are you doing?'

'I need some air.'

'Don't lean out like that.'

'You can't stop me.'

'Abbie, don't. Stop messing around.' She leaned out further. 'You'll fall.' Abbie turned to her. 'I don't care,' she said. And then she was gone, and the window banged back against the frame.

Sasha woke, her neck jerking back, her heart pounding. She looked down at her hands and they were outstretched, as if trying to catch something. Leaning forward, she concentrated on breathing normally, willing her heart to stop racing. The book which had lain in her lap fell forward onto the floor of the plane with a dull thump. She tried to grab it. It would wake Nic and Katie, who were sleeping either side. She must have slept awkwardly, her neck was stiff and she had no feeling down her right-hand side. Slowly, she opened and closed her hands. Her palms were sweating. She wondered if she had called out 'No!' But everyone around her was still sleeping, the slack-jawed, uncomfortable sleep of aircraft flight. She laid her head back against the seat, and tried to clear her mind. But still she saw Abbie's beautiful face, cold, angry, rejected. Felt the lurch forward as she tried to stop her, then the falling, drowning, helpless sensation once she had gone. She had failed to save her. She stared at Katie, willing her to wake up, but she was unconscious to the world, her eyelids flickering as her eyes moved in a dream. Sasha closed her eyes again, but did not hope for sleep. Variations on the dream would come again, and again, as her subconscious fought to find an answer.

'Just our luck to lose our bags,' Katie said, as they stood by the carousel.

'Maybe yours was too heavy,' Nic said.

'Why mine?'

'Oh, no reason,' she smiled.

'Look, there they are.' Sadly, like a dismal after-thought, their clump of bags appeared, shunting towards them.

'Thank Christ for that. If I don't get home and into bed I am going to collapse. I need to sleep for a week,' Katie said.

'Lucky you,' Nic said. 'I've got to go back to work tomorrow.'

And I have to tell my husband I no longer love him, Sasha thought. I know which I would prefer. They heaved their bags off the carousel, and loaded them onto two trolleys. They seemed to have amassed a ridiculous amount of stuff, with all the things they had bought in Cusco. Katie had had to buy a whole new bag to put all hers in.

Wearily, they pushed the trolleys through the big sliding doors, into a sea of unfamiliar faces. 'I always think I'll know someone,' Katie said. 'It seems so odd to see so many people and not know anyone.'

I do know someone, Sasha thought. I know him. Alistair was standing slightly apart from the crowd. He was wearing the suede jacket she'd bought him two Christmases ago, and a pair of dark green moleskin trousers she hadn't seen before. Clutching his hand tightly was Emily, and Abbie stood behind him, as tall as his shoulder. He'd been chatting to Emily when she first saw him, and then he looked up. And saw her. Their eyes met. She stood stock still, and in that moment before Emily ran forward, she decided.

Chapter Eighteen

'This is the best one,' Abbie said, holding the painting up to the light streaming through the studio window. Sasha had turned what had been a big dusty attic over the garage into her art studio, and the walls were stacked with canvases. It was the perfect place.

'It really has the feel of the mountains,' Abbie said. 'You can feel the sun because of the reflection, but you can't actually see it. It's really clever.'

'Oh,' Sasha said, grinning, 'you can't frame the sun. It's too powerful and intense.' She squatted back on her heels. 'So you think that one – and these over here – for the exhibition?' It was only a local exhibition, in the village hall, but as Alistair said, it was a start. Who knows, he said, where she might go from here? He was thoroughly enjoying the kudos of having an artist for a wife, if it did mean he had lost his chief cook and bottle-washer.

Nothing was ever going to be perfect, but then nothing ever was. Only now there was love. Not red-hot, whirlwind love which could not be sustained, but a love which had acknowledged faults and mistakes, parcelled them up and shut the door. A love which let them be their own person, not the person the other wanted them to be. And out of that acceptance and letting go of blame had come passion, a new-found passion which had taken them both by surprise in its intensity. And once that connection had been made, many other connections returned. Like laughing about silly things, and surprises, and touching.

Sasha hugged her knees. Only a year, a year since she had returned, and so much had changed. This, and the good fortune of Alistair securing a new backer willing to pump money into the company, which had turned it around. But most of all they had just looked at each other, and decided that they liked more than they disliked, and they had both realized that it is too easy to fall into the spiral of repetitive, destructive patterns of behaviour and hang onto them as security and justification for unhappiness.

In the car on the way home from the airport they hadn't talked much. Emily had chattered on about what she had been doing, how lovely Helga the au pair was, how Daddy had forgotten her games kit on Monday morning and how they had a new girl at school who was useless at spellings. Abbie had stared moodily out of the window. Halfway home Alistair, without taking his eyes from the road, reached over and took her hand. He let their entwined palms rest on the edge of her seat and she looked at them, amazed. It was the first time he had voluntarily touched her for years. What a grown-up you are, she thought.

Chapter Nineteen

The hand which held the newspaper flat and smooth was tanned, with a smattering of freckles on the back, the freckles partly hidden in the creases which had just started to appear. She didn't worry too much about them – there was no real point in worrying, you'd just drive yourself mad because there was nothing you could do about it. Anyway, if you were both growing old together then it didn't matter much at all, as long as you deteriorated at the same pace. She took a sip of her coffee. At her feet Rob, Bob's son, thumped his tail. It was nearly time for a walk, and he kept glancing sideways at the lead which was hanging off the dresser. Sasha stretched. Ten o'clock. She really ought to get into her studio and finish that commission. But there was plenty of time, she thought. Plenty of time to stand, and stare.

The sun was shining, it was a lovely bright autumn day. First she would take Rob out, and walk through the woods where the leaves were just starting to fall. She thought of Emily, and how she'd loved kicking her way through them. Emily, about to set off for university. Abbie, grown-up and gone. Even Katie's daughter was nine now. Which reminded her. She must ring Nic, and tell her they could come to France at Easter, to stay with her and Tim. Not a perfect life, she thought, glancing at the clock again. But quite enough for her. The sun came, and went, and you couldn't spend your life wishing for it.

She turned the page of the newspaper, idly, and there he was. She looked at his photograph, surprised that she wasn't surprised. He was standing on the steps of parliament – the Municipal Building in Lima, she saw from the caption – waving and smiling. He had hardly aged at all. Same wavy dark hair standing up from his high forehead, same faintly teasing smile, same broad shoulders, same air of arrogance. Peru's charismatic new president, according to the headline. No wonder he was so popular, it was a landslide, she read. Her eyes scanned down the page, knowing what she searched for. There. He was married, with three children. She smiled to herself. He would never be faithful, but if you adored him, you would turn a blind eye.

Gently, she put down her coffee cup, and then she put that hand on the newspaper, her fingers sliding up the page. They came to rest against his cheek, and the paper, caught in the sunlight, did not feel cold and inanimate, but warm, life-giving. She sat back, her heart beating. Warm. Like human skin.

THE END

A SELECTED LIST OF FINE WRITING
AVAILABLE FROM BLACK SWAN

77084 1	COOL FOR CATS	*Jessica Adams*	£6.99
99822 2	A CLASS APART	*Diana Appleyard*	£6.99
99821 4	HOMING INSTINCT	*Diana Appleyard*	£6.99
99933 4	OUT OF LOVE	*Diana Appleyard*	£6.99
77185 6	SIZE MATTERS	*Judy Astley*	£6.99
77105 8	NOT THE END OF THE WORLD	*Kate Atkinson*	£6.99
99863 X	MARLENE DIETRICH LIVED HERE	*Eleanor Bailey*	£6.99
77136 8	ONE DAY, SOMEDAY	*Lynne Barrett-Lee*	£6.99
99947 4	CROSS MY HEART AND HOPE TO DIE	*Claire Calman*	£6.99
99990 3	A CRYING SHAME	*Renate Dorrestein*	£6.99
99954 7	SWIFT AS DESIRE	*Laura Esquivel*	£6.99
77001 9	HOLY FOOLS	*Joanne Harris*	£6.99
77110 4	CAN YOU KEEP A SECRET?	*Sophie Kinsella*	£6.99
77164 3	MANEATER	*Gigi Levangie*	£6.99
77104 X	BY BREAD ALONE	*Sarah-Kate Lynch*	£6.99
99939 3	MY SECRET LOVER	*Imogen Parker*	£6.99
77106 6	LITTLE INDISCRETIONS	*Carmen Posadas*	£6.99
77004 3	DO YOU COME HERE OFTEN?	*Alexandra Potter*	£6.99
77088 4	NECTAR	*Lily Prior*	£6.99
99952 0	LIFE ISN'T ALL HA HA HEE HEE	*Meera Syal*	£6.99
77087 6	GIRL FROM THE SOUTH	*Joanna Trollope*	£6.99
99903 2	ARE YOU MY MOTHER?	*Louise Voss*	£6.99
99864 8	A DESERT IN BOHEMIA	*Jill Paton Walsh*	£6.99
99723 4	PART OF THE FURNITURE	*Mary Wesley*	£6.99
99834 6	COCKTAILS FOR THREE	*Madeleine Wickham*	£6.99
77101 5	PAINTING RUBY TUESDAY	*Jane Yardley*	£6.99